DAWN OF MAGIC

SEA OF FLAMES

TREE OF AGES BOOK SEVEN

SARA C ROETHLE

THE TREE OF AGES

The Northern Wilds

Uí Néid

River Cair

Port Ainfean

The Melted Sea

Migris

The Sand Raod

Badenmar

Greenswallow

Sormyr

The Blood Forest

The Marshlands

Garenoch

Finn

Finn's skin was slick with sweat. She rolled over in bed, reaching out for Iseult, but the space where he should have been was empty. She turned over and stared up at the ceiling, illuminated only by the moon shining through the high window. She could still feel the flames licking at her skin as they engulfed the forest. An entire sea of flames.

She worried her dream portended what was to come. More dragons were sure to arrive within the realm. While none had returned to attack the burgh, she could distantly sense them waiting, and *hunting*. She used to feel the trees and the earth. Now she just felt fire, ice, death and destruction. She'd given up her magic to save Naoki, and in so doing, had cursed herself with dragon blood.

The door cracked open, revealing a shadowy figure.

"You should rest," Iseult's voice soothed.

"I had the dream again."

He stepped into the room. A shred of moonlight glinted on his black hair, for just a moment lighting his gray-green eyes. She noted the sword at his hip despite the late hour. He rarely went without it these days. He sat beside her on the bed, leaning forward to brush a sweaty strand of hair from her face. "It was only a dream. Tomorrow you will wake, and there will be no more flames."

The remnants of the dream hit her again, more distantly this time. Heat and death. "You don't know that."

He continued to stroke her hair, bringing with his movements the smell of dying grass from outside. He'd been patrolling again, despite the mages guarding the burgh. "No, but neither do you."

She reached for him, pulling him down to lie beside her. "If you believe there is no immediate danger, then why were you out?"

"Because I like to be sure."

She turned on her side and nuzzled her face against his neck. They should have been safe within Garenoch. Safely guarded by mages, assassins, and the few Aos Sí who'd remained loyal to Eywen. The faie were all outside the walls, and dragons had not been sighted since the harvest season began to dwindle. But she knew they were out there, and so was Belenus. He might have failed to watch her die once, but next time, she knew she might not be so lucky.

Iseult wrapped his arm around her back, pulling her close. He hummed softly, a song from his childhood. He never hummed around anyone else—those who knew him would never believe her if she told them—

but once he'd learned it soothed her, he did it whenever she needed comfort.

She snuggled closer. "I should just get up now. There is much to do. We need to discuss sending scouts to find Oighear—or Keiren. Their insight could prove invaluable."

"I think you should leave them wherever they are. Neither Keiren nor Oighear can be trusted."

"But they may be my only hope of reaching that snowy realm. Even with Naoki's help, I cannot seem to find it."

"Perhaps you are not meant to."

She resisted the urge to squirm. The thought of trying to reach that other realm—the realm where people and places went when they disappeared—terrified her, but she had to keep trying. She'd sworn to Kai she would save his family, and she'd meant it. She would not let him down, not while her chest still held breath.

Iseult began to hum again, and sleep tugged at her. She had been sleeping so poorly, she knew she'd be exhausted by tomorrow night, there really was no need to wake up now. Her real reason for wanting to do so was just to avoid another nightmare.

Against her will, sleep came, and the land was engulfed in fire.

Anna

At dawn, Anna sat on the roof of one of the many buildings in the rear courtyard of the estate. She'd taken to sitting up there every morning as the sun rose. It was the only time she found true solitude, something she'd depended on in her many years on the road. She opened the waxed cloth in her lap and stuck a slice of dried apple in her mouth. *Very* dried apple. And mealy too. With chaos and war shaking the countryside, and the meager harvest season all but over, food had grown scarce. Ealasaid was confident she could feed and clothe everyone within Garenoch, but Anna was not so sure. She tended to see the harsh realities where others would not.

"I thought I'd find you up here," Kai's voice said behind her.

She turned. She hadn't heard his steps. Despite the shadows of his black cowl, he still held a hand above his eyes, shielding them from the gentle rays of dawn.

She turned away. "The sun will be up soon. You'd better hurry inside."

Instead of doing as she bade, he stepped carefully across the roof and sat beside her, tugging the hem of his gray breeches down to remain tucked inside his boots. "I can stand a bit of sun. It isn't that bad."

Finally, she smiled. "Liar."

His hand still lifted, he turned his gaze northward.

"Every day I expect to see another dragon swooping in."

She shrugged nonchalantly, though she expected the same. "The walls have been repaired, and we know of the threat now. The mages have a plan for dealing with them."

He scoffed. "As if you trust that plan."

She laughed softly—*tiredly*. He knew her too well. "I just wish there was more we could do."

His expression was serious as he turned back to her. "As do I, but we do not have magic like Finn, not even like Keiren or Ealasaid. There is little we can do."

She shoved his shoulder. "Oh stop feeling sorry for yourself."

She turned her gaze to the courtyard below as a young girl she recognized as a messenger hurried across the dying grass. She didn't stop to greet the few mages already milling about, tending beds of herbs and chopping wood for fires. Instead, she hurried directly toward the building Anna and Kai sat atop. An educated guess told her who the messenger sought.

"Something for Finn," Kai echoed her thoughts. "Let's see what it is."

She stood and followed him across the roof. Messages for Finn were *never* good, especially when the messenger carried them so urgently. However, she was never one to shy away from bad news. She liked to face her problems head on.

Thinking of Eywen, she corrected her thoughts. *Most* of them anyway.

〰️

Finn

Finn dashed across the courtyard. Spotting her, Naoki, leapt off the building she'd been resting atop, bounding down to prance circles around Finn like an excited dog. Heedless of her size, her gleaming white talons tore up soil, and her ivory horns came a little too close to taking down ornamental shrubs. She never came close to hitting Finn though, she always seemed keenly aware of her mother's location. The echo of a door shutting behind her reached her ears, signaling Iseult following close behind.

She probably should have waited for him, but the news was just too exciting. She had to reach the gates at once. Tugging her breeches up, she sprinted around the eastern end of the main estate, catching sight of Kai and Anna as they hurried toward her.

"We saw the messenger!" Anna shouted. "What is it?"

Finn waved them off, not wanting to stop and explain. Things had seemed so wrong for so long, could something, even just a small thing, be right again?

They fell into step on either side of her, easily pacing her with their longer legs.

She frowned, but kept running. Her body had grown hard and fit over the course of her adventures, but Kai and Anna had been fit all their lives. She'd never outrun them, especially Kai, now that he was no longer human.

Kai swerved a little closer. "Care to chat and jog?" Only a hint of exertion was evident in his tone.

Iseult caught up to their backs as she reached the main estate gates. She slowed, waiting for someone atop the walls to open them. "Àed is here. He awaits us at the inn."

Anna snorted, tossing her long dark braid behind the shoulder of her loose white blouse, cinched in at the waist and bodice by a simple tan corset. "So he's still alive then?"

Finn glared at her, shifting her feet impatiently across the soggy dead grass. "Of course he's still alive. Why wouldn't he be?"

"We haven't heard from him in over a year," Anna huffed.

Finally, one side of the well-oiled gates opened with barely a sound, just enough for them to pass through. Instead of replying, she hurried onward toward the main road bisecting the burgh. She'd feared the same as Anna—that Àed was dead. Dead and forgotten, left out for the wolves. What other reason would he have for staying away so long? Surely Garenoch was the most sensible place to be once the dragons arrived.

Kai fell back as Iseult moved forward to walk at her side, his expression pensive. "You must prepare yourself, it might not actually be him."

"But the messenger said—"

"She's never met him. It could be an imposter, just be on your guard."

She pursed her lips and kept walking. A few burghsfolk watched them as they passed, but not with much interest. Most recognized each of them by now. If Naoki had followed, there would have been more of a startle, but she knew to stay within the estate walls. While she'd never attacked anyone, the burghsfolk were understandably wary of dragons.

Finn's jaw clenched. If only they knew what blood ran through her own veins. They'd fear her too.

It didn't take long to reach the main inn, and she couldn't help a small smile. This was the place she'd first met everyone currently accompanying her. Who could have ever imagined how things would end up? It seemed a fitting place to finally be reunited with Àed.

Kai nudged her shoulder. "Are we going inside, or are we just going to stare at the doors?"

She grinned. Iseult was wrong, it would most definitely be Àed inside, and she couldn't wait to see him.

As if reading her thoughts, Iseult entered the inn first, letting the door swing shut behind him.

Anna smirked, her eyes on the gently swinging

door. "Better get in there before he decides Àed is an imposter in disguise and slays him."

At the thought, Finn hurried forward, pulled open the door, and went inside. She scanned the bustling common room, her eyes finally landing on a round table near the back corner. At first she only saw Iseult's tall back, then beyond him, Àed and Bedelia.

Kai reached her side and followed her gaze. "He looks . . . older. If that's even possible."

Ignoring his words, and the few waves of greeting from others within the common room, she ran toward Àed and Bedelia.

Bedelia rose to greet her. Her pin straight brown hair was uncharacteristically long, reaching her shoulder blades, and she was in plain clothing, a tunic and breeches, instead of any armor. It made her much easier to hug. Finn squeezed so tightly she might have squashed a less-sturdy woman.

"Oh I've missed you," Finn whispered in her ear.

"And I you," Bedelia said as she pulled away. "But I fear this cannot be an entirely joyful meeting. We've come to you for help."

Finn looked between Bedelia and Àed, who was yet to speak. "Is it the dragons? Or the faie?"

Àed's back hunched further, making him seem small. In fact, he was actually smaller than he used to be, not in height, but in bulk. His parchment-thin skin seemed to sag from his bones. His long silver hair hung limp across his dirty blue traveling cloak, and his stubble-coated cheeks were hollow.

Finn jumped as Iseult's hand alighted upon her shoulder. He'd likely already deduced what she was just beginning to realize.

Her throat felt tight, and her eyes threatened tears. "You're ill, aren't you?"

Àed's sky blue eyes finally met hers. They seemed duller than before, almost as if a thin film coated them. "Aye, lass. In a way, at least." He half shrugged. "It's to be expected at my age. I would have been content to die in peace, but the lass here insisted I come to see ye." He gestured to Bedelia, towering over him in his seat. "After a bit of bickerin', I had to admit, she was right."

She wanted to ask them both a million questions, but in that moment, there was only one that truly mattered. She sat beside him on the bench pulled up to the table and took his bony hand in hers. "What can I do?"

Àed looked past her to Bedelia.

"Tell her," she insisted.

Àed sighed, giving Finn's hand a light squeeze. "Ye can show me to me daughter, so I can make me goodbyes."

Finn shook her head, stunned. Sure, he seemed older, and weak, but that didn't mean—this could not be happening, not now. When he was missing, she could console herself with the idea that maybe he wasn't dead. To lose him, for sure and for good, it was too much for her to bear in that moment.

Dizziness overcame her. She abruptly stood, dropping Àed's hand, feeling like she might vomit. The common room seemed to spin, slowly at first, then more quickly. She wanted to tell him she didn't know where Keiren was, but could not form the words to speak. The last thing she saw was Kai and Anna eyeing her with concern.

Strong hands caught her as she fell back, back into oblivion, then there was only darkness.

Finn woke with a roaring headache, not remembering going to sleep. The entire day's events seemed hazy, but more troubling was the icy feeling of her body. She couldn't feel her fingertips.

She tried to remember what had happened. If she was asleep, she had to be in her room, but she couldn't quite force her eyes to open. Iseult must have forgotten to tend the hearth, but why? She struggled to sit up, bracing with her hands, which crunched through fresh snow. She recoiled, her eyes snapping open. She rubbed them with damp palms, swiping moisture back through her tangled hair to push it out of her face.

She blinked rapidly, waiting for her eyes to come into focus. Wherever she was, it was dark. She could see traces of stars overhead, illuminating the sky in frayed bursts of purple-blue light, but they were mostly obscured by clouds, leaving the snowy expanses around her in colorless shadow.

With a groan, she stood. At one time, she would have been terrified waking in a strange place, but this seemed to happen to her time and again. She couldn't be in the in-between—that had been destroyed . . . although Branwen had managed to bring her somewhere just like it once. But no, this wasn't that place, though this frozen land was something like it, and she had been here before—her back broken, on the verge of death. She felt she should be glad she'd finally made it here—maybe she could locate Kai's family—but all she could think in that moment was, why was she here now?

Steps crunched up behind her, followed by a hot huff of breath. She turned, then sagged with relief. She hadn't seen Loinnir since the day she healed her. It was the last time she'd seen Belenus too. Hopefully she wasn't about to repeat *that* experience.

She stroked Loinnir's soft white muzzle, edging her palm up toward her glistening horn and silky mane. She leaned to one side to peer into the unicorn's glittering eye. "You didn't happen to bring me here, did you?"

Loinnir huffed an emphatic *no*.

She hadn't really thought so. She glanced around their expansive icy surroundings. Perhaps she'd been caught up in one of the shifts that could swallow entire burghs, displacing them to this unknown realm.

"Well," she shrugged, turning back to Loinnir, "I believe I'm stuck here until Naoki comes to find me. I do not know how to return on my own. Perhaps we should look around a bit."

Loinnir walked to her side, then bent her front legs into the snow, making it easy for Finn to climb atop her warm back. Once she was in place, Loinnir straightened, then started walking.

Finn hunkered down, greedily absorbing Loinnir's heat. She had not been prepared for a winter stroll . . . though it had come at a fortunate time. She now remembered what had sent her spiraling. Àed had come with ill tidings. She was not quite ready to hear what he needed to tell her. She might never be.

They walked through the snow for a long quiet while, her thoughts distant. Usually in these circumstances, Naoki would come to find her, but she might be asleep, or off chasing squirrels, not yet realizing her mother was gone.

She narrowed her eyes at an orb of light in the distance. "What is that?" she asked, knowing Loinnir was unable to answer, though she was quite sure the unicorn could understand her words. "Let's go over there."

Loinnir obeyed, and soon more lights came into view. Not floating orbs after all, but torches. Had she actually stumbled upon inhabitants of this strange land?

She had almost reached the settlement, could even hear voices, when a shiver went down her spine. Sensing her sudden distress, Loinnir halted. Finn looked over her shoulder, observing a hunched, hooded form. She didn't have to see his face to know who he was.

"What do you want, Arawn?"

Arawn pulled back his hood, revealing his shadowed face. He was in his younger form, looking more masculine than his older one. She knew his voice could sound like a thousand different voices all at once, or just like one. His true voice.

His smile was barely visible in the darkness. "Just wanted to see what the dragon girl was doing in this realm."

"Dragon girl?" she questioned.

"Yes, a tree girl no more. You know as a dragon, you are no longer off limits to Belenus. You are little more than an animal. He can kill you with barely a thought."

"So why hasn't he?" she growled.

Arawn lifted his hands. "I see your dragon blood has brought out your temper." He tsked. "You'll need to rein that in, lest you become too . . . beastly."

"What do you mean?" All she could think about in that moment was that Arawn had been the one to curse Iseult, and he'd tried to trick her into sacrificing herself to save him. She had not seen him since the day she faced Belenus at his castle.

"Isn't it obvious?" Arawn laughed. "The blood of a dragon changes you. You must feel it?"

Her dreams of fire flashed through her mind. "I have no idea what you're talking about."

"You do, I can read it in your eyes. Now tell me, how do you intend to defeat the dragons now that you're one of them? Will you slay your own kind?"

A gust of icy wind lifted tendrils of her long hair. She slid from Loinnir's back, her boots sinking into the snow, then approached Arawn.

His deep-set eyes widened, just a touch. Did he really think she'd still be afraid? That she'd run instead of coming toward him?

She stopped walking. Why *wasn't* she afraid of him? He was a *god*. What was wrong with her?

He seemed to read her thoughts. "I think you not long for this world, dragon girl. And once you are gone, your mages will perish."

She took another step toward him. "I will not just lie down and die for you. Belenus and I had a deal."

"You call naming your terms and jumping off a ledge to escape striking a deal?"

She just watched him. Belenus might have tried to stop her from leaving, but they all knew her plan was the only option they all had, as long as she was around.

"Fine," Arawn huffed. "Try to enact your plan if you

please. The faie will no longer heed you in this form. Perhaps they will kill you and save us the trouble."

That gave her pause. Could he be lying? She hadn't seen one of the faie—besides Kai and the Aos Sí—in quite some time. Not even a pixie.

"You hadn't realized it?" he taunted. "Oh that is rich —" There was the thumping of wings above. He turned at a flurry of snow as Naoki touched down only a few paces away from him.

Finn didn't so much as flinch at the sudden intrusion. Naoki's energy was more familiar to her than almost any other.

Arawn straightened, moving his glare from Naoki to Finn. "You could have warned me."

Naoki stretched out her long neck, lowering her sharply-pointed maw toward the snow, catching faint hints of starlight on her four ivory horns. Her lilac eyes watched Arawn like he might be good to eat.

Arawn stepped back. "I suppose this means you'll be leaving. Your ride is here, after all."

He was right. She needed to get back. Given the place from which she departed, she was likely far from Kai's family—if that was how traveling between realms worked. Plus if she really had been caught up in a reality shift, she needed to make sure everyone she'd left behind was alright. "Tell Belenus to stay away from Garenoch. Any armies he sends will be swiftly put down."

Arawn edged backward through the snow, farther

from Naoki. "Do not fear, Belenus will let the dragons wear down the mages before he comes in for the kill. The beasts are cautious for now, but their hunger will not remain at bay forever. They must be fed, or they will fade."

Had she feathers like Naoki, they would have prickled, or had she a pelt, it would have raised. The sudden predatory instinct was entirely new to her. She walked toward Arawn, who now watched her warily, sensing something had changed.

"You've gone on about me being a dragon girl," she mused, a sudden revelation coming to her. "At first I was a bit offended, but now I'm beginning to wonder just what that means. Correct me if I'm wrong, but don't *dragons* eat gods?"

"Only the most powerful of dragons," Arawn countered. "Not some half-breed." His words showed no fear, but she didn't miss his step back.

She closed the space between them again. "Care to test that theory?" She wasn't quite sure what she was doing, except following her instincts. Instincts quite new to her.

He took three more steps back, lifting his hands, palms out. "Not particularly, no. And if you are wise, you'll leave me be. You may need my help in the future. For now, I simply came to see why you are here."

Help? What on earth was he talking about? She still didn't know why she was here, but she wasn't about to tell him that. "That settlement," she said, gesturing behind her. "Are they from my realm? A village caught up in a reality shift?"

He nodded. "If that's what you want to call it, yes."

"So all those lost. They are still alive?"

"Look around you," he sneered. "This is a barren landscape. They may have survived thus far on supplies brought along, and a bit of wood and plant matter foraged here and there, but they will not last indefinitely."

A pang sliced through her heart. Kai's family. They'd been transported with only their home and the belongings within, not an entire village. Their supplies would not last them for long.

Arawn had continued backing away, and was now nearly encapsulated in darkness.

She reached out to stop him. "One last thing!"

He stopped. "Yes?"

"Tell Belenus I want to meet with him. It can be at a time and place of his choosing."

Arawn seemed caught completely off guard. After a moment of thought, he nodded. "Very well. I shall relay your message, but I can guarantee no such meeting." With that, the darkness surrounded him entirely, and he was gone.

She turned to Naoki, still watching the space where Arawn had been. With him gone, Finn felt more herself again. She wasn't entirely sure what had come over her, but she didn't like it. And just what had he meant by *help*?

She reached out to stroke Naoki's smooth feathered neck. She debated going to the settlement and speaking to those there, but knew it would do little good. Naoki could bring her to other realms because they both shared dragon's blood. They couldn't bring anyone back with them—not even Loinnir—just as they could bring no one else here.

Loinnir nudged her shoulder as she stared off into the darkness, deep in thought. She reached back and stroked Loinnir's forehead. "I wish you could tell me why I ended up here, and how to bring you back."

Loinnir pressed her muzzle against Finn's back, as if to say *go*.

She would go, she knew she had to, but she silently vowed she would be back. Not just for Loinnir, but for all those trapped here. None of whom had much time left.

inn woke up in her bed, though she wasn't sure how she'd gotten there. Candlelight dimly lit her room, necessary with the pitch darkness beyond the window. A familiar scent was nearby, but that wasn't right. She shouldn't have been able to *smell* her friends. She wasn't a wolf.

Assuming her mind was playing tricks on her, she lifted her head. Her nose had been right. Kai sat on the edge of her bed, hunched over a book held close to a candle on the bedside table. She'd never noticed his scent before, soil and soap, but underneath that a hint of the sea, all swimming with faie magic.

He turned to her, catching her staring. "About time you woke. Iseult and the others are pulling their hair out trying to figure out what happened at the inn."

She pushed away a tangled lock of hair, still damp from melted snow, as thoughts of scents fled from her mind. "Where did you find me?"

He set his book on the bed and turned further toward her. "When you just disappeared like that, we figured Naoki would be the only one who could find you. We returned to the courtyard and woke her from her nap." He visibly shivered. "You'll never wake a sleeping dragon if you know what's good for you. She was crankier than a newborn babe with colic."

Ah, so that was why Naoki had taken so long to find her.

"She brought you back," Kai continued, "but you were unconscious. And none of us speak dragon, so we've been waiting to hear what happened to you. It was like another reality shift, but only you were affected. The inn is still standing."

A tension in her shoulders eased. The inn was alright. Everyone else was alright. "I'm not sure what happened. I was feeling terribly overwhelmed. My emotions got the better of me. I lost control."

He lifted a brow. "So you brought yourself there? We thought for sure it was Belenus, which set Iseult to plotting like a madman with the others."

She shook her head. "No, it wasn't Belenus, though I did see Arawn there." She scooted toward him across the bed, then sat on her knees. "Kai, there was a village there. A whole village swept away to that other realm. I think if I can go there again better prepared, then maybe I can find your family." She hesitated. "I'm not sure how to bring them back . . . but I could at least deliver supplies."

She'd thought her words would bring him hope, but his shoulders remained hunched, like the weight of living was slowly crushing him. "We've no way of knowing if they even live, or how to find them. And what about Belenus? You said you saw Arawn?"

She chewed her lip, wondering how much to tell him. "He said because I gave up my magic, my immortal blood, to save Naoki, that the faie will no longer follow me. Without them—"

"That can't be true!" he blurted. He gently grabbed her arm. "Without the faie . . . "

She nodded. "I know. If I cannot contain faie magic, Belenus *will* kill the mages. He'll let the dragons pick us off one by one, then an army from Sormyr will finish the rest."

He shook his head, just as stunned as she at the realization. "What are we going to do?"

"I don't know. Even without Belenus' threat, something has to change. The land is too unstable."

He dropped his hand from her arm, seeming to calm himself. "What about Niklas? He orchestrated the barrier breaking. He had to have foreseen the consequences."

She shrugged. "If you come across him, ask him for me, won't you?"

He scowled. "You're filled with dragon blood now. Don't dragons track magic?"

Her lips parted, but no words came out. She hadn't thought of that. "It's a possibility, I suppose, though I wouldn't even know where to start. Perhaps with Naoki's help . . . "

"Is your loss of magic the reason we haven't seen any pixies?"

She sighed. She had hoped it was just the presence

of so many mages. "Yes. They would have been a lot more useful in finding Niklas than I'll be."

He gripped her arm again, this time offering a comforting squeeze. "I'm sure you'll manage. Should we be expecting an attack from Belenus in the meantime?"

She appreciated his faith in her, however misguided. "Not according to Arawn. He claimed they'd wait for the dragons to attack us again, but I think it might be something else."

He went still, watching her carefully, the flickering candles the only movement in the room. "Go on."

She thought back to her meeting with Arawn. It was only a feeling, she could be totally wrong, but . . . "I think, now that I am . . . what I am, he may be a bit frightened of me."

"You were far scarier before."

She shoved his shoulder. "I'm being serious. The one thing the gods seem to fear is dragons, because dragons can eat their magic. I'm wondering—" she paused, finding the idea a bit absurd.

He seemed to follow her thinking. "You're wondering now that you're part dragon, if you can eat magic too?"

The idea made her shiver. "It's possible, don't you think? I can travel to that other realm because of the dragon blood. Only gods and dragons can travel back and forth freely. Would it not stand to reason that I would inherit other dragon traits as well?"

"Is there a way to test this theory?"

She frowned. "Maybe, but I wouldn't want to risk hurting anyone."

"Try with me. I have some magic in me, don't I?"

"That's beside the point! Have you gone mad?"

He moved closer to her. A lock of chestnut hair fell across his eyes, doing little to dampen their sudden intensity. "I'm a willing victim. Just try it."

She wrapped her fists around her bedding, her entire body suddenly singing with tension. "No."

He crawled further onto the bed, mirroring her position, sitting on bent knees. "Do it."

Her cheeks flushed with annoyance. "Why are you so intent on this?"

He leaned closer, looking deep into her eyes. "If you can harness your new magic, you may be able to defeat Belenus. You may even be able to *eat* faie magic, restoring balance, whether they want you to or not. You may be able to travel to other realms and bring my family back alive. But you have to try. I know you're scared, but—"

"I'm not scared," she hissed. "I'll try it, but not on you."

He pulled away, sitting more casually. The surrounding candlelight swayed across the stone walls with his movement. "Fine by me, as long as you try."

She dropped her wadded up bedding and crossed her arms. "You're infuriating."

He smirked. "You're welcome."

She sighed. He really did know her too well. He knew she'd be scared of embracing this new magic, but he'd instantly seen a possibility she hadn't. A possibility to restore balance and protect the mages. It was worth the risk.

"The Dearg Due," she decided.

Kai lifted a brow. "What about them?"

"If I must try to eat faie magic, I would try it on them. They would kill me and steal you away if they could. I will feel little guilt over their demise."

Kai watched her for a long moment. "You want to hunt down the Dearg Due and eat their magic?"

Suddenly she felt like an idiot for even thinking it, but, what other choice was there? She would not risk harming Kai. She forced herself to meet his gaze. "You think it a foolish plan?"

He let out a slow breath. "Yes, but I also cannot argue it. The only point I can argue, is that I'll be going with you."

"Who says I would argue such a point?"

He stared at her, and she quickly gave in to the obvious. She would have argued, just like she would argue when Iseult insisted on coming. There would be a formal discussion of this new plan later, she was sure, but for now, she at least had something to focus on.

Unfortunately, that something would entail becoming more like a dragon. First hunting her prey, then devouring it.

Resigned to her fate, she tossed herself back against

her pillows. "Thank you," she grumbled. "I would have struggled to come to this realization otherwise." She stared at the flickering candlelight on the ceiling for a long moment, then propped herself up on her elbows. "Is Àed really dying?"

Kai's smug expression fell. "I think so."

Her body seemed to melt into her covers. There was so much more to face than testing out dragon magic.

The bed shifted, then Kai stood over her. He offered her his hand. "You'll regret it if you don't see him before it's too late. Hear what he has to say, and what he needs from you."

She stared at his hand for a moment, then took it, allowing him to pull her to her feet.

They stood for a moment hand in hand. She stared at the closed door, then sighed. "I'm not going to thank you for this one."

"I wouldn't dream of asking."

She held tight to his hand as they walked toward the door, opened it, then went out into the hall. She felt absolute fear, *terror* really. Far more so than she'd experienced when facing Arawn, Belenus, or anyone else.

The door creaked open at Finn's touch. First she saw Iseult, waiting just within, back straight, right hand hovering near his sword. Seeing her, his stance relaxed. His normally impassive expression held so many things he wanted to ask to her, revealing just a hint of softness guarded by his warrior exterior.

She nodded subtly. There would be time later. "Kai can explain."

Iseult clenched his fists, but nodded, then walked past her out the door, pausing only to give her arm a reassuring squeeze. She could sense Kai's eyes on her back through the doorway, but she couldn't turn to look. If she did, she was bound to run away.

As Iseult and Kai left her, she finally turned her gaze to Àed, sitting on one of three small wood-framed beds in a bare-bones room meant for newly arrived mages.

Àed, hunched and appearing about a million years old in his tattered gray cloak, looked not at her, but at the now closed door. "Ye've managed to bring out the heart in that lad."

She almost smiled at Iseult being referred to as a *lad*. "Probably because my behavior is so maddening to him. He had to break eventually."

He laughed at her joke, and the feeling of dread within her eased. He might be ill, but he could still laugh. He wasn't dead yet, and that meant he could still be saved. Without thinking, she walked across the room and sat beside him on the bed.

"What happened? Tell me everything."

He huffed, puffing out his hollow cheeks. "I think yer the one who should be regalin' me of your experiences."

She eyed him sternly.

His shoulders slumped, trailing limp silver hair forward to obscure his face. "Alright, lass. Alright." He blew the hair from his cheek with a scowl. "It was one of them dragons. I could sense it huntin' me for some time. I did me best to evade it, but when it finally found me, there wasnae much I could do. It didn't eat me, like I'd expected. Instead it seemed to suck the life from me. It drank me magic like a dram of the finest whiskey. Would have finished the job too, if that foolhardy Bedelia hadn't attacked it like a goddess of war. We were fortunate the beast was young, she was able to scare it off. I imagine its size was the only reason it didnae attack me within the port."

Finn swallowed the lump in her throat, able to picture the scene in her mind. She knew the dragons were sentient beasts, but hadn't realized they were wise enough to not attack where they might be defeated. Perhaps that was the reason Garenoch had not suffered another attack since the first two dragons were put down. "And what the dragon did to you, this is why you'll . . . die?"

He nodded. "As ye know, me daughter crippled me long ago. I began to age more hastily after that, but this, this will end me in short order."

She shook her head. "I don't understand. You're not immortal. Why did you not age before?"

"Me daughter and I aren't like the mages runnin' all over the place. She's a sorceress, for lack of a better term. Legends call me a conjurer, but I'm more of a sorcerer. I don't conjure spirits, but both of us, we walk with one foot in other realms. That type of power gives us unnaturally long lives. Without it, all me years are catching up with me."

His gaze had dropped to his lap. She reached out and placed her hand gently on his bony arm. "But Keiren, she can help you? Is that why you want to find her?"

He laughed, but it was choked with tears. "Nay, lass. I want to say me goodbyes."

She resisted the urge to squeeze his arm, to shake him, anything to convince him to not give up so easily.

As if reading her thoughts, he turned to her. "It's me time, lass. I've no desire to live forever, and you and Keiren can take care of yerselves. Now that I've brought Bedelia back to ye, I know she'll be looked after as well. Ye need to let me go."

Though tears stung her eyes, she refused to let them fall. If he could face death so bravely, the least she could do was hear him out. She took a shaky breath, then forced her voice steady. "I understand. We'll try to find her, but we've been searching for a while already, so I fear I can make no promises."

"Trying is enough, lass. I know ye've got bigger problems to worry about. Iseult told me about yer dreams."

She leaned back, surprised. "I hadn't realized he was worried about them. He insists they are merely dreams, and not portents."

"It's ye we're talkin' about, lass. Surely they are nae *just dreams*. What ye did to save yer white dragon, it changed ye. Even with little magic left to me, I can see that."

She hunched forward, bracing elbows on knees. "Even if that is so, there is not much I can do about it."

"Not much we can do about a lot of things, lass. Best we can do is keep fightin'."

She nodded, then leaned her shoulder against his. Her thoughts wandered to the arguments soon to come. She *would* go after the Dearg Due to test her new magic. It would be dangerous, and would perhaps end in disaster, but she had no other plan for defeating Belenus. It had to be done.

Àed patted her hand, seeming to read her dread, though he did not speak. They sat like that for a long while, with her hand resting lightly on his arm. For the moment, it was enough. The rest—she'd deal with it when the time came.

Iseult

The clang of Bedelia's blade against his sent a thrill up Iseult's arm. It had been ages since he'd sparred with a worthy opponent. Maarav was strong and agile, but he preferred to spar with daggers, and Iseult's weapon of choice was the sword.

Their feet kicked up bits of soil scented heavily with moisture, flinging dying grass, slick and difficult to gain steady purchase upon.

Bedelia struck again, and Iseult met her smoothly with a parry.

She lowered her blade and stepped back, wiping the sweat from her brow with her sleeve. Her breath fogged the air.

He lowered his sword. "You should rest. You've had a long journey."

She shook her head, swiping sweaty locks of hair from her face. "Rest? With gods and dragons running amok? Now is no time to be resting on our laurels."

Her mention of dragons stiffened his spine. He'd been so concerned over Finn, he hadn't taken the time to ask of Bedelia and Àed's travels. He didn't even know why they were traveling together in the first place. His discussion with Àed had revolved around Finn.

She seemed to read his expression. "Yes," she answered his silent question, "we've seen the dragons. Though not up close until that little red one attacked Àed. It went for him like it knew he was special."

He sheathed his blade, now having more interest in Bedelia's story than her swordsmanship. "Where?"

She smirked. "A man of few words, I see little has changed in my absence." She sheathed her blade down her back, then walked by his side toward the path bisecting the front courtyard. "We encountered the dragon a day's ride south of Port Ainfean. We had been living at the port, working as we could."

Her answer surprised him enough that he blurted, "Living together?"

Bedelia shrugged, keeping a casual pace at his side. "It worked well for us. Originally we'd both simply intended to travel to the port together, then go our separate ways. Àed's journeys had depleted much of his coin, and I was in even worse shape, really. Once we arrived, we paid a local inn for use of a storeroom as lodgings." She shrugged again. "Then we just never left. We both prefer to be left alone, so the arrangement was comfortable, only paying for half a space with none of the hassle of communal living."

Thinking of the hassle of living within the large estate, he could understand her motives. He'd much prefer a small home for just him and Finn to live out their lives, to perhaps have children.

He pushed away his thoughts. That was not a life for him, and it was a life Finn had already lived once.

Bedelia's eyes were on him as if trying to interpret his thoughts. He was confident she could not, for those who knew him would never guess he considered such things.

He felt his expression shutting down as they reached the main estate. He held open the door for her. They'd go through the main hall then back toward the kitchens to find her something to eat.

As the inner warmth of the estate enveloped them,

he stopped and turned toward her. "The dragon, it's the reason Àed will die?"

"Figured that out already?" She continued walking, knowing the estate from her previous time there. "Yes, it's the reason. He says it ate what little magic was left to him. It was what sustained his unnaturally long life, and without it, he will soon perish. Keiren maintained contact with us for a while, but we haven't seen her in months. He wants to find her again before he dies. We'd hoped she'd be here."

Iseult matched her confident gait. "We don't know where she is, and Ealasaid has searched as much as she is able. Scouts sent west don't return, and those sent north rarely fare much better."

The smell of fresh-baked bread hit them, drawing them across the burgundy rugs of the back corridor the rest of the way to the kitchens.

Bedelia stopped before they could make it inside. "Iseult, our lives are in shambles, what are we going to do?"

Her blatant honesty gave him pause, almost as much as the hint of dread in her voice. "We will wait for Finn and Àed to finish their discussion, then we will learn what happened to her at the inn."

The corner of her mouth ticked up, a phantom of a smile. "One step at a time, eh?"

"I'm glad you've returned," he said as he walked past her, leaving her shocked and blinking after him.

Her voice carried through the doorway. "I think that's the nicest thing you've ever said to me."

Finn

A heavy pall hung over the evening meal, a direct effect of the preceding discussion. A discussion Finn had been right to dread.

After she met with Àed, she'd told everyone else what had happened in that other realm, and what needed to be done. She'd told Iseult privately, knowing he'd not react in a positive way. She'd expected anger, or at least an argument, but in the end, he'd hardly reacted at all. He'd been as stony-faced as ever since.

Yes, arguments had been made, but in the end it was Finn's choice. She would venture into the woods at sunrise, and would not turn back until she found the Dearg Due. As expected, she would not be going alone.

Now, around a long wooden table within the main estate, she sat with Iseult, Kai, Anna, Àed, Bedelia, and Maarav. Eywen, Ealasaid, and her general Sage would join them soon. Maarav cradled his son, Elias, who slept soundly in his arms. Finn hadn't let herself focus on the small child. He left too many questions in her mind of what she might want if things were different.

Finn scraped her fork across her plate, avoiding the hunk of roast grouse and the small boiled potatoes—

thinking about others in the outer burgh who would have only potatoes, if that. The depressing thought was almost preferable than the stony-faced man at her side. He'd argued least of all, which had come as a surprise.

Perhaps he'd been unable to form a reasonable argument against her plan. She *needed* to find the Dearg Due and see if she could steal their magic and bring them to heel. Perhaps it was not a wise plan, and she was betting too heavily on being able to eat magic like a dragon, but what other plan did she have?

Iseult leaned near her shoulder. "You should eat."

Were his words clipped, or was that just her imagination? He couldn't be happy she wanted to run off again, to take the weight of the land on her shoulders, but what other choice was there? She was the only one who could set things right, and Kai's family was running out of time. She wondered if she was simply trying to justify it to herself.

Tuning out the hushed conversations of her companions, her mind looped back yet again to her talk with Iseult, bringing her gaze involuntarily to his cheek, then his shoulder. With her fork in her right hand, she reached the left under the table and took his hand.

His grip was limp for a moment, then he gave her fingers a squeeze. He'd help, as always, but he didn't have to like it.

Feeling slightly better, she stuck her fork into a potato and took a bite. She could not afford to place

Iseult's feelings above the fate of so many others. She couldn't even afford to consider her own. Maybe if she were able to eat magic, and ate enough magic, she could bring Kai's family home, and even Loinnir.

She realized Kai was watching her, while Bedelia spoke softly to Anna, and Àed stared at his plate. Maarav dragged Iseult into conversation, distracting him.

She often felt like Kai knew her every thought. Maybe he did. He *did,* after all, seem to know her better than anyone else. He had supported her arguments fully, always seeming to be on her side.

She met his unwavering gaze. She'd given him the option, whether he wanted to face the Dearg Due with her, or stay behind. He'd chosen to come. She hadn't doubted for a moment that he would.

The sound of voices echoed through the distant hall a moment before Ealasaid, Sage, and Eywen joined them. Ealasaid's shoulders were slumped with fatigue, her finely woven lilac dress seeming out of place with the puffy blue skin beneath her gray eyes, and the grim set of her mouth. Finn would do well to remember the weight of the land was not on her shoulders alone. Ealasaid had many mouths to feed, mouths that would soon be without food if the faie weren't pushed back from the surrounding farms, and if the trade-ban with Sormyr weren't put to an end.

The trio would be staying behind to deal with Garenoch's more pressing needs. Only Finn, Iseult, Kai,

Anna, and Bedelia would go to face the faie. She could only hope what she was about to do would draw Keiren and Oighear in from wherever they were hiding. Keiren, to say goodbye to her father, and Oighear—Finn was reluctant to admit—because she could really use her knowledge, and her help.

What conversation took place during the rest of their meal, Finn could not recall. Her mind was focused on what was to come. On knowing that in leaving Garenoch, even just for a night or two, she took the risk of never returning from the faie-ridden forests, or more frightening still, of returning only to find nothing but a ruined city littered with corpses and ash.

Anna

*A*nna tied shut her satchel, then set it aside on her dresser. Candles flickered in the night-darkened room, stirred by the cool air coming in through the open shutters. Her hair was damp from her bath, already pulled back in a tight braid. "It's late, I need to rest if we're to leave at first light."

Tension sang through her at Eywen's light touch on her shoulder. "I'll come with you. All you need do is ask."

She glanced over her shoulder at him. His black hair was back in a clasp, revealing his pointed ears, the same pallid color as the rest of his skin. He looked anything but human, especially with those deep sapphire eyes, but the more Anna was around him, the less faie he seemed. While he'd been alive in one state or another for centuries, he still felt love, grief, joy . . .

She shook her head, forcing her expression to soften. He'd done nothing but what she'd asked of him. He'd given her space to come to terms with her thoughts. To decide if she truly wanted to be with him, or if it was just the chaos of her life that drew her toward someone safe and strong. "Ealasaid needs you here. You know more about the faie than most others. You can keep Garenoch safe."

He reached out as if to touch her hair, then dropped his hand, giving her that cursed space.

She felt such a fool. She took his hand, enjoying the hint of surprise in the slight widening of his eyes. "Kai doesn't have anyone to watch his back. Not like Finn has in Iseult." She gritted her teeth, then relaxed her jaw. "And not like I have in you," she finished. "I must face this with him. He is more traumatized by his time with the Dearg Due than he will admit."

Eywen's fingers laced with hers. His hand, impossibly smooth for a swordsman's, was warm and real in her own. "You are a good friend."

She laughed half-heartedly. "That's about all I'm good for, it seems."

His expression remained serious. "Listen to your instincts. You may try to ignore your gifts, but you see more than others do. It is a blessing. Do not hide from it."

She was too tired to argue. Not physically tired, but tired of everything else. She missed traveling the countryside with Kai in a time before the faie had returned. Before gods and dragons. Before *Finn*. She had an odd sort of love for the tree-brained woman, but there was no arguing that Finn had changed her life forever. She'd also saved it a time or two, so she supposed she couldn't continue being sour about it all.

Eywen watched her closely, looking for some hint of her mood. He was profoundly skilled at noticing the slightest change of expression, the barest sag of the shoulders, or straightening of the spine.

She turned to fully face him, stepped forward, and leaned her forehead against his chest.

He didn't move. She wasn't even sure if he was breathing.

"Don't get any strange ideas. It's just that I'm venturing into the forests from which most do not return. Kai and I will be with Finn, and Naoki will be nearby, but I'm a realist at heart. You and I . . . may never see each other again."

His hand cradled the back of her head, the other lowered to her back. "We will see each other again. Fate did not bring me to you, just to see us part."

"I don't believe in fate."

"I have enough belief for the both of us."

Remaining close, she turned her gaze up to him. "You'll grow tired of waiting eventually."

He stroked her hair. "Anna, I was a prisoner to the Snow Queen for centuries. I was locked in an eternal slumber with nothing to do but wait."

She smirked. "So what are you trying to say?"

"That I'm very good at waiting."

Their eyes locked, and she wasn't sure what else to say.

"May I have a kiss, since we must part?"

His words startled her. She wanted to look away to

hide her blush, but couldn't quite manage. She was utterly confident in other areas of her life. She could venture into battle without fear—she'd stolen from nobles, escaped the hangman's noose, faced faie and dragons—so why did Eywen make her so humiliatingly nervous?

At her expression, he stepped back. "I should not have asked."

Her heart lurched. She did not want him to step back. Perhaps he was not as adept at reading people as she thought. She closed the space between them, then tilted her head upward. It was the most she could manage.

He hesitated for a moment, then gently pulled her close, and lowered his lips to hers.

As their lips met, lightning crackled through her. Not her first love, Yaric, nor any man or woman who'd flitted through her life in between, had *ever* made her feel like that.

It was absolutely terrifying.

Eywen was the first to pull away. His sapphire eyes sparkled, and she wasn't positive, given his skin tone, but she was quite sure he was flushed.

It made her smile. He might fluster her to no end, but perhaps she flustered *him* more than he let on.

His palms slid from her waist to take both her hands in his. "May I see you off in the morning?"

Her words felt oddly distant. "I'm sure you'll be there no matter what I say."

He raised one hand to his lips, dusting her knuckles with kisses.

Alright, she was wrong. *She* was the only one flustered. She tried to be brave, but soon had to avert her gaze.

Eywen lowered her hand, then stepped away. "I'll see you at first light." His words were cheerful, almost as if he found her amusing.

How terribly vexing. "If you must," she said as he walked toward the door.

She'd meant to leave her back to him as he departed, but turned at the last moment.

He held the door open, but had turned back too. Their eyes met.

She glowered. "You know you're infuriating, don't you?"

"My dear Anna, don't mistake one emotion for another." He exited and shut the door.

She was left blinking after him, her heart fluttering. Suddenly she regretted that she must leave in the morning. She was beginning to *need* him, and that simply wouldn't do.

She didn't need anyone, and no one needed her.

She knew the words were no longer true. She needed quite a few people, and for some reason, they felt the same. She was wanted here amongst her friends, and by Eywen.

What a lot of idiots.

Ealasaid

Ealasaid's curly blonde hair gleamed as she walked past a candlelit wall sconce in the hall of an estate back building, the one filled with all her friends. She was bone-tired, but she couldn't rest just yet. She passed a small window and glanced out at the east end of the courtyard, spying the structure where the original estate owners, Lord Gwrtheryn and Lady Síoda, now lived. She wouldn't venture within *that* structure for all the honey bannocks in the land, and the pair seemed to feel the same way about her. They hated magic, and the faie, *and* the dragon in their courtyard, but they'd been kept safe. It was more than most could say.

She reached Finn's door and was about to knock, but realized it was open just a crack. Afraid something was amiss, she pushed it open, her magic just a thought away.

The room within was empty, lit only by a glass lantern by the bed. The door to the adjoining balcony stood open, revealing only star-speckled blackness.

Keeping her steps light in case there really was an intruder, she walked across the room and peeked out.

Finn stood alone, wrapped in a gray woolen blanket, her gaze distant. She looked somehow harsh in the moonlight. Different than how she used to be. She was just as kind as ever, but the day she'd rescued Naoki, she returned with something *sharp* about her. Ealasaid cringed, hating to admit, she'd avoided Finn because of it.

She was quite sure she hadn't made a sound, but Finn abruptly turned toward her.

She stepped fully out onto the balcony, bracing herself against the biting air. "I wanted to bid you a proper farewell now, since it's sure to be chaos in the morning."

Were Finn's eyes glinting in the moonlight, or was she seeing things? No one else seemed to sense this massive change in the woman that for so long they'd called friend. If they did, they surely hadn't voiced it.

Finn smiled softly, easing Ealasaid's tension. "I appreciate you coming. We've had little time to talk, and I know you're busy with the mages. And with Elias."

The mention of her son warmed her heart. It always did. "There does always seem to be one emergency or another. It's exhausting."

Finn wrapped her blanket more snugly around her shoulders. She seemed nervous, which in turn raised Ealasaid's hackles.

Finn chewed her lip, fidgeting for a moment, then blurted, "I've been meaning to apologize."

Ealasaid's jaw gaped, but before she could reply, Finn finally made eye contact, halting the words on her tongue.

"I've been avoiding you," Finn sighed, "and I didn't mean to."

Ealasaid could barely breathe, fearing Finn had seen the hesitance in her eyes, reflecting her true thoughts. Was she about to be confronted?

Finn went on, "It's just that, it's hard sometimes, being around a child, seeing him with two parents ready to protect him. Though I lost my daughter long ago, it doesn't really *feel* like that long, and when I defeated the Cavari, I lost my mother too." She bit her lip, as if she'd said too much.

Ealasaid gave a small sigh, relieved that Finn's words held an apology, and nothing more. She lifted her hand to her chest. "I had no idea you felt that way!"

Finn stepped toward her. "It's not your fault, not at all. It's just something that's difficult to face. You and Maarav have managed something in this chaos that Iseult and I have not. It's simply difficult to face not only what I've lost, but what I may never have."

Guilt welled up from Ealasaid's chest, tickling her throat. Here she'd been silently judging the changes in her friend, when she'd been walking the halls of the estate in real pain. Pain she might not have expressed to anyone until this moment.

She closed the distance between them and rubbed Finn's arm through her woolen blanket. "There's no reason you can't have it too. Have you and Iseult—"

Finn shook her head before she could go on. "It

wasn't long ago that I faced a god and leapt from a tower onto a dragon's back, and Iseult was asleep, under a curse. So no, I don't think either of us have even considered anything more. And with how things are now . . . " she trailed off, turning her gaze back to the courtyard.

"Eala," she began anew, glancing toward her, then back to the courtyard, "something changed inside me when I gave Naoki my blood. She kept some of herself, she remained a dragon at heart, but I—" she hesitated, "I was dying. I was perhaps even closer to death than she."

Ealasaid was utterly still. "Finn, I know you took on some of Naoki's blood, but are you saying you're actually part dragon now?"

She shrugged, her panic seeming to settle into resignation. "The black dragon called me dragonkin, and the other morning, I could have sworn I scented Kai before I even opened my eyes. Things are shifting inside of me. I don't know what it means to be kin to dragons, but I do know that dragons are consumed by the need to eat magic. They are hunters. Bringers of destruction." She stepped forward, bracing her hands against the railing. "I fear what will become of me." She shook her head, tossing her long hair to trail down her billowing blanket. "No," she corrected, "I fear what *I* will *become*."

It was a bit surreal to Ealasaid, having her own fears voiced by the one who'd elicited them to begin with, but Finn didn't need agreement, she needed a friend.

She squeezed Finn's shoulder. "You're still you. You still care about the same things you cared about before, else you wouldn't still be here. And you have the rest of us to help you figure out everything else. Maybe once we find Oighear or Keiren, one of them can tell us more. Keiren has *the sight*, she might know more than any of us."

Finn stood a little straighter at her words. "You're right, of course you're right. And I promise you, I *will* defeat Belenus. I will set things right, but finding the Dearg Due, seeing if I can rein in their magic, and eventually the magic of other faie, is the first step. We have to right the imbalance. There will be no point in saving the land from the gods if there isn't any land left to save."

Ealasaid smiled, though she still felt a bit uneasy. "See? You're still you, and once Belenus is gone, you and Iseult can consider what you both want for the future."

Finn nodded a little too quickly, not seeming to fully consider her words. Still, she replied, "Thank you. I was being short-sighted."

Ealasaid wasn't so sure about that. In fact, she thought Finn was being quite rational in considering the long-term implications of her condition. While she had done her best to comfort her friend, she wasn't really sure if Finn ever would be able to live a *normal* life, because she just wasn't normal. As the rightful Queen of the Dair, she'd been an anomaly from the start, and now she was an immortal woman with dragon blood running through her veins.

So no, she could not say what the future held for her dragon-blooded friend, nor for the man she loved. All she knew for now, was that Iseult was a *very* brave man.

※※※

Branwen

On a rooftop above the balcony, the hem of a black cloak fluttered in the wind. Branwen's jaw grew more tense, having overheard the conversation. These utter fools, focusing on the faie and this blasted imbalance. Didn't they realize that the root of all their suffering was the Ceàrdaman? Didn't they realize Niklas had been pulling their strings all along?

She shook her head. *Just as he'd pulled hers.* When Iseult was cursed by Arawn, it was *she* Niklas sent to meet Finn in that place that had seemed so torturingly like the in-between—where she'd been trapped half-alive for far too long. It was *she* Niklas sent to confront the Snow Queen herself, convincing her that her interests were best served by aiding Finn in breaking Iseult's curse. And when Finn learned that it was *she* who had sent Oighear to break Iseult's curse, she hadn't given that a second thought. However, had she known Niklas was actually behind it, she would have suspected further manipulation. After all, the Travelers never did anything for free.

Branwen gritted her teeth, quelling her annoyance. Niklas had played Oighear just as easily, knowing the Snow Queen would never have trusted one of the Ceàrdaman. But a wraith, someone too weak to harm her, too stupid and human to manipulate her? Well, that was far more clever. Oighear had jumped at the opportunity to have Finn in her debt, but where was the Snow Queen now? Niklas probably knew, but he'd never tell.

Just like he'd never admit to killing her brother.

Branwen crouched down on the roof with her hands pressed against her stomach. Thoughts of Anders demise still sickened her. Niklas was unaware that she knew he murdered her brother. This knowledge exposed him as her enemy, and now she was his. But keeping that secret from Niklas was difficult, so she needed to take him down quickly.

If Niklas' death withdrew the magic which animated her . . . well, this half-life was really no life at all. She and Niklas would both leave the realm of the living together.

She leaned forward, peering over the roof's edge. Finn was now standing alone on the balcony. *Finn*. Not such a great friend, really. Not anymore. She sucked her teeth, recalling the moment she'd told Finn what really happened to Anders, even at the risk that Niklas might have been spying—though she had not sensed him, and she *always* sensed him when he was near—but for what? Finn had barely reacted, not with surprise and certainly not with care. She'd thought Anders got what was coming to him for having trusted the Travelers in the first place.

Casting her thoughts aside, she leaned forward. She waited impatiently for Finn to leave, but she remained on the balcony alone.

"Where are you, Keiren?" Finn muttered under her breath.

Branwen went utterly still, bracing herself at the roof's edge. Keiren had been the one who told her that Niklas killed her brother, in exchange for whatever she knew about Niklas' plans. The sorceress was apparently the only intelligent one of the bunch, keeping an eye on the Travelers' moves instead of gawking at gods.

Unfortunately, neither she nor the sorceress knew what Niklas was doing now. He'd sent Finn after Belenus, but why? The gods couldn't touch Niklas, him not being mortal, and not even of this realm.

Finally, Finn went inside. Branwen rose from her crouch, her black cloak billowing in the wind. At least Finn was finally prepared to act, even if she was concerning herself with the wrong thing. For now, she could continue to watch, and she'd do what she could to guide Finn in the right direction.

She began to turn away, but hesitated. Once upon a time, Finn had been her friend, someone she could have spoken to earnestly about her troubles.

She shook her head, then made her way across the roof. That was a lifetime ago, and they were different people now. Finn hadn't helped Anders when he needed it. She was as much to blame for his death as Niklas. She was needed for now to defeat the Travelers, but once that was done, if Finn perished in the final battle . . .

Branwen's mouth sealed into a bitter line. Yes, if Finn was brought down along with the Travelers, she'd not shed a single tear.

She was about to leap from the roof onto the high wall when a throat cleared behind her. She whipped around.

A tall, thin man stood behind her. Onyx black hair shadowed deep set eyes and a hooked nose. She recognized him, though she'd only watched from afar. The god Arawn.

Arawn stepped toward her. "Greetings wraith, I've been looking for you."

She stepped back, but he was suddenly at her side, holding onto her arm. "What do you want?" she choked.

"The same thing as you, my dear. Now let us be off."

Anna

They departed on an unusually sunny morning, riding straight to the forest west of Garenoch. Anna's hackles were raised in anticipation, despite the ambiance of bird-filled pine trees with sunshine gleaming through their branches. Scouts who ventured into the forest rarely returned, and she wasn't sure her group would either. For it was within the deep forest, after nightfall, that they would find the Dearg Due. She hoped the search would take but one night, and a single encounter, after which they could retreat to the burgh and the relative safety of the walls. She'd rather not venture too far, for she feared there were even mightier faie within the forest than the Dearg Due.

She glanced around, assuring herself none of her companions had been lost, her memories of the Blood Forest still all too clear. Finn and Iseult rode ahead, Kai next to her in the middle, and Bedelia at the rear. Naoki was off in the woods somewhere, doing who knew what. Her nearby presence made Anna feel safe, she could admit . . . at least, safer than she would have without her. The dragon was large enough to scare off most faie, but she wasn't as big as the black dragon, nor the bronze or green they'd battled at Garenoch.

Kai's voice interrupted her thoughts. "Do you see anything?"

She shook her head. She'd been watching the forest for lights, anything that would give away faie magic, but had seen none save the dappled sunlight filtering through leaves and needles.

She absentmindedly patted her gray mare's neck, then froze mid-motion. A hint of shimmering light caught her eye, duller than Finn, but still noticeable. "On second thought, I take that back. There." She pointed past Iseult.

Hearing her words, Finn and Iseult stopped ahead. Finn looked back to Anna, but Iseult trained his gaze in the direction of the lights only Anna could see.

"So soon?" Finn asked. "We're only half a day's ride from Garenoch."

A dark-haired figure came into view ahead. At first Anna thought Eywen had come to accompany them after all, but that hope quickly vanished. This Aos Sí, though nearly as tall as Eywen, was female, and watched them with impassive eyes, bow raised, aimed at Iseult. Anna nearly yipped as Bedelia's horse moved to her other side. Bedelia could be so quiet sometimes. Anna had nearly forgotten about her.

More Aos Sí could be seen behind the lead, deeper in the trees. They were all female as far as Anna could tell, some in tattered dresses and some in loose breeches.

The lead Aos Sí spoke in the common tongue, "We have claimed this forest, mortals. You'd best turn back."

Kai's gaze darted to Anna, the most obvious question clear in his eyes. *They didn't recognize Finn?*

Finn cleared her throat and straightened in her saddle. "As Queen of the Dair, anything that belongs to you, belongs to me."

The lead Aos Sí snorted, flicking her head back to toss aside one of the small black braids hanging near her cheek. The back of her hair hung loose down to her rump. "You do not shine like the Dair. Name yourself."

The other Aos Sí behind her muttered amongst themselves. They didn't seem overly hostile, except for the bow still aimed at Iseult.

"Were any of you at the fortress in the marshlands?" Anna asked, wanting the bow to lower before someone lost an eye. "Surely you remember her?"

"They weren't at the fortress," Finn answered for her. "Eywen said many of the females disappeared once they were free from Oighear."

Finally, the bow lowered. "Eywen?"

Please be friends and not enemies, Anna thought at the recognition in the woman's tone.

"Yes," Finn answered. "He has remained with us since the barrier fell."

The bow dropped to the woman's side, and Anna heaved a sigh of relief. It would have been rather pathetic for them to get killed their first day out, and not even by the Dearg Due.

Some of the other Aos Sí stepped forward while the lead observed Finn, as if memorizing every detail. "You truly are the Oak Queen who freed us from Oighear the White? I know Eywen would not willingly follow any other. Unless you tell us falsehoods."

Anna's horse danced nervously beneath her, probably sensing her burning questions. Was this an old lover, perhaps? "How do you know him?" she blurted.

Kai grinned at her. "Is that jealously I sense?" he whispered.

She glared, but the Aos Sí answered. "I am his sister."

His sister, not his lover, Anna thought, the small pang in her heart disappearing.

Eywen's sister nodded toward the deeper woods. "Now come, you will be guests at our camp. Tell us of your plans, and why you're here, and we'll decide if you truly know my brother, or if you are imposters and must be killed."

Anna watched Iseult and Finn lock gazes ahead. Finn nodded encouragingly, and with a heavy sigh, Iseult dismounted.

Finn was down next. "Lead the way."

Anna looked to Kai, who shrugged, and Bedelia, who'd already dismounted.

Bedelia looked up at her. "I don't see that we have much choice, unless we want to battle them here and now. They outnumber us, and we know how fast the Aos Sí can move."

With a groan, Anna climbed down from her saddle. Though mildly curious to know Eywen's sister, she preferred to just find the Dearg Due, do what they must, and get on back to the estate.

"Bloody dragon," she muttered to herself, "never around when you need her."

Eywen's sister looked over her shoulder as she turned to guide them. "What was that?"

"Nothing."

The Aos Sí flanked them as they walked, and Anna ended sandwiched between her horse and Eywen's sister, effectively trapping her.

Her discomfort was strong enough that she clenched her horse's reins until her knuckles turned white.

The Aos Sí cleared her throat, then once she had Anna's attention, asked, "How do you know my brother?"

Oh, what to say? Anna opened her mouth, then closed it. *Friend* didn't seem the right word.

"They're lovers," Kai answered from the other side of her horse.

"We are not," she hissed. "Just, something in between."

The Aos Sí lifted her highly arched black brows at her. Now that she was so near, Anna could see a slight resemblance to Eywen in the gentle slope of the nose, and the arches of the lips. Lips that were now grinning.

"Lovers? Truly? I never thought I'd see the day Eywen thought of anything besides service to one queen or another." Seeming to note Anna's blush, the Aos Sí nodded to herself. "Well then, I suppose we should get to know each other."

Anna was glad Finn and the others had begun conversing with the other Aos Sí, and thus would not likely overhear the embarrassing conversation. "Eywen never mentioned a sister."

"It hardly matters. We've been separated for centuries. Oighear favored the male warriors, and treated the rest of us poorly. He probably doesn't even remember he has a sister."

"Then why get to know me?"

She grinned. "I didn't say I didn't still *care,* and I never thought in a million years he'd end up with a human woman." She narrowed her eyes. "Though you're not quite human, are you?"

"I am human," she grumbled, glad Kai was talking to one of the other Aos Sí and could not interrupt.

"Have you bonded with him?"

She assumed *bonded* meant what Eywen had once mentioned. It was something akin to what Finn had done with Iseult and Kai. Sharing blood and immortality in exchange for becoming a bit more human. Eywen had offered her such an exchange willingly, but she was inhuman enough as it was. She didn't need to feel any stranger.

"Ah," the woman observed, "not quite to that point yet, eh?"

Anna's face burned furiously. "What is your name?"

The Aos Sí laughed. "Alright, I'll let it go. My name is Syrel."

"I'm Anna. How far is your camp?"

Syrel's eyes glittered with good humor, much unlike the other female Aos Sí Anna had encountered. Those who'd suffered Oighear's torments all seemed a bit . . . odd. They rarely spoke, and glared openly at any who tried to engage them.

"Not far." She gestured to the forest ahead.

Anna would have noticed the camp herself had Syrel not distracted her. There was more magic ahead —more Aos Sí—but not as many as she'd feared. In addition to the ten surrounding them, likely only a handful more, judging by their faint glow of magic.

"You'll be safer here than anywhere else in the forest," Syrel explained. "The lesser faie do not bother us. I won't let anything happen to Eywen's *lover*."

Anna stared at her boots as she walked. "I'm not his lover."

"If you say so."

Anna could hear Kai snickering on the other side of her horse. She'd be sure to give him a good smack once they were alone, that was, if they made it out of the forest alive.

Bedelia

Bedelia's nerves were as tightly strung as Syrel's bow. She sat rigidly on a roughly hewn log, dragged close to one of several fires. Most of the Aos Sí in the camp glared at them coldly, though a few had warmed up, if not as much as Syrel. Apparently Syrel's conversation with Anna had satisfied her that they were who they said they were, but now she seemed set on wringing every last bit of information out of them.

Bedelia stared down at the alcoholic beverage she'd been given in a tiny, roughly carved wooden cup. The liquid was reddish brown, and had probably been fermented in a hollowed out stump. It was slightly sweet, but burned all the way down. After the first sip, she'd decided on politely holding it until she found a moment to dump it in a shrub.

Syrel had been stunned to learn their group sought the Dearg Due. Her exact words had been, "Who would want to spend time with those pale, blood-reeking fiends?" She didn't seem to realize the Aos Sí were nearly as pallid as the fiends in question.

Finn and Iseult now sat off by the fire, conversing with Syrel, and Anna and Kai argued quietly amongst themselves. Darkness was coming, and they hadn't even managed a full day of riding. Of course, if Syrel could help them locate the Dearg Due, they were better off being near the safety of the Aos Sí camp.

Bedelia was so deep in thought she yipped as Syrel plopped down beside her. She'd seen her swill two of the small drams of rotten liquid already, though she didn't seem bladdered. Bedelia would have been off her seat and in the dirt if she drank that much.

"What is your tale?" Syrel asked. Her body was at ease, no weapons in sight. "I've spoken to the others, but you've remained mute."

Bedelia cursed the others for pairing off and leaving her alone. Perhaps she should have joined into one of their conversations earlier. "I've no tale to tell. Finn is a friend. I'm happy to help her in any way I can."

Syrel leaned in toward her shoulder, bringing with her the scent of the forest with a tinge of woodsmoke. "But what's in it for you?"

Bedelia stiffened. "She's my friend."

"But you must have your own goals. Clearly you're an adept swordswoman. I can tell by the way you hold yourself. The swordsman loves the Oak Queen. Anna loves my brother. And Kai is infected by the Dearg Due."

Bedelia's spine jolted straight at the mention of Kai's curse. "W-what?"

Syrel laughed. "You think I couldn't tell? Look at his eyes, the way he moves. It's as clear as day, though it makes little sense to me. Most of the infected turn into slowly rotting, mindless monsters."

Memories of Sativola flashed through her mind, of what she'd had to do. She clutched her stomach, feeling ill, and looked past Syrel toward Finn and Iseult, willing them to come save her, but they were deep in conversation with one of the other Aos Sí. Kai and Anna seemed to have gotten over their argument, but they showed no signs of leaving the fallen log they'd seated themselves upon. Not even the horses would beckon her for care.

Syrel watched her closely, suddenly serious. "I've made you uncomfortable. I forget sometimes that most mortals fear us. I'd assumed since you know my brother well—"

"It's not that." Though really it was, at least in part. "I'm not uncomfortable around you. Just a bit . . . out of place." She was always out of place, wasn't she? And always burdened with tasks which hurt her heart.

Syrel looked to some of the nearby Aos Sí gutting freshly caught fish and throwing their innards into the fire. "I know how you feel. When we escaped Oighear, I thought I'd feel free. Instead I hide in the woods with this lot. Some of them have come around, but most are just broken."

"Broken?" Bedelia asked, thinking how much she related to the word.

Syrel nodded, her gaze on the other Aos Sí. "Most are much older than me. They suffered even more under the reign of Oighear's mother. I think it unlikely they'll ever fully recover. Being around them is . . . difficult."

She was surprised to hear Syrel was so uncomfortable with her own kind, age difference or no. Though she supposed that would be the same as Syrel believing all humans should get along with each other, regardless of their life experiences.

"So now that we've established your lack of discomfort around me," Syrel began anew, "will you tell me your tale? This is the first real excitement I've had in ages."

Bedelia shrugged. "I suppose I cannot tell you because I don't really know. I don't know much of *anything*, I'm afraid. I'm a bit lost." She bit her tongue, surprised at how candid she'd been.

Syrel turned her knees toward Bedelia's, facing her more fully. "My new friend, as long as there is ground beneath your feet, you can never truly be lost."

"You can if you don't know where you're going. If you don't even know what you're looking for. Isn't knowing those things the point of life?"

Syrel grinned. "And here I thought you didn't know much of *anything*. You may not know what you seek, but at least you have the sense to look. Speaking of looking, you should look behind you."

She whipped around. The sun had nearly set, but it wasn't yet full dark. The Dearg Due shouldn't be out yet. Her eyes widened at tiny lights, flashing in unison all throughout the trees and on the ground.

"Faie?" she gasped, ready to reach for her sword.

"Don't tell me you've never seen firebugs."

Bedelia felt so idiotic she could have curled up in a ball and died right there. "Firebugs, of course. I've seen them before." *Idiot, idiot, idiot.*

She turned back to catch Syrel's grin. "You're on edge, it's understandable."

She was surprised Syrel wasn't poking fun at her. Keiren would have called her a whimpering babe for catching such a fright over firebugs. "Yes, none of our scouts have returned from this forest. It has made me wary."

Syrel nudged Bedelia's arm with her elbow. "Don't worry, human, I will not let anything happen to you. Any friend of my brother's lover is a friend of mine."

Bedelia found the statement oddly comforting. She was usually the one doing the protecting, not the other way around. But if Syrel was anything like Eywen, she knew she was outmatched.

Syrel nodded past her. "Here comes your Oak Queen. I believe it's time to go in search of the Dearg Due."

Any comfort Bedelia felt quickly evaporated. It was time to venture into the quickly darkening woods, in search of monsters more fearful than her worst childhood nightmares.

More fearful than the adult ones too.

Finn

Night insects chirped and hummed, filling the dark forest with their songs, oblivious to the danger the companions faced. Walking under a half-moon, shedding only the faintest light, Finn gripped Kai's hand tightly in hers. She would not risk the Dearg Due taking him before she could react. Before her magic changed, they had agreed to leave him be, but now, everything was different. The Aos Sí had not recognized her as the Oak Queen, so the Dearg Due weren't likely to either. Their treaty no longer stood.

Iseult walked on her other side, and Bedelia, Anna, and Syrel behind them. She'd been surprised Syrel had wanted to accompany them. None of the other female Aos Sí were willing to risk their necks for strangers. They remained huddled by their fires, on guard and ready to defend their camp.

Naoki was with them too, though far out of sight. She would come if called, but Finn had done her best to communicate that she should stay away, lest the Dearg Due remain in hiding.

As her boots crunched over dead leaves, Finn looked past her hot breath steaming the air, searching for the shine of eyes in the dark. The Dearg Due could travel faster than most faie, save the pixies. With the amount of ground the creatures could cover in one night, they might be difficult to locate. Their only hope was that they'd see the weary travelers as prey in a forest where prey had long since learned to hide away at night.

She gripped Kai's clammy palm more tightly. He'd walked into the forest bravely, but she knew the fear he felt deep within. Perhaps that's why they understood each other so perfectly. Deep down, at the core of their beings, was fear. If she couldn't drink down Dearg Due magic, they would all perish. Her weakened magic and one Aos Sí would not be enough to save them. Naoki would kill a few, but she was small for a dragon. If the pack—Finn could only think of them as a pack, like wolves—was large enough, there would be no stopping them.

"They watch us," Syrel whispered.

"Yes," Anna replied softly.

Finn focused, and noticed a shift in the air, a slight whisper of power. She could sense their magic too. The Dearg Due were near.

"Why haven't they attacked?" Kai hissed, his words barely audible.

"Assessing the risk," Syrel replied.

They stopped walking. Gripping Kai's hand tightly, Finn raised her voice, "Reveal yourselves!"

Kai inhaled sharply, but nothing moved. Only the sounds of their breathing, and the gentle breeze ruffling the leaves overhead could be heard.

"They retreated," Anna murmured. "But why?"

Syrel shook her head, her skin a ghostly gray in the moonlight, while her black hair seemed to meld with the shadows. "Too close to camp, most likely. They prefer weaker prey."

"Should we go further?" Kai asked.

Finn squeezed his hand for being brave. While part of her wanted to press their luck, she knew patience was needed. "No, they know we are here now. We will return to camp and wait them out." She glanced at Kai. "I have little doubt they will come for you, now that they know you are here. Let it be on our terms, not when we are tired from tromping through the dark woods far from the camp."

"Wise words," Syrel answered, her tone more relaxed. "Let them brood awhile, and we will try again tomorrow night."

Finn hated the idea of waiting another night, but if they could lure the Dearg Due closer to the Aos Sí camp, it was worth it. Anything that might make the Dearg Due hesitate to attack was worth it. She'd need time to test her new magic, time that would already be too little when lives could be lost in the blink of an eye.

The next morning, Finn and Iseult ventured on foot away from camp, leaving their companions in relative safety. It was a risk, but Finn needed a break from the Aos Sí, and even from Kai, Anna, and Bedelia. She could not recall the last time she and Iseult had a quiet moment alone.

Now if only that moment weren't filled with such tension.

Though the air was chill, birds still sang overhead, and flashes of sunlight warmed her cheeks. It should have been a nice moment, perhaps even romantic. "I know you don't want to be here," she sighed.

Iseult stopped walking and lifted a brow. "Why would you think that?"

"You don't agree with what we're doing."

He shrugged and kept walking. "That has never mattered much."

She hurried to catch up with him. "It does matter, you know it does."

He shook his head slightly, his eyes on the patchy forest path ahead. "I was not seeking pity. I know my concerns cannot be placed over the safety of an entire burgh. I feel no bitterness. I only wish things were not as such."

She took his hand. "Just because things must be as they are, does not mean your feelings don't matter."

Finally he turned to her, the phantom of a smile on his lips. "Little good that does me."

She relaxed at his tone and they started walking again, hand in hand. "Maybe once Belenus is defeated, it will finally be the end of this madness. We can both fade into obscurity and live out our lives together."

"I have faith that will be the case, some day. Though I may be an old man by that time, and you may no longer want me."

His words halted her once more. She blinked up at him. "Is that truly what you believe?"

He tilted his head. "I will grow old, you will not."

"You have some of my immortal blood. You may live longer than you think."

He shrugged, then tugged her hand to keep walking. "We cannot know what will be—with any of it—so I simply must hold out hope."

"Hope," she muttered, her mind lingering on the ideal she'd clung to for so long. "Yes, I suppose there's that."

"It is more than most have."

"I suppose it is." She slowed her pace, beginning to feel wary traveling so far from camp. While the Dearg Due would not attack them in full sunlight, there may still be other faie about. "We should return to camp and rest. I want everyone clear headed when we face the Dearg Due."

Iseult dropped her hand as they turned and started back the way they'd come. "Most of us are no match for them, you do realize that?"

The tension they'd started out with seemed to return. Iseult rarely expressed doubt when it came to battle. She stared straight ahead as they walked. "I know that. You can stay at camp if you like. Anna and Bedelia too."

"You know none of us will agree to that."

She sighed heavily. "Yes, I'm not the only one impossible to reason with."

He laughed. She realized it had been quite some time since she'd heard his laugh. Though many others had never heard it at all, so she counted herself lucky. She could only hope that luck would hold.

The rest of the day went by painfully slow. Finn had been unable to rest at all, though they'd had little sleep the previous night. If the Dearg Due were truly clever, they would wait them out for several more days until they were all so sleep-deprived they wouldn't put up any fight at all.

Finally setting off into the slowly darkening woods was a relief—though it was a relief filled with fear and anticipation. She knew the Dearg Due would return to watch them again this night, they'd probably watched the camp from afar last night too.

Finn squeezed Kai's hand. Iseult had been right, none had volunteered to stay behind, so it was her, Kai, Anna, Bedelia, Iseult, and Syrel, walking through the dark once more.

"Stop," Syrel hissed, sensing something the others could not.

Finn stopped. Her pulse thudded rhythmically against her throat as she scanned the trees. It didn't take long for her to catch the first flash of reflective eyes.

It was more than they'd seen the previous night, yet they didn't attack right away, which was a good sign. Maybe they recognized her. Or maybe they just recognized Kai, and were planning to kill everyone around them. Either way, that they'd let themselves be seen meant a confrontation was at hand.

"Don't look into their eyes," Syrel muttered. "They can entrance you."

Long white hair, dull like spider webs, caught the moonlight. The woman who stepped forward wore all black. Shapeless tattered clothing, little more than rags. She walked toward them, stopping well out of reach. The glinting eyes of her sisters could be seen through the trees all around.

"Few mortals walk these woods at night." Her voice was dry, like the hiss of boots through tall grass. She glanced past Finn to Syrel. "And the Aos Sí travel only in herds, afraid to face us alone, though they boast of being great warriors."

Maintaining her grip on Kai, Finn took a step forward. "Do you recognize me?"

The woman's pale face transformed with a menacing smile. "Oaken Queen, Dair no longer. This earth no longer heeds your call, nor do we. We almost didn't recognize you last night, didn't care to kill you."

Finn's throat went dry. It really was true. The faie no longer recognized her as queen. "Then why speak with us now?"

"You are of little consequence to us." The Dearg Due looked to Kai. "You, however, we have been waiting for. Watching, always watching. You are a rare occurrence. Too rare to let go."

Finn jumped as Kai snorted with disdain, though his hand trembled, his fingers tightly laced with hers. "I'm sure any man to survive your curse runs far and long from you. I will continue to do the same."

The Dearg Due's rasping laughter was echoed by her sisters. The sudden eruption of sound made Finn realize all the night insects had fallen silent. Nothing around them moved.

The Dearg Due turned her eerie gaze back to Finn. "Tell me, fallen queen, why have you made it so easy for us to take him? I would like to know before I kill you. My sisters watch the Aos Sí camp. If they come to rescue you, they will be killed."

So that's why they'd waited until tonight. Last night

was just a small hunting party, but now they'd summoned more of their kind. She couldn't very well tell them the reason she'd been stupid enough to enter the dark woods, or they'd attack immediately. Which meant it was now or never. She had to eat their magic. To do just what that dragon had done to Àed. If it could be done, there might just be hope in restoring balance to the land. She could bring the faie back under her control, and grow strong from those who would not kneel.

She focused her senses on the Dearg Due around them, and the forest beyond, searching for any hint of energy she could use. She could feel the Dearg Due's pulsing magic, but it was wholly contained inside them. There were no frayed edges to pull at.

"Finn—" Kai began.

"You will not tell?" the Dearg Due asked, clearly not even noticing Finn's efforts. "Then you will die now."

Her sisters swarmed forward, too fast for Finn's eyes to follow. She held tightly to Kai and focused her thoughts on Naoki. Curse her foolishness, she should have practiced! She was too terrified to risk Kai with a preliminary attempt, and now he would suffer a fate worse than death.

Bony fingers, stiff and sharp like cracked branches, wrapped around her arms from behind, then just as suddenly fell away. She turned to see Iseult's sword tip protruding from the woman's chest. The darkness drained the color from the blood now speckling Finn's sleeves.

She spun around, realizing she'd lost her grip on Kai, but Syrel was there. The movement of her blade was a graceful dance, felling the Dearg Due trying to reach Kai. Syrel's body and blade consumed the battlefield, herding Anna and Bedelia inward. Trees crashed off to Finn's right as Naoki touched down from the sky above, letting out an ear-splitting shriek.

All went still and silent, even Syrel. A rumbling growl echoed from deep within Naoki's long neck.

"Dragon!" one of the Dearg Due hissed.

"Only a small one," another said. "Cut it down."

"She'll eat your magic!" Finn shouted desperately. "Do not come near her."

Several of the Dearg Due laughed, though Naoki's presence had at least shown them caution. "Dragons may eat our bodies, but they can not suck out our magic. We are faie, magic is what we are. We cannot be separated from it. Even in death, our magic will seep into the earth and filter back into our people."

Finn couldn't seem to inhale. Keeping her hand low, she flailed it toward Kai until he took it. Her hand tightened into a desperate grip. She'd promised to keep him from the Dearg Due, and now that promise would be broken with her death. If neither she nor Naoki could steal faie magic, the Dearg Due would feast upon them.

Despite the woman's words, she knew she had to

try. There was nothing left to do, and she wasn't just a dragon. A fraction of her old magic must yet remain. If they were going to die anyway . . .

She dropped Kai's hand, gesturing for him to stay back as she walked around Naoki and toward the Dearg Due.

"Finn, no." Iseult started forward.

"Back!" she hissed. She didn't wait to see if he obeyed. She could waste no time. She had to strike while the lead Dearg Due was waiting, watching with her head tilted like a curious bird.

Finn's entire body trembled as she strode up to the creature. Her air stuck in her chest, rendering her unable to suck in a full breath past her fear. She reached out and placed a hand over the surprised Dearg Due's heart.

At the touch, something dark and slithering was called forth from within her. Something that wanted blood, death, and power. The world fell away in the face of that sudden hunger.

She no longer had to guess at what to do. She innately knew. She pulled at the Dearg Due's magic. It was just as the creature had said, her magic was entwined with her very essence, her life force, but Finn didn't care. She ripped what was inside the woman apart, pulling that dark light into herself.

Her arms erupted in goosebumps at the thrill of it. Her vision swam like she'd had too much wine.

The Dearg Due dropped to her knees, and Finn

went with her, keeping her hand pressed over the woman's heart.

"How?" the Dearg Due rasped.

She didn't die, and because of the close link Finn now shared with her, she knew that to the Dearg Due, it was a fate worse than death. Now weak, she would be abandoned by her sisters. Left to starve in the forest, or to be killed by other faie.

As one, the other Dearg Due dropped to their knees.

Lights danced in Finn's vision. She pulled her hand away, then stood.

The Dearg Due curled in a fetal position at her boots.

Finn tried to relax, but she couldn't seem to focus beyond the surrounding creatures. Their magic called to her. Now that she knew what to do, she was sure she could drain them without touch. Kai and Syrel's magics were a distant echo, not as tasty as the dark faie.

She smiled, a smile she was quite sure she'd never smiled before. "You will swear fealty to me. Bind your magic to mine. The only other choice is death."

The Dearg Due bowed their heads, acquiescing, though it did not please her. She could sense their tendency toward betrayal. They would never truly answer to her, but for now, the knowledge of what she could do was enough.

She could feel her friends watching her. She could feel their sudden fear, perhaps even revulsion. Soft feathers grazed her fingertips. She reached out and stroked Naoki's cheek. She realized that Naoki should have been eating magic like the other dragons, but her mother simply hadn't taught her. Now she had learned, and with that knowledge, could grow big and strong.

Dizziness overcame her in a sudden wave. The world began to spin. She collapsed, and all went dark, cold, and icy around her.

Finn knew where she was the moment she felt the snow beneath her back, slowly dampening her hair as her warmth caused it to melt.

Judging by the hot breath on her face, someone was leaning close over her, but she knew it was not one of her companions. She could sense this man's magic like a second pulse thrumming in her head.

Her eyes opened to a familiar face hovering over her. "Belenus," she said, her voice sounding oddly distant.

"I see you've figured it out. You reek of faie magic. I know what you're trying to do, but you will never accomplish it in time. The land has become too unstable."

She sat up, forcing him back.

He stood. His white hair appeared impossibly soft, though she'd never want to touch it. It fluttered around his silver-embroidered coat, the tiny tendrils dancing with gusts of snowflakes. His blue eyes looked nearly white in the moonlight.

Finn rose, expecting to feel weak from passing out, but she felt amazing. The Dearg Due's magic still coursed through her. "Why have you brought me here?"

"I didn't bring you, you came yourself. And you asked me to meet you, or did Arawn lie? I'd thought perhaps you were ready to surrender. I'd not be wasting my time otherwise."

She'd brought herself here again? It seemed to happen whenever she felt overwhelmed, but why would this be the place she'd come? "I will not surrender. I will defeat you."

"You're making a mistake you will not come back from."

She pushed back her sweaty locks of hair, growing stiff with cold. "Why do you care? You've wished me dead from the start."

He flicked his fingers as if shooing an insect. "You are an abomination. Eating magic like dragons. Those beasts do not belong in your realm."

"Yeah? Well neither do you."

His laugh cut her like rough shards of glass. "Foolish girl. The gods bring prosperity to the mortals who follow them. You saw Sormyr. Food is plentiful. The crops grow better than ever before. The people of the city are safe, warm, and happy. With what you are becoming, you would bring them only darkness and death. Put an end to your madness while you still can."

His words made her hesitate. He was right, she'd seen Sormyr's bounty with her own eyes, but that didn't mean that she would only bring ruin. "You're lying. You're just afraid I'll win."

"I'm not afraid of you, silly dragon girl. I am a god."

She walked toward him, her boots crunching through the snow. "Then why do you stand so far back?"

He blinked at her, seemingly shocked by her aggression, but did not step away. She too was shocked. To be so openly threatening was uncharacteristic of her.

His stunned expression melted into a smile. "I see you're already changing. It will get worse, the more magic you steal. Soon you'll become a beast, just like Ashclaw. Driven by hunger, and nothing else."

"Ashclaw?"

"The black dragon, the one who wanted to eat you, not very long ago."

She clenched her fists. "Then so be it. If it is the only way to restore balance without harming my friends, I have no other choice."

"Then it will be a race." Belenus turned partially and extended a hand behind him.

A woman stepped forward, looking so similar to Belenus—down to the silver embroidery in her white dress—they could easily be noble siblings dressed to awe their subjects.

"Oighear?" Finn gasped. "Why?"

Oighear's face could have been etched from porcelain, her expression was so lacking. "I told you what I was meant to be. My grandmother was a goddess. Belenus has agreed to raise me back to what I should have been. I will reclaim the faie and place them under my rule, limiting their powers."

Finn furrowed her brow. "Wouldn't that be enough to restore balance?" She turned to Belenus. "Why threaten the mages with such a simple solution at hand?"

Belenus was glaring at Oighear, as if offended she had chosen to speak. "It is not enough, simply as it should be. The mages have too much power. They must be culled."

Oighear snorted. "Or the Queen of Wands could simply bind them."

Finn's teeth were on the verge of chattering. With the shock of seeing Oighear, her adrenaline had subsided, leaving her damp and uncomfortable. "Even if she could manage that, it would make them easy prey to dragons. Nothing will be set right if the dragons remain in this realm."

Belenus lifted a hand before Oighear could speak, though his eyes were all for Finn. "Would you give up your precious pet? And the life you have forged for yourself? Lest you forget, neither she nor you belong here. You never have."

Finn was beginning to lose her patience. "Why are we here? What good does it do any of us to argue?"

"As I've already told you, it is your own fault you are here. Your very magic is unstable. This realm closely parallels your own. When you already have one foot in other realms, you need only take a single step to come through, and this one is nearest."

She crossed her arms, not wanting to show him how much she was grasping at every thread of information. "What do you want, Belenus? You will not make a deal, and you cannot harm me. According to Arawn, you are content to sit back and wait for the most opportune moment to strike. So why come to this meeting at all?"

He walked toward her. Perhaps she'd been wrong in thinking he feared her. He stood so close they were nearly touching, gusts of snow swirling around them both. She had to crane her neck upward to look at him, but she refused to back down.

"You must stop this nonsense with the faie," he said evenly. "Draining their magic into yourself still leaves the magic in your realm. It is not what we agreed upon."

She lifted her brows. "So we did have an agreement then, that you wouldn't attack if I could rein in the faie?"

"The time for agreements has long since passed. Continue your folly if you so choose. Gather more magic, and it will only attract the dragons. They will do my work for me."

"Dragons don't eat faie magic, and they don't eat other dragons."

Belenus leaned his head down to hers. "But you are neither. Not really."

Oighear stepped into view beyond Belenus. "Finnur, you know what you're doing is wrong. How can you harm the faie?"

Finn felt her gaze growing distant and cool. Something large and dark swam up inside her. Something that hadn't been there before. "They made the choice to no longer follow me. They brought this upon themselves."

Both Belenus and Oighear stared at her in disbelief.

She smiled. She was tired of being kicked around by gods. So what if the dragon magic was slowly changing her? Perhaps it was finally making her what she was always meant to be. She'd turned her own people, even her own mother, into trees, and she'd do far worse to the faie. She had failed in protecting her daughter. This time, she'd do whatever it took. Even if it destroyed her.

Belenus watched her for a moment longer. "So be it." He snapped his fingers, and both he and Oighear disappeared.

Finn stared out into the cold darkness for a long while after that, waiting for Naoki to find her and bring her home.

Branwen

Branwen's head throbbed, which was odd, because physically, she felt very little these days. She sat up. She was in a dark cellar, lit only by a single candle. Large mead barrels lined one wall, and straw dusted the stones beneath her.

The man who'd taken her—no not a man, a *god*—leaned against a small wooden table, arms crossed over black robes most commonly worn by scholars. "Did you have a nice rest?"

"What do you want from me?"

His dark eyes glared. "To stop your meddling. You're dangerously close to getting in my way."

She stood, brushing straw from her black cloak and wild russet hair. There was only one door that she could see, presumably locked, though it didn't matter much to her. Since she'd become a wraith, she'd become rather good at escaping, at running away without anyone noticing, and at spying from rooftops.

Arawn sneered. "You truly believe you can escape a god? You will remain in this place until I want you to leave."

"And what might prompt such a desire?"

He pushed away from the table and stepped near. "You help me, and once my goals have been achieved, I'll help you."

She gave the room a final glance, but she supposed she had little choice in the matter. She looked to Arawn. "Go on."

"I want Finnur to become powerful enough to defeat Belenus. She has already discovered much without interference. She must not be derailed."

Branwen sucked her teeth, considering his words. "You want her to bind the faie. To drink in their magic?"

He nodded, casting his hooded eyes into shadow. "It is the only way. Once she is strong enough, she will drink down Belenus' magic."

"But why? Is he not your ally?"

Arawn leaned his back against the wall and crossed his arms. "We are simply both victims of the same circumstance. It is not as Belenus chooses to claim. He is too prideful. We did not come here to restore balance. Coming here was our punishment. The gods were content in fading away, but not I, nor Belenus. We were determined to make mortals believe once more, in any way we could. This was before this land was sentenced to death. Due to our previous . . . meddling, the fading gods used the rest of their magic to punish us. They bound us to this land to die with it."

Branwen's jaw gaped. "Why are you telling me all of this?"

"Because I can. I'm quite sure you will see reason and join me. You stand little chance of succeeding on your own. The Ceàrdaman are worthy opponents. Not even I can locate them, nor can I divine what they plan."

She stared at him.

"Yes, I know they are your target. I am not just the god of curses. I know your deepest fears. Your desires. I took no risk in bringing you here, because you *will* join me."

She crossed her arms. "Let me see if I understand. You want me to make sure Finn continues on her path, stealing magic from the faie until she is strong enough to defeat Belenus?"

He nodded.

"Why can't you just guide her yourself?"

He huffed. "She does not trust me. It is better, for now, that she believes I still work with Belenus, for she would only suspect trickery otherwise."

She lifted her brows, not sure what he meant.

He rolled his eyes. "If I tried to guide her, she would make it her goal to thwart me, even to her own detriment."

Branwen nodded slowly. "Alright, so you need me, because you think me more likely to gain her trust. But that leaves one thing unexplained. What's in it for me?"

He rubbed his brow, gently shaking his head, then lifted his gaze. "You're terribly dense, aren't you? I will grant you your revenge."

"But you said it yourself, you cannot even locate the Travelers."

He lowered his hand and stepped toward her. She

could feel his sudden anger like ants marching across her skin. His face seemed to hold a million different faces. Young, old, male, female. "Belenus plans on saving the non-magic mortals. He grants them plentiful crops and safe walls. He desires their worship, for that is what gives gods their power. Once he is gone, that power will be there for me to take, and once I have it, none shall be able to hide from me. You will be owed a favor from the only god in existence. Does that not sway you?"

She realized she was cowering, and forced herself to straighten. "I suppose it's as you say, I don't really have a choice, do I?"

"No, you do not, but it is in your best interest to assist me willingly."

She held out her hand. "All I want is vengeance for my brother. Grant me that, and I will do whatever you ask of me."

He looked at her hand like it was a putrid rodent covered in grime, then up to her face. "Go to Finnur. You were friends once. Convince her you are there to aid her."

"Why? She's already doing what you want."

"Because when the time comes, she'll need to trust me too. She'll need my help to defeat Belenus. Until then, you will not mention me."

She let her hand drop. "Fine."

"Good girl." He turned away, and in a sudden eruption of shadows, was gone.

Branwen took one last look around the cellar, wondering exactly where they were, and how far she had to travel to find Finn. It didn't really matter. Arawn had given her a better plan than she could have ever conjured. She didn't really trust him to keep his promise, not for her sake, at least. But the death of a god would draw the Ceàrdaman out of hiding. Whenever history was being made, the Travelers liked to be nearby to tug at the threads and shape them to their will. She would gladly use those threads to hang them.

Ealasaid

*E*alasaid's soft boots barely made a sound as she paced across the stone floor. Her dress swung gently with her steps. She cradled Elias against her chest, fast asleep. She'd heard horror stories of other mothers with babes up at all hours of night, but Elias had been a sound nighttime sleeper as soon as he was able to go a full night without feeding.

It was well he was asleep now, lest he sense the growing tension in the room.

Standing near the crackling hearth, she turned toward the long table where the others were seated. Maarav, Eywen, Sage, and Slàine all waited for her to speak. Waited for her to make a decision that felt impossible to make—not without great risk.

"We cannot just depend on Finnur," Slàine reiterated. "We need food. Resources. We *must* expand."

Sage glared at her, then swiped a palm nervously over his short dark hair when the glare was returned. They'd gotten along less and less—the general of the mages, and what equated to the general of the assassins

—but Sage was no fool. Slàine could easily cut him down before he could send a stream of fire her way.

Watching them both, Ealasaid shook her head. "I know we must expand, but how? The forests to the west are out of the question because of the faie. To the east, the river and impassible cliffs limit space."

"To the north, then," Maarav suggested.

She looked to Eywen to see if he agreed, but his gaze was on his hands. He'd barely spoken all evening. Was he thinking of Anna, or was there something else she didn't know?

"To the north," Slàine agreed, obviously, since Maarav had been the one to voice the idea.

Ealasaid looked to Sage. "What do you think?"

Sage rubbed his furrowed brow. For someone just as young as she, he looked like he'd seen far too much, and had barely lived to tell the tale. "It's all well and good to say we'll expand north, and with our magic, walls can be erected quickly, but what of supplies? What of food to feed the workers?"

"We'll send a scouting party toward the northern burghs," Slàine decided. "We may be banned from trade with Sormyr, which cuts off the costal port towns, but there are smaller ports along the River Cair. We'll trade with them. We've a surplus of weaponry, and the relatively unprotected ports will jump at such items. While that party is out, plans will begin to extend the burgh walls."

Maarav snorted. "You were cooped up within *Àit I*

Bhfolach for too long. You wildly overestimate the supplies these port towns will have. Even before the barrier fell, they were largely dependent on trade with Migris. Now," he shook his head, "Àed and Bedelia came from Port Ainfean. While the port still stands, and they have not yet starved, trade with other ports was limited. They could perhaps provide us with fish from the river, which we could do ourselves if we protected enough of its banks to set up larger nets."

Ealasaid didn't bother mentioning that Garenoch's river was too shallow to provide enough fish to feed an entire burgh, and he was right, Slàine had spent too many years in the safety of her small hidden city far north, where attacks were few, and fish were plentiful from the sea. Protecting the river banks here was a last resort, if nearby game ran too low. What they really needed was protected land for livestock.

Elias whimpered in his sleep. Ealasaid gently bobbed him in her arms, soothing him. These meetings were always like this. Suggestions made and cut down. Only this time was different. They had to act. They'd hidden within the safety of the walls too long, and she'd overestimated how long supplies would last. Her people were going hungry, having to ration supplies, and it was *her* fault. There was no other choice but to act.

Her body radiated tension. "What about further north than Ainfean? Do any other cities still stand?"

Slàine sneered. "Perhaps the ruins of Uí Néid are still inhabited."

"By reivers," Maarav added.

She remembered Conall and his band of reivers all too well. Fueled by grief for her lost kin, she'd almost been fooled into joining them. She pursed her lips. "You know, it's an idea."

"Reivers?" Maarav balked. "You *do* remember our encounters with them?"

"They are barbarians," Slàine said plainly. "They would sooner cut us down than trade with us."

Ealasaid walked toward the table, then handed Elias to Maarav. Her arms free, she moved toward the open space at the head, then leaned forward against it, palms splayed across the smooth wood. "The reivers are fierce warriors. They have extensive lands in the Northern Wilds, and presumably crops and livestock to feed their people. Soldiers and food. The things we need most."

Slàine shook her head. "You're mad."

Maarav grinned. "That's the thing I like about her."

Eywen finally seemed to startle into awareness. "What of the dragons? It would take weeks for a scouting party to reach the Northern Wilds. A handful of mages away from the protection of the burgh would lure dragons like moths to brightly burning flames."

"Then only mortals will go," Maarav suggested. "If they stick to the eastern woods, they could easily travel undetected. Once they reach one of the ports, they could perhaps gain passage along the deeper part of the river."

Ealasaid smiled at him. Not that she particularly enjoyed the inherent risk of lives in such a plan, but at least it was a feasible suggestion.

Slàine glowered. "Of course, it will be *my* people who go. The only non-mages who are also skilled fighters. Skilled enough to cut down stray faie, should they be encountered."

Maarav's eyes glittered with mischief. "Do you not think they can make it? Have they grown soft?"

Slàine stood with a huff, scraping the legs of her chair across the stones. "Fine. I will prepare a scouting party." She whipped her glare to Sage. "But your mages better start working on expanding the walls and planting crops. I want it all finished upon our return."

"You're going with them?" Maarav interrupted.

Slàine glanced at Elias. Ealasaid was well aware she considered him her grandson, and was reluctant to leave him. "I cannot ask others to go in my stead. I have asked far too much of them already."

Maarav stood, towering over Slàine. Elias all soft and peaceful in his arms was the only thing that kept him from looking utterly menacing in that moment. "You'll do no such thing, old woman. The younger ones are more able-bodied than you, and you are one of the few people we trust to watch Elias when we cannot."

Surprisingly, after a moment of hesitation, Slàine nodded. Ealasaid had noticed long ago how the years had begun to take their toll on her. Her mane of silver hair had begun to thin, and sometimes on cold mornings, she walked like it hurt to move. To those who knew Slàine, these changes had been apparent, but Ealasaid had assumed the stubborn old woman would be the last to acknowledge them.

Sage and Eywen both stood.

Sage looked to Ealasaid. "I suppose the two of us will begin planning the expansion in the morning. We'd be useless as scouts."

Slàine huffed. "Stating the obvious."

Eywen, seeming lost where he stood, finally looked to Ealasaid. "Some of my people could go. I do not think the dragons would track the Aos Sí as they do mages. They seem less concerned with the faie."

It seemed he had missed parts of the conversation, but Ealasaid daren't comment. If he was so worried about Anna, why hadn't he gone with her?

Sage shook his head at Eywen's suggestion. "You have innate magic. Whether the dragons want you or not is of little consequence. You would still draw attention to an otherwise untraceable party."

Eywen didn't argue.

Ealasaid watched him closely for a moment, but he gave nothing else away. She supposed it wasn't entirely her business either way, so she let it go. "Let's all get some rest. We'll get started in the morning."

Nodding and muttering amongst themselves, everyone left the room except for Maarav. Hoisting

Elias up more securely, he approached her, then leaned down and kissed her forehead. "Do not let these new developments weigh on you, wife. We do what we must."

Her shoulders slumped with her long exhale. She turned and stared into the fire. There had once been tapestries with Gwrtheryn's clan crest hanging on either side of the stone hearth, but now those spaces stood vacant. Garenoch no longer had a crest, nor a heritage. Its inhabitants came from all across the land for protection. They hadn't known they'd starve.

She took a steadying breath. "I know trade with the reivers is unlikely, and enlisting some as soldiers, even with the protection we can offer, even less so. Perhaps Slàine's party will find enough trade in Ainfean . . . "

Holding Elias against his side with one arm, Maarav reached out the other, pulling her back against him. "We won't let them starve, Eala. This is simply how things go in wartime. It is not your fault supplies have grown low."

"Isn't it?"

"No. It's not. Most here would be dead if it were not for you."

His words gave her little comfort. Even if Finn was successful in her plan, Belenus still needed to be dealt with. The soldiers in Sormyr still waited, ready to attack Garenoch on his order. She wondered just where Keiren had gone. Though the sorceress had been a thorn in her side at times, she had come to depend on her for insight. Now Keiren's own father was wasting away in the estate, and she was nowhere to be seen. Did she know that he was dying? Did she care that the mages needed her?

Unlikely on both counts. Whatever Keiren was doing, she was acting on her *own* interests, just as she always had.

❦

Keiren

"Can't you move any faster!" Keiren growled, stumbling over loose rocks on her way up the steep mountainside. The clouds shrouding the moon made it difficult to navigate every step.

"I'm twice your age, woman!" Óengus growled back. "And carrying all our supplies besides!"

"You're not twice my age," Keiren muttered, though she knew what he meant. Though she'd been alive longer than him, physically Óengus was older. He would have been a total burden if he hadn't regained his abilities when the barrier fell . . . and if he hadn't been so easy to persuade on the matter of carrying their supplies.

"Do you *see* anything?" she asked, wanting to change the subject before he made her carry one of the heavy satchels slung across his chest on either side.

"Not a glimmer," he panted. "I don't think we'll find them up here."

She trudged onward, her eyes on the distant crest. She'd spotted smoke plumes before the sun had set that day. There was *someone* up there.

She scanned the cliffside above, pondering the puzzle it presented. "There is no magic to be felt in this area," she muttered. "Not a drop. No faie, no mages, *nothing.*"

"So?"

She rolled her eyes, though Óengus could not see. She turned toward him. "So? Does it not seem a trick of the Travelers? To remain undetected by gods, dragons —by you and I?" She hated to admit that Óengus probably *saw* more than her. It was a gift of those with a measure of Traveler blood in their veins, those who originally hailed from Clan Liath.

Óengus stared at her, his silver beard bristling in irritation. "You believe they hide their magic in plain sight?"

"Yes," she said, then turned and kept climbing. Almost immediately her boot slipped on a rock and she nearly fell. She cursed, then kept going. This area—this strange, magic-less area—neutralized her magic too. She was utterly defenseless, as clumsy as any mortal climbing up the steep mountainside. It was a risk coming here, but she was out of options. She'd searched for the Travelers high and low, and had even convinced Óengus to aid her—not that he'd been doing anything better, besides drowning his sorrows in whiskey in Ousepid—but Niklas had eluded her.

She knew if there was anyone who could outwit the gods, who could outwit the fates themselves and restore her father's magic, it would be Niklas. He'd managed to play puppet-master with her, with the Snow Queen, and who else was anybody's guess. She had no doubt he was still playing that role now, in some way.

She *had* to find him. If that meeting was to occur here, in a place without magic, she'd wring his skinny little neck with her bare hands until he told her everything she needed to know.

Her father's life depended on it. He would be too proud to ask for her help. He probably assumed she didn't even know what had happened to him. But she knew, and she would not stand idly by while old age took him.

She'd been unable to bring back her mother. She'd squandered Bedelia's love. She would not lose him too.

inn

The gentle light of sunrise tugged Finn into consciousness. She lifted a hand and rubbed her brow, slowly remembering where she was. Her bedroll was tugged up to her chin, hard ground beneath her, horses snuffling nearby.

Her spine shot straight as realization dawned on her, eliciting a jolt of pain in her skull. She hunched forward and lowered her chin until the throbbing in her head subsided, then, eyes squinted, looked around. She startled, finding Iseult seated to her right, then relaxed.

He watched her carefully with his calm, gray-green eyes. His black clothing wouldn't show bloodstains from the battle, so she wasn't sure if he'd changed or not. "What happened?" he asked.

She rolled her tongue around in her mouth, but it remained bone-dry.

Iseult handed her the water skin laid on the ground beside him.

She took a swill, nearly choking on it. What was wrong with her? She shouldn't have felt *this* bad from a short trip to the other realm. "You tell me first. Is everyone well?"

He nodded. "Naoki remained with us until the Dearg Due departed, though I believe they had no intention of attacking after—" he cut himself off, and for that she was grateful. In the crisp light of morning, she found herself unwilling to face what she had done. "As soon as we returned to camp, she disappeared," he continued, "then eventually returned with you. And that is all I know."

At the mention of camp, reality finally clicked firmly into place. They were still in the woods, possibly in danger. She glanced around across other bedrolls, the smoldering embers of the fire, and a few female Aos Sí off in the distance, standing guard. She looked in the other direction, near the horses, and found Naoki curled up like a cat in a space between the trees barely large enough to contain her.

She stretched her neck to either side, doing little to lessen its stiffness, then turned back to Iseult, deciding there was nothing left but to tell the truth, despite the worry it was sure to cause. "Belenus and Oighear were both there. Oighear still believes she can rule the faie, and Belenus has agreed to give them to her. If I continue on this path, she will once more become my enemy."

"She always was. Her alliance only lived as long as it suited her."

She lifted both brows. "But you trusted her to help us."

"When it was in her best interest. You trust too easily."

She hung her head. He was right. Even after all the betrayals she'd suffered, she wanted to believe people could change. She'd seen so many people change, but perhaps ancient faie queens were not quite *people* to begin with.

"What else did Belenus say?" Iseult pressed.

She told him, wanting to get it all out quickly. Once finished, she let out a trembling sigh. "It changes nothing, except that we must move faster. As I am, I am not sure I could face Oighear and defeat her, especially not with Belenus aiding her—"

Iseult looked up toward the sky at a distant thrumming, and her jaw snapped shut, before opening again to ask, "What is—"

He held up a hand as a shadow moved across the sun, blocking the early morning light. She looked for the source, then her stomach dropped. A massive dragon circled overhead. While she could not judge its color from such a distance, the sick feeling in her gut told her which dragon it was.

"Ashclaw," she rasped.

Iseult was already on his feet, drawing his sword, as if he'd face the dragon on his own. The camp had begun to stir. Naoki lifted her head with an inquisitive chirp.

Iseult looked down at Finn, then to the rest of the camp. "Deeper into the woods! Now!"

Finn felt rooted to the spot as a thousand thoughts coalesced into one solid notion. She had acquired many different enemies, but what was the one thing gods, faie, and mortals alike feared?

Dragons. This one especially.

She launched to her feet and ran past Iseult toward Naoki.

"Finn, no!"

Iseult's words barely reached her. Naoki was already up and moving. Finn dove onto her dragon's back just as she launched herself skyward. She had a moment where it felt like all her organs had sunk to her belly upon Naoki's white feathers, then they were in the sky, cold wind whipping by almost painfully.

She didn't dare look down at the camp, at those calling out to her. Ashclaw had noticed her. He veered off course, circled once, then gave chase as Naoki made for the edge of the forest, her wings pounding frantically.

In Finn's last encounter with Ashclaw, he had spoken into her mind, then left her alive for Loinnir to heal her. He'd called her dragonkin, not his enemy.

Would that truce hold now?

She was about to find out.

Bedelia

Bedelia shot up in her bedroll to the sound of frantic shouts and running feet. A flash of white caught her eyes as Naoki grew small in the sky above, Finn atop her back. Awestruck, her jaw dropped, then instinct kicked in and she was out of her bedroll, tugging on her boots then strapping her sword across her back.

Her next thought was to look for Iseult, who she turned to find rapidly approaching her back.

A rare show of emotion creased his brow. His sword was out, for what little good it would do. "Saddle the horses. We must follow them."

Kai and Anna arrived on either side of her, then moved on, reacting more quickly to head toward the horses. She forced her dizzy thoughts to quiet and rushed past Iseult to aid them.

She had just tugged her horse's belly strap tight when a hand alighted on her shoulder. She turned toward Syrel, already outfitted with her quiver and bow strapped across her back.

She gripped Bedelia's shoulder so tightly it almost hurt. "Let me come with you."

Bedelia glanced around, confused. The other Aos Sí had already dispersed into the woods.

"Wha—"

Syrel's blue eyes were wide, pleading. "Hiding in these woods like a coward is as bad as being trapped under the rule of the Snow Queen. Please, do not leave me here. Take me with you."

The others had already climbed into their saddles. She had to go. "It is too dangerous! We're chasing a dragon!"

Syrel clung to her. "If the world is to stay as it is, I do not want to live in it!" Her voice lowered. "Please, I long to be free. Let me help."

"Bedelia!" Iseult shouted. "Now!" With the reins of Finn's horse looped on his saddle, he turned his horse and galloped off, followed shortly by Anna and Kai.

She pulled away from Syrel and hoisted herself atop her saddle. "I have to go!"

One last look at Syrel's pleading eyes made her decision a split second before she acted. She offered Syrel a hand, then tugged her up into the saddle behind her as she kicked her horse to a gallop.

Syrel clung tightly to her waist, letting out a shout of excitement, followed by joyous laughter. Laughter at heading away from a safe existence and into danger.

Bedelia found that odd, and decided her initial impression of the female Aos Sí was correct. Their time with Oighear had driven them utterly mad.

Finn

Finn clung to Naoki's neck, keeping her belly pinned

low across the dragon's back to avoid being ripped free by the wind. Their aim was the Sand Road past the edge of the forest, where both dragons could comfortably land.

Naoki slowed as they passed the last of the trees, touching down gently for her, but for Finn, the momentum was too great. Her body kicked upward, flipping her over Naoki's neck. Her breath left her as her back hit the hard-packed dirt road.

She groaned, then sat up, wincing at a ground-trembling thud as Ashclaw touched down some ways off. For some reason, her mind had made him smaller —likely because she couldn't quite comprehend how large he actually was—but now she could not deny it as his looming shape cast her in shadow. His glistening black scales, cracked the last time she'd seen him, had repaired themselves. Perhaps he'd shed his skin like a snake, though Naoki had never done so. Of course, she had feathers, not scales.

Ashclaw stalked toward her, steaming saliva dripping from fangs the size of her forearm. One had been cracked at their last meeting too, but was whole and terrifying once more.

Naoki stood over her protectively as Ashclaw's words hissed through her mind. "Brazen girl. I may have left you alive once, but 'tis foolish to believe I'd do so again. Dragons may not eat other dragons, but we kill each other for territory often."

She scrambled to her feet, then placed a hand at the

base of Naoki's neck, worried she'd charge Ashclaw and they'd have no chance to talk. "I think if you simply wanted to kill me you would have caught us in the air."

"I like to play with my food."

He was getting too close. One blast of flame and— "Wait!" She held up her free hand. "I think you'd like to hear what I have to say."

He took one step closer, then sat back on his haunches, curling his tail around his feet. He towered over her, blocking the sun's warmth. "Do go on."

She stepped forward, pressing her trembling hands against her thighs to hide her fear. "What happens to the magic you eat?"

"I thought you had something important to tell me."

"I'm getting there, I promise."

Ashclaw tilted his spiked head, then huffed a cloud of acrid smoke. "I digest it. It sustains me."

"So what happens when *I* eat magic?"

"How should I know? You are an anomaly."

"What if I told you I can eat faie magic?"

"That is useless to me. The faie are not tasty. They are deeply bound to their magic, and so I must consume their bodies. They offer little sustenance. Trust me, I've consumed many varieties."

"What if I could give you Belenus and Arawn? You've had trouble catching them, haven't you?"

Smoke spewed forth from Ashclaw's nostrils as he craned his neck down toward her. "Do you taunt me, girl? I will catch the gods eventually."

She smiled coyly. "Or, I could *give* them to you. Unlike you, I can take magic from the faie. When I am strong enough, I will use it to defeat the gods—they speak to me regularly. If you're willing to make a deal, I will give them to you instead of killing them."

She felt ill at her own words. She was no killer, and feeding anyone to a dragon just seemed *wrong* . . . but Belenus had started this. He wanted her dead, and would not stop unless she killed him.

Ashclaw seemed to consider her words. "What sort of deal?"

This part made her feel more ill still, as it came to her suddenly without time to consider consequences. She hoped she did not regret it. "Protect the burgh of mages from Belenus and his soldiers so that I can be free to travel and consume faie magic. Once I am finished, you will get Belenus and Arawn."

"Or I could just eat you and your little dragon now, and find the gods myself. It is only a matter of time."

She shook her head, desperately searching for a reason for him to help her. "This world is unstable! You say it is only a matter of time, but what if time runs out before you achieve your goal? What if you are forced back to your realm?"

He huffed smoke again. "Me? The mightiest of dragons, protect puny mages? They aren't even powerful enough to make a good snack. Only lesser dragons would bother with them." He lifted his snout, but she could tell he was finally interested in what she had to say.

Her body was so filled with tension she thought she might burst. She needed to finish this before Iseult and the others reached them, for surely they were already on their way.

"It is good you do not wish to eat the mages, because you *cannot* eat them. Eat one single mage, and the deal I offer is off. Harm them, or refuse me, and I will kill Belenus and Arawn in another realm, and you will never get to feast on their magic."

Ashclaw leaned forward, slamming his front talons into the earth. She braced herself against the sudden reverberation. His neck slunk toward her like a snake until his humungous snout nearly touched her face. His breath smelled like rotted meat and ash.

Her body began to tremble against her will.

Naoki breathed heavily, crowding toward Finn, ready to face down the much larger dragon without a hint of fear.

"Fine, dragonkin, you win."

Her shoulders relaxed with a subtle exhale.

"I will protect your mages," he continued into her mind. "Tell them I will come so they do not attack me. You have ten risings of the sun to complete your task. Provide me with at least one god, weakened for the kill. Fail, and I will eat the mages. I will steal their magic and use it to become strong enough to find Belenus and Arawn on my own."

"Finn!" Kai's voice sounded somewhere far to her right, near the edge of the forest. She was out of time.

She heard hoofbeats thundering near.

"Ten suns. Ten moons." The force of Ashclaw taking flight knocked her from her feet. She fell back against Naoki, who curled her wings forward, sheltering her.

She steadied herself, watching Ashclaw growing small above her as she waited. Iseult and the others would reach her soon, and they would return to Garenoch to tell Ealasaid what had transpired. The mages would be protected, so she could venture far from Garenoch and not worry about Belenus attacking in her absence. He would not be able to punish her for rallying the faie despite his warnings, or for consuming the magic of those who would not obey her. Everything would all be alright. She had ten days. Ten days to change everything.

She clung to Naoki, and shook her head. *Ten days* to change the entire balance of the land, bring all the faie under her rule, and capture two gods. She couldn't forget about saving Kai's family, and the others trapped in that secondary realm.

With that thought in mind, ten days suddenly didn't seem like a very long time at all. Iseult was the first to reach her, and it was then that it became clear what a massive mistake she'd just made, because she dreaded telling him her plan. She might have bought ten days of protection, but she might have also bought a death sentence for them all.

8

Bedelia

Since they were one horse short—the Aos Sí women had no mounts to spare Syrel—Syrel rode with Bedelia back toward Garenoch. They kept to the Sand Road, the fastest route, despite the inherent risk of bandits, other dragons, or soldiers from Sormyr. Bedelia's mind still spun from what Finn had done. That black dragon—Ashclaw she called it—was so massive . . . it could easily destroy the burgh. It might be put down eventually with so many mages around, but many lives would still be lost.

She clenched her reins, looking ahead to Finn, Iseult, Kai, and Anna—plotting, as usual. They'd all quietly conversed the entire day's ride. Now night had nearly come again, but at least the torches lining the walls of the burgh were within sight. They would be safe soon, at least for the next ten days.

Syrel leaned forward, placing her mouth close to Bedelia's ear as they both gazed at the nearing lights. "Are we sure it's wise to enter a burgh that's now allied with a dragon? Finn's plan seems a bit mad."

Bedelia secretly agreed with her, but thought it best not to say so out loud. When Finn had divulged her plan to feed Belenus to a dragon, she'd thought for a moment Finn had turned fully dragon herself. "If you remain near Finn long enough, you'll grow used to these things. Much of her life is spent walking along a frayed rope through chaos, above a pit of untimely demise."

"And here I thought power made life better."

Bedelia sighed. "I've never met a man or woman with power who was truly happy. Not once. If you're having second thoughts about joining us—"

Her breath was warm on Bedelia's cheek. "No. No second thoughts. I told you, I will pay any price to be free. The life I've lived thus far, well, it can hardly be considered a life at all. Anything is better than that."

Bedelia couldn't help but be pleased Syrel would stay. She was pleasant to be around, and seemed to actually care about her thoughts and opinions. Not that Finn and the others didn't care, they just tended to be busy with other things.

As they neared the gates of the burgh, she thought of Àed, hoping he yet lived. She was sure he'd like Syrel despite her lineage.

"Do you think we'll see my brother this night?" Syrel's voice pulled her out of her thoughts.

"Are you worried?"

Silence weighted the air, then Syrel spoke, "It's just

been a long time since I've seen him. I'm not sure how he'll react."

She was quite sure there was more that Syrel wasn't saying. Perhaps an old grudge? Had Syrel done something to upset Eywen? Given the character of each, she thought this the most likely scenario, and not the other way around.

"We may see him, but he will likely be quite concerned with Anna."

"He really loves her?"

"I believe so."

She seemed to relax, slumping lightly against Bedelia's back. "Then perhaps he is not the brother I remember. I look forward to meeting his new self."

Well now she was wildly curious. "New self?"

"We all suffered under Oighear's rule, in different ways. Spending so long . . . it changes you. I'm glad to see some of those changes can fade over time, and can perhaps be reverted entirely."

Thinking of her own traumas, suffered in such a short time compared to Syrel and Eywen, she hadn't the heart to convey her doubt that such wounds ever truly heal. You could learn to be a different person, but the hurt would always be a part of you, in one way or another.

Anna

With the horses stabled, and her companions safe in their chambers, Anna stalked through the dark streets of Garenoch. Maarav had pointed her in this direction, letting her know Eywen had been overseeing the construction of a new wall to the east, as far as the forest and distant cliffside would allow. Since they'd come in from the west after nightfall, they hadn't noticed the construction.

Though Eywen would likely be back to the estate soon, she was eager to find him. *Why* did he never mention having a sister?

What else did she not know of him?

She found the group of mages, a few assassins, and Eywen as they were admitted through the gates. The mages shoulders were slumped. She'd learned previously that using magic to erect entire walls exhausted them. Many would sleep through the next day, and some likely beyond that.

Eywen brought up the rear. Despite the black hood shadowing his features, she could tell it was him by the way his tall form gently shined to her eyes alone.

She waited for the tired mages to pass, then went to him.

He noticed her immediately, and waved off the few inquisitive mages who'd noticed he no longer walked behind them.

He gripped her arms gently. "You're back so soon? Has something happened?"

She wanted to embrace him, but resisted, even

though with his features shielded from the humans, it likely wouldn't draw much notice. The non-magic mortals of the burgh had grown comfortable enough with the occasional presence of Aos Sí, but they treated Eywen much like they did Naoki—they wouldn't outright attack him, but they tended to scurry in the opposite direction.

She took a step back. "Finn drained the magic of the Dearg Due, bringing them to heel, and has allied the burgh with the black dragon, but we have other matters to discuss."

Eywen blinked at her, his features barely visible in the ambient light from windows, along with a few outdoor lanterns and torches. "We have *other* matters to discuss?"

She nodded, then glanced around the quiet road leading into the burgh. Her bones ached for her comfortable bed, but sleep would elude her unless she first spoke with Eywen. "Yes, I'll answer your questions about Finn, but there are some questions you must answer too. But not here."

"Have you eaten?"

She shook her head. They'd had some slightly stale bannocks on the road, but little else.

"Then let us go to the inn. We'll each have a nice meal away from the interruptions of our companions."

"Don't you think people will stare?"

"Since when have you cared what anyone else thinks?"

She laughed. However, despite his bold words, his hood remained up when they entered the inn's common room, and he led her to a far corner table, then sat with his back to the few burghsfolk present.

Once they both had wooden mugs of hot herbal tea —peppermint with oatstraw—and sad meals of under-sized trout and brown-spotted boiled potatoes, Anna couldn't quite bring herself to ask the questions she'd been so intent on having answered.

After taking a sip of his tea, Eywen leaned forward, trailing a lock of black hair out of his hood. "We were able to erect a good portion of wall today, but it will take many days to complete it, and far beyond that for any winter crops to fatten the burgh's food stores."

She looked down at her plate, then back up to him. She had not involved herself much in burgh business, too busy with the constant chaos that was Finn. "Things have grown quite dire, haven't they?"

He nodded, his sapphire eyes serious. The other patrons within the warm bustling inn seemed far away and not quite real to her. "No one is starving yet, but if something doesn't change, that point is not far off."

She scraped her fork across her plate, suddenly feeling a bit guilty for not wanting the unappetizing portion before her.

Eywen reached across the table and put a hand on her arm. "While I am eager to hear what you meant about allying the burgh with a dragon, you said you had something you wanted to ask me."

She tried to summon some of her earlier indignation, but it seemed to have left her tired and sad. Her eyes remained on her plate. "We brought your sister back with us. Why did you never tell me about her?" Finally, at a small spark of familiar anger, her eyes raised to his. "Why have you told me almost *nothing* about yourself, when I have told you everything?"

His arm dropped back to his side. "My *sister*? Syrel?"

"What, do you have more than one?"

He shook his head. "No, just the one, I'm just surprised. Where did you find her?"

"You didn't answer my question, why didn't I know about her to begin with? Why do I know nothing else about you? How am I supposed to trust you at all?"

His shoulders slumped. She hadn't meant to empower her words with so much emotion, but it had all come tumbling out.

He met her gaze. "My past is lengthy and very painful, and with the long slumber of the faie, much of it has faded from my memory. Only the time since I awoke, since you and your companions were taken prisoner by Oighear, seems real to me. And you know everything of that time."

"But your sister. She has not faded from memory?"

Finally he smiled, a sad, almost wistful smile. "Though it is true Syrel is my sister by birth, we were never what one of your upbringing might consider a family."

"My upbringing did not include a family, but go on."

He inclined his head, acknowledging her point. "Oighear treated male and female Aos Sí very differently, and her mother before that as well. Lads were trained to be soldiers from childhood on. Women were little more than slaves. I barely knew Syrel beyond our youngest years, and the times I did encounter her—" He shook his head. "Well, I cannot tell you what sort of trouble you've brought to this burgh. Nothing malicious, mind you, but I promise, there will be trouble."

She listened intently to his story, realizing she'd only been looking for a reason to be upset with him. She could understand why he did not speak of his more distant past. "I apologize for bringing all this up. I shouldn't have made you talk about it."

He reached out and touched her arm again. "You can ask me anything you please. Just know, I do not speak of that time because it does not seem real to me. My real life is here, with you, and it has only just begun."

"And it's likely to end in roughly ten days too, if Finn doesn't feed a god to the black dragon."

His eyes widened for a moment. When he recovered his natural calm, he gestured to her plate. "Eat your meal, and tell me everything."

She stabbed her fork into her trout, then ate a bite. It wasn't as bad as it looked. Both the fish, and *other* things. "You should eat too. We're going to be here a while."

He grinned. "I'm glad you're back. I found my

thoughts constantly with you, and was unable to focus on much else."

She frowned. "I was gone less than two days."

"Two days into danger. I would rather not face such worry again."

She blushed, then quickly stuck another bite of fish into her mouth, stifling what surely would have been an embarrassing reply. This life may have been new to him, but it was just as new to her, at least the part where an ancient faie warrior could make her blush like a maiden at her first Ceilidh.

Branwen

Branwen crouched in a dark corner created by two adjacent estate buildings. The trees close to the outer wall had been cut down, preventing anyone from climbing up from the outside, but she didn't need that easy route of entry to move about unnoticed. In fact, it seemed she was *noticed* less and less by the day. There had been a few moments on her way in when someone walking by should have spotted her, but they looked past the space where she stood, as if something compelled their eyes away. Perhaps their minds just didn't want to comprehend what she was, an abomination. Her body should have been long since dead, but remained animated by all the in-between magic now coursing through the land.

Shaking her head, she turned her attention back toward the courtyard. Now was not the time to ponder her mortality, or what might happen to her in the future. She had one goal, and one goal only.

Finally, those she awaited came into view. She'd watched them enter the burgh too, but thought they might feel more secure within the estate.

Finn and Iseult talked quietly, too soft for her to hear, still in their traveling cloaks, but now without their horses, satchels, and bedrolls. Jealousy boiled in her stomach as she watched them, Iseult leaning close, Finn trusting him with her life, though he was a rather dangerous man. Why did Finn get to be with the one she loved after all she'd done? Finn knew who killed Anders, yet she had continued to work with Niklas. She'd protect all of the nameless faces of the burgh, but would see to no vengeance for someone who'd been her friend.

Bolstered by her anger, she straightened and walked across the courtyard, wondering if Finn's eyes would avert from her like all the rest.

She approached their backs, noticing as Iseult's spine stiffened. That dratted man's senses were too keen for his own good. He touched Finn's shoulder, then gestured for her to turn with him. They faced Branwen as she finished her approach, though the way they watched her made her feel like she was walking through thick, slippery, mud. One wrong move and she'd slip into the muck, and might not be able to rise.

As Iseult's gaze was the more intimidating of the two, her eyes remained on Finn. She smiled sheepishly as she reached them.

Neither spoke. She'd expected Finn at least to have a reaction, to wonder where she'd been since their last meeting, but she supposed she really didn't matter to *anyone*.

She resisted the urge to look down at her boots.

"Why have you come?" Iseult asked finally.

She took a deep breath. "I wish to end my cowardice. I've been hiding all this time, hoping things would get better and I could perhaps return to the archives, but things only seem to be getting worse. Some of the archives have even disappeared."

They both watched her, neither acknowledging what she'd said. When had Finn grown so cold?

Branwen hoped her expression looked pleading, belying her rage. "I want to help now, in any way I can. I'm a wraith, I can travel far, and I'm good at going undetected. Please, forgive me my cowardice and let me help." *Or do it because you owe me*, she thought. *You brought me into this mess to begin with.*

Finn's expression softened slightly. "Why now?"

She clenched her fists, hidden beneath her black cloak. "I fear that my family's Archive might disappear too. I can't let that happen."

Finn took a step toward her, compassion clear in her expression. She should have known from the start that family would be the key to Finn's heart. This would be far too easy. She dared a glance at Iseult, and had to resist the urge to cower. Perhaps not *that* easy.

"How did you get into the estate?" he asked. "Did someone let you through the gates?"

Ah, perhaps she'd made a mistake in confronting them here. "I—" she swallowed a very real lump in her throat. "I apologize, it is not hard for me to slip about. People don't seem to notice me. It's how I know I can be useful. Please, just let me prove myself."

Finn, seeming to have an idea, patted Iseult's arm. "We need someone to find Keiren," she turned to Branwen, "do you remember who she is? She must be brought here straight away."

"The red-haired sorceress?"

Finn nodded.

"Alright, I'll do it. Do you have any idea where she is?"

"No, that is why no one else has been sent."

Did they take her for an utter fool? Was Finn just trying to get rid of her? "Thank you. Thank you for allowing me to help. I'll search for her high and low, and I'll report back every so often."

Finn smiled, if it could be called a smile. It was more an upward tilting of her lips conveying sadness and exhaustion. "Be careful."

Did she really care? Branwen nodded with mock

excitement, then hurried off before Iseult could think of more questions to ask her.

Fully within their sight, she scaled the nearest estate building, hopped the dangerous distance to the top of the wall, then turned and waved.

They both watched her, Iseult, like he was considering fetching a bow to shoot her down. *His* trust would be the most difficult to gain.

She hopped down, gripping the outer wall's edge with her fingertips. Her intention had been to wait until they went to their chambers where she could return to listen outside their window, but their soft words carried on the wind.

Finn's voice, "What do you think she's up to?"

Then Iseult's, "It is not important. We must focus on the task at hand. We only have ten days."

Ten days? Ten days to what? Branwen remained hidden on the other side of the wall for a long while, but no more words came. No matter, she'd find out everything soon enough. She had no intention of leaving the burgh. She'd wait, and watch, checking in every few days to gain Finn's trust. According to Arawn, Finn was already on the right path. Therefore, her task was to simply ensure Finn did not stray, and when the time came, everyone would play into *her* plan for once. They might hardly notice her anymore, but they'd all come to regret it. Sometimes the unseen things were the most important detail of all.

Naoki

Naoki stalked through the forest outside the burgh, pleased to be able to hunt freely. When her mother was in the woods, she was too concerned with protecting her to completely focus on the joy of pouncing rabbits and swallowing them whole.

She wove through the trees, then abruptly halted against her will. Something was tugging on her, or maybe she was tugging on it. She craned her neck back to find her rump had become wedged between two trunks. She chittered in annoyance. She'd grown too big to comfortably stalk in the deep forests where the rabbits liked to dwell.

She gave her rump a shake, cracking one trunk until she was loose, then continued on her hunt, wings tucked in tightly to not get damaged.

Her large round eyes caught movement, and the scent of rabbit. She crouched down, waiting for the perfect moment to leap.

The sound of tiny wings, then something fell upon her back. She jumped with a shrill shriek, trying to shake whatever it was loose. A piece of cloth? No, a net? The net pulled taught, pinning her to the ground. She thrashed and spewed ice crystals from her maw, unsure of what was happening.

One of the trees she'd hit with ice animated before her. Its knobby nose and craggy features crumbled the ice coating it. The trow smiled at her. "Apologies, dragon, but the trees of this forest are no strangers to cold."

Naoki blinked at the trow, confused. The tree faie liked her mother, why would they harm her?

More trow ambled into view, and surely more were pinning the net around her. She heard a faint buzzing noise, and felt something tickling her belly, and suddenly the sound of tiny wings made sense. Flashes of color, dulled by the moonlight, danced around her. She snapped at the pixies, but they were too fast for her to catch. She spewed ice all around, coating the trow, but missing most of the pixies.

The ropes continued to wind, and she couldn't move. Soon she was entirely bound with thick ropes, wound too many times for her to snap. Finally her head was pinned, and her beak bound.

She blinked at the trow who had spoken, wishing she could ask *why*.

The trow seemed sad, though it was hard to tell with the rough bark coating his face. "Tree Sister has done something bad, dragon. She ate faie magic. She will come for us all soon, we think. We like being free, and we will not give it up. Once Tree Sister swears with her blood not to harm us, we will give you back to her."

Naoki struggled at his words, but the other trow barely seemed to notice. They began dragging her through the forest, having to stop frequently as she became wedged between trees. She shrieked and cried through her sealed beak, but to no avail. She was too far from the burgh for her mother to hear her. They'd never been separated before, not like this! Not where she couldn't run through the trees and different realms to find her mother once again. She had to fly to reach that other realm, and bound as she was, she could not even walk. If her mother went there . . .

She let out one last muffled wail. This time, her mother would have to come to her. She would come, wouldn't she? She wouldn't let the trow keep her.

Would she?

Late that evening, under cover of full darkness, a red-winged pixie alighted upon a particular windowsill. It hadn't been difficult to find. She could sense the *monster* within, their Oaken Queen no longer. Tiny fingers trembling, she tugged the rolled parchment from her belt, glad to be rid of it as it impeded her flight. She slipped the parchment through the window shutters, waited one breathless moment, then took flight.

They'd taken a massive risk in stealing the dragon,

but they could see no other way. To be bound again like they once were, or to have their magic eaten . . . well, it simply couldn't happen. Every creature deserved to be free. Those with wings, most of all.

Finn

For Finn, the next morning brought with it a relative sense of peace. At least she had a plan now, an end in sight. Iseult had risen before dawn, like usual, leaving her alone in their chambers. She washed her face in her basin, then dressed in thick leather breeches and a gray woolen tunic, a little too big for her small frame. The breeches, crafted by Slàine's assassins—though she hardly thought of them as such any longer—were meant for swordplay. Despite her better mood, she wanted more than anything to feel safe. *Protected.* Perhaps it was because Ashclaw would likely arrive that morning. Or perhaps it was because of what she must do next. Either way, no one would care what she wore, and the breeches made her feel better.

As she ran a comb through her waist-length hair, she approached the shuttered window. She had set the comb aside, prepared to open the shutters, when she noticed a tiny roll of parchment on the stones near her stocking-clad feet. Curious, she retrieved and unrolled it, then scanned the words hastily scrawled on one side. They were almost illegible, as if written by a child.

Her face grew hot as she read. By the time she reached the end, her hands were trembling. She read through the note again, growing angrier by the second. Her body quaked with rage. She crushed the note in her hand, then tossed the crumpled parchment at the wall. It pinged off the stone with hardly a sound.

Forgetting she was yet to don her boots, she stalked across her chamber, flinging the door open before storming out into the hall. She rushed down the stone corridor, not really sure what she intended to do—except murder any faie who had harmed Naoki. The note said her dragon was captured, but alive—she better be alive—else Finn would burn the entire forest to the ground.

She was so blinded by the hot rage coursing through her, she didn't even notice Kai as he came around the corner. Reacting just before she would have barreled into him, she darted aside, then continued on.

"Finn!"

She ignored his words. Nothing must stand in her way.

She heard footsteps following after her, then felt a hand around her arm, spinning her around.

Kai's face held plain concern. "Where are you storming off to, woman?"

She blinked back tears, but wouldn't let them fall.

She liked the anger better. "I'm going to kill every last faie in the forest."

His eyes widened. "What in the Horned One's name are you going on about?"

The tears threatened again. She forced them back. "Naoki. They took Naoki. Did you not notice she is not in the courtyard?"

He tightened his grip on her arm, then lowered his voice. *"Calm down.* She's probably just out hunting."

She wished she hadn't crumpled and tossed away the note. "The faie took her. They want me to swear a blood oath to not harm them, and they will give her back."

His eyebrows lifted. "So your solution is to kill them all?"

The rage returned like a flaring ember in her heart. Molten metal flowed through her veins. She tugged away from him. "They took her!"

He grabbed her again. "Finn, calm down, I think I know what's going on. This is the, for lack of a less silly term, the dragon blood in you."

His words quieted her rage, just enough to listen.

"You got emotional, didn't you? And you didn't react how you normally do. You didn't worry, or cry."

Was he right? Would she have normally reacted in a different way?

He watched her expression shift. "There now, it seems you're beginning to see reason."

Her limbs went weak. What had she been thinking?

If she'd directly attacked the faie, Naoki might have been killed. She fell to her knees, then looked up at him. "How did you know?"

He joined her on the floor in the middle of the hall, kneeling in front of her. His chestnut hair, longer than it used to be, draped forward over one eye. "Because I went through the same thing after the Dearg Due infected me. The Dearg Due are hunters, as are dragons, driven by instincts and . . . hunger. You must not let those instincts entirely overwhelm your rational thoughts."

She blinked at him. He was absolutely right. She was feeling instincts she had never felt before. Well, that wasn't quite true. She felt them when her daughter was killed too. They had always been a part of her, only now they seemed . . . amplified.

Kai watched her cautiously.

Her trembling voice seemed distant to her ears. "When did you become so wise?"

He gripped one of her hands in his, and patted her shoulder with the other. "I've always been wise. Now let's return to your room and get your boots, and we'll figure out a plan to get Naoki back. But first you must meet Ealasaid at the gates. I heard some screams earlier, so I imagine the black dragon has arrived."

Ashclaw. She'd nearly forgotten about him. She let Kai help her to her feet, then they walked side-by-side back toward her room.

As they reached her door, she turned to him.

"Dragon instincts or no, if they harm Naoki, I will kill them all."

He opened the door, gesturing for her to go inside. "I know, and I will help you. But for now, boots, Ealasaid, then we'll make a plan."

She walked into her room and went for her boots. When things were calm—if they were ever calm again —she'd ask him what he'd meant by *hunger*. The Dearg Due drank the blood of their victims, did that mean Kai was craving blood too? Did it mean that, like the dragons, she would begin to crave the magic of others? Was it possible she did already?

Her head spun as she sat on her bed lacing her leather boots. She could still feel a deep well of rage within her, ready to be unleashed. Perhaps this change had taken hold the moment she'd exchanged blood with Naoki, but Naoki wasn't a wild beast, and she didn't steal magic. Why had this change affected her in such a drastic way?

Kai watched her, his expression still cautious, as if he could read her every thought. She turned away from him as she stood. If there was something different in her eyes, something that hadn't been there before, she didn't want him to see it. She didn't even want to see it herself.

Ealasaid

From atop the high wall near the gates, Ealasaid watched the black dragon stalking across the field beyond the western road. He was so much larger than the green and bronze dragons that had attacked the burgh. If he turned against them, she was not sure the burgh would survive.

"This is utter madness," a voice sounded behind her.

She turned to Maarav, his black hair lifting gently in the wind. "What isn't madness these days?"

He lifted a brow. "You are glad it is here?"

Was she glad she'd had to tell the people she'd sworn to protect that a dragon would guard them for the next ten days? Hardly. She'd left out the part that after that, the dragon may well kill them. Yet most still cowered in their homes, and would likely not emerge for many days.

She sighed, then turned her sights back to the dragon, its winged back facing away from the burgh. It did seem to be protecting them, *for now.* "I think the dragon would sooner kill us all, but for the time being, this is the situation we are in. We should use its protection to expand the burgh and plant winter crops, to perhaps even hunt and fish deeper into the woods."

"And if the scouts sent north return with supplies, or worse yet, with reivers, and the dragon doesn't realize they belong here and eats them before they can reach us?"

She rolled her eyes. "Well, perhaps Finn can tell it not to."

He laughed. "You've grown hard, woman. A year ago you would have shrieked at the sight of a dragon guarding your burgh."

She smirked. "Well I have to live with you every day. Surviving that has enabled me to survive *anything*."

They turned at the sound of footsteps as Finn, Kai, and Iseult reached the top of the stone stairs behind them, their eyes searching for the dragon beyond the wall. Ealasaid could tell immediately that something was wrong—*more* wrong than the humongous beast lurking nearby. Finn looked frail in her oversized woolen tunic and thick breeches, with Iseult and Kai twin pillars on either side—though one was a bit shorter, and slightly less stony-faced despite his pallid skin and red-rimmed eyes. Though it was not particular sunny, Kai had his omnipresent black cowl shading his features.

Finn glanced at the black dragon beyond. "Naoki has been taken. Kai and I are going to find her."

For a moment, Ealasaid was at a loss for words. It was not the greeting she had expected. She looked to Iseult for a reaction, but he showed no signs of one. "Just the two of you? Who took her?"

"Who *takes* a dragon?" Maarav added.

Finn still watched the dragon beyond, her eyes never quite settling on the group even as she spoke. "The faie. I will defeat them. Kai and I will bring Naoki back. It would be senseless to risk taking any others when the faie will not be able to harm me."

She wasn't so sure. She'd heard what happened with the Dearg Due, but if Finn faced them again, they'd be prepared. They would not fall so easily. She shook her head. "So Kai will come because you think this is the Dearg Due's doing, and he can lure them out?"

Finn nodded. "I can think of no others who would make so bold a move but the Dearg Due. They will come for Kai, but they will not kill him as they would anyone else." She looked to Iseult as she added, "Having anyone they might kill is more dangerous for me than going alone. I must not be distracted."

A rare flicker of frustration showed in Iseult's features. This had obviously been a topic of argument between them. Frankly, Ealasaid was surprised Finn had won, though she agreed with the reasoning.

Maarav put a hand on Ealasaid's shoulder, his eyes still on Finn. "What of that big black beast out there?" He gestured with his free hand behind them.

Finn shifted her weight in her knee-high boots, clearly impatient to depart. "For the next ten days he will protect everyone here. I advise you continue with your plans to expand."

"And when the ten days are up?" Maarav persisted. "He kills us all?"

She shook her head, tossing her long hair over her shoulder as she stood a little straighter. "I will not fail. I swear it."

Ealasaid held up her hand before Maarav could speak further. "We only have ten days, and we are wasting time here." She looked to Finn. "Find Naoki, do what you must. Just make sure you come back and warn us if we need to prepare to fight a dragon. We did it before, we can do it again." She didn't add that this dragon was twice the size of the others, and she worried the burgh would not survive. It would do no good to worry. All they could do now was move forward.

Finn turned to leave, but hesitated. "We'll return as soon as we are able. Kai and I will try to find the daytime resting place of the Dearg Due to face them while they are weakened. There are only so many caves in this area large enough to conceal a dragon."

"Oh!" Ealasaid said at a sudden idea, stopping Finn before she could hurry off. She hated the look in Iseult's eyes, and the thought of him having to worry while Finn was away. "Find Sage," she instructed. "He should be in the front courtyard with the newest mages by now. Take him with you. I know you do not want to risk others, but he is fast with his fire, and most faie, especially the Dearg Due, seem to fear it."

At her words, Iseult's shoulders relaxed, ever so slightly.

Finn hesitated, then nodded. "Very well." Her eyes seemed intentionally diverted from Iseult. It must have been *quite* the argument. Instead, she gripped his arm for a moment, still not looking at him, then turned to leave.

Kai gave them all an apologetic shrug, then followed

after her, back down the stone stairs and into the burgh.

Left behind, Iseult stood rigid as a pole for several tense heartbeats, then turned and followed after Kai and Finn.

Maarav sighed as his brother's back slipped out of view down the stairs.

"Go on," she said with a small smile, already knowing what he was thinking.

He kissed her cheek, then hurried down the stairs after his brother. For a one-time assassin, occasional smuggler, and a bit of a con man all around, Maarav had become a rather loyal sort. She liked to think she'd had something to do with the change.

She smiled at the thought until she turned around and caught a glimpse of the black dragon, leading her to imagine her husband, her child, and all the burghs-folk below, falling victim to its fire.

She stared at the dragon for a long while, cool wind tugging frizzy curls free from her braid, and fluttering the hem of her dress. Despite her better judgement, she wished Keiren was with her, if only to give advice, as she always seemed full of that. For as things stood, she could think of no better plan on her own than to just wait and see what would happen.

Maarav

Maarav and Iseult walked through the burgh toward the estate, though Maarav could tell Iseult was eager to leave him behind. He was quite sure he knew why.

He glanced at Iseult, willing him to meet his gaze, but his eyes remained forward. "You're going to follow her, aren't you?"

Iseult did not reply, but his stony expression was telling.

"Her plan is wise," Maarav pressed. "Bringing Kai to lure out the Dearg Due is risk enough. I have no doubt if one of those blood-suckers manages to disarm you, Finn will do anything they say to keep you from coming to harm. You will be a hindrance, not an asset."

"She can drain their magic. I've seen it. They will not stand against her, and they already have the dragon's life as leverage."

Maarav rolled his neck, cracking joints stiff from sparring with Slàine. "You have a point there, I suppose. I imagine you told her this as well?"

"She feels Naoki is of hardier stock than I. She is not quite the hostage I would be."

"And yet you're still going?"

"Yes."

Realizing he was running out of time to make Iseult see reason, he grabbed his brother's arm.

Iseult stopped, eyeing him coolly.

Maarav nearly let go at the look. Though he knew Iseult cared for him, brotherly love might not be enough to prevent an attack, not where Finn was concerned.

He spoke quickly. "Brother, you must learn to trust her. Ealasaid is stronger than me, it is something I have had to accept. I can watch her back as much as I please, but in the end I must trust her judgement. She knows better than I of what she is capable, and if she needs my help, she will ask for it." He was glad most the burgh dwellers were hiding in their homes, leaving the street near-desolate, preferring not to be overheard on this subject.

Iseult seemed to ponder his words for a brief moment, then shook his head. "Finn is too self-sacrificing. She would let the Dearg Due kill her if it would save the dragon."

"I assure you, she would not. Can you not see how much she has changed?"

Iseult was silent. Maarav had a feeling he had indeed seen how much she had changed, but was refusing to process it.

Confident he would at least not hurry off, he released Iseult's arm. "She loves you. She will not leave you behind."

Iseult surprised him by actually acknowledging his words. "But if she becomes something else, something else entirely, is that not as bad as losing her?"

"You don't want her to take the faie magic, do you, even if it will save us all?"

"It should not be her task to save everyone. She has never known peace in her existence."

Maarav lifted a brow. "Well neither have you."

"It is not the same."

He sighed. "Unfortunately brother, it doesn't really matter. You and I are mere pawns in this game. We are simple mortals. We cannot hope to outplay the gods. All we can do is support those who can. Do not risk yourself, because I assure you, if something happens, Finn will blame herself. She will utterly unravel, and we will all die. You hope to protect her physically, but that is not what she needs from you, not anymore. Protect her heart, and she will handle the rest."

Iseult stared at him for a long, uncomfortable moment. "Our mother would have been proud of you."

Maarav's jaw dropped. Unable to handle the sincerity of Iseult's statement, he grinned. "Our mother also sold me to assassins."

Iseult did not return the grin. "Thank you, brother."

Maarav watched Iseult as he turned and left him behind. Had he actually managed to get through to him, to sway the most stubborn person he'd ever met from his path?

He was quite sure he had. The world really must be ending. It was the only explanation.

Finn

Finn, Kai, and Sage walked through the forest bordering the western side of the burgh in pursuit of the Dearg Due. Finn hoped they would not have to go far—the worry would probably kill Iseult if it did. It never took the Dearg Due long to track Kai, so if they were nearby, perhaps they would emerge, even in daylight. If not, Sage would lead them to search the nearby caves.

Bringing Anna would have been wise as she could easily detect the Dearg Due magic, but the fewer present to witness what might happen when she faced Naoki's captors, the better. She glanced at Kai and Sage, glad they were her only accompaniment. While she hadn't lied about her worry for Iseult's safety, that was not why she'd willed him to stay behind. Her new instincts might overcome her again, and *that*, she did not want Iseult to see—ever. He'd fallen in love with a much different person from what she was now, and she would not risk him viewing her differently.

Kai nudged her shoulder as their boots crunched across a mixture of needles and dead leaves. "Pay attention now. Sage might be quick with his fire, but you're far more effective against the faie."

Finn glanced at Sage on her other side. He didn't comment, maintaining the drawn out silence. The only sound he made was the gentle hiss of his boots, and light tapping of his long oaken staff, used like a walking stick. She hadn't spent much time with Ealasaid's general, and it showed. They hadn't spoken a word to each other since they'd left the burgh.

Sage stopped walking and pointed southwest. "The first cave is over there, if you would like to search it."

Ah, so he had been paying attention. She'd halfway thought he'd forgotten he was the one who was supposed to guide them to the few nearby caves.

"You know this area by heart?" Kai questioned.

Sage's eyes seemed to hold a bit of the fire he could summon in a heartbeat. "What kind of general would I be if I did not? We may have to flee the burgh with that black dragon lurking outside the gates."

Finn mulled over how to reply. Perhaps her plan to enlist Ashclaw had not been well thought out, but it was too late to go back now. "I'll enter the cave first. You two stay behind and watch my back."

A rumbling voice startled her. "I'm pleased you came, Tree Sister."

Sage was the first to react, lifting his staff defensively. Pixies swarmed around them, tiny sharpened sticks and occasional stolen sewing needles in hand. She knew how fast they could move. They could poke out an eye before one could blink.

Confused, Finn turned to face four trow. Beyond them, more trow were rooted, appearing almost like normal trees, though she had learned to tell the difference. Above their skyward-reaching branches flitted more colorful pixies. "Why have you come?" she asked them. "You should not linger here. We seek the Dearg Due."

One trow's heavy, rough brow lowered over his leaf-green eyes. His companions watched on silently. "You have not come to swear your oath to us?"

"You?" Kai gasped. "You sent her the note?"

The thought was so ridiculous, Finn could hardly comprehend what the trow was saying. Stunned, she waited for the trow's response, no longer feeling safe beneath the shadows of its mighty boughs.

"You have crossed a line etched deeply in the earth, Tree Sister. To rob the faie, any faie, of that which makes them what they are—it is evil. We could not risk that you would do the same to us."

She cleared her throat, silently warring with a waterfall of emotions crashing together in her heart. "You are the ones who took Naoki?"

"I assure you, the dragon has not been harmed. Swear a blood oath to us, ensuring you will not take our magic, and she will be returned to you."

Kai glanced at her, seeming to note her tenuous grasp on remaining in rational control, and took the lead. "How did the lot of you manage to capture a dragon? Just trow and pixies?"

The trow straightened its spindly legs, the only way it could stand taller with its trunk too rigid to bend. "Trow are not so easily felled, not by the cold, nor by gnashing maw or swiping talons."

Finn fought to keep her voice steady. "The trow fear

fire more than cold." She stepped forward, away from Kai and Sage. "I cannot give you what you want. I must restore balance to this land. Return Naoki to me now, and I will allow you to flee. Perhaps you will manage to avoid me in the future."

The pixies darted up for the cover of inanimate trees, but the small group of trow stood their ground, hauntingly still for several drawn-out moments.

Finally, the lead trow spoke, "Harm us now, Tree Sister, and your dragon will be killed. She is not here with us."

His threat made her temper rage. Words spilled from her lips without a second thought. "I will raze this entire forest if you do not return her *now*!"

The trow's eyes widened, but he did not step away. "Just what has happened to you, Tree Sister? You are not as I remember."

With her hands clenched into fists at her sides, she stepped toward the trow. "I will drain the magic from you one by one until Naoki is returned. Send a pixie to tell those who hold her captive, if they wish to save any of you, they will hurry."

"Finn—" Kai's hand on her shoulder didn't feel quite real. She couldn't banish the thought of Naoki's fear from her mind. She was probably heavily bound, her wings pinned, when she never hurt anything more than rabbits and a few of the more destructive faie.

She shrugged Kai's hand away and closed the

distance between her and the lead trow. She raised her hands from her sides. "You will be the first to go."

Pixies swarmed around her, but did not get too close. She could feel bursts of heat from Sage's fire at her back, keeping them away.

The trow's face fell. Tears glittered at the edges of his green eyes, dampening the bark below. The other trow stepped away. The pixies overhead whispered frantically.

"What has become of you, Tree Sister?"

"Finn." Kai's voice sounded behind her. "Think about what you're doing."

It was the trow's tears that finally got to her. If he would have reacted violently, she wouldn't have been able to stop herself. But the trow were peaceful, even kidnapping a dragon had been so thoroughly against their nature.

She looked at the tears leaking down his bark and fell to her knees, shaking her head over and over. Her rage was still there, so thick she could taste it. "I cannot give you what you want," she rasped. "If I do not steal the magic of the faie, everyone I hold dear will be killed. I must restore balance to the land, and I must defeat Belenus before time runs out."

Kai knelt by her side, but it was Sage who spoke. "Why must you shoulder such a burden alone? Why is it your task to restore balance to this land, when you are just one life upon it?"

Her head hung lower. If the trow attacked her now,

she probably deserved it—though she didn't think Sage or Kai would let it happen. "I am the only one who can do it. The only one who can take magic from the faie, and use it against Belenus."

Sage's voice again. Closer this time. "Weren't you their queen once? Can you not use them against the gods *without* robbing them of everything?"

Blinking away tears, she looked up at the trow before her, then over her shoulder to Sage. "Even if they would fight for me, that would not restore balance to the land."

Sage leaned against his staff, seeming unworried the trow might attack, not after Finn's threats. "I'd say that's a problem for a later time. You brought that black dragon to us, and limited yourself to only ten days to defeat Belenus. Let us face that problem first. The rest can be figured out later."

"He's right," Kai agreed. "Listen to him. Think about what you are doing."

She gnawed her lip, considering, then shook her head as she looked to Kai. "But your family. I must restore balance before it is too late for them."

Kai hesitated, then slumped his shoulders and shook his head. "It may very well be too late already, but if they can be saved, it will not be like this. You will save them because of who you are, not what you're in danger of becoming." He offered her his hand.

Her fingers trembled as she took it, then together they stood. She felt ashamed of what she had almost done. The trow had helped her so many times. They were kind and peaceful, and now, they were only trying to stay alive.

She forced herself to meet the lead trow's eyes. "What say you? Will you join me in my fight against the gods?"

The pixies hissed and muttered from the branches above, none daring to move closer. It seemed they were all as wary of Sage's fire as they were of Finn's magic.

The trow took the opportunity to step away from her, far enough that she could not quickly reach him. "Swear an oath to never harm us, any of us, and we will aid you. We want only peace with the mortals of this land. An end to being hunted."

Finn opened her mouth, then closed it. Swearing such an oath would negate the only plan she'd managed to come up with. She was not strong enough to face the gods as she was, not without more faie magic, but could she really have gone through with it in the first place? Could she have survived what she would have become?

Even so, she could not doom them entirely. "I will swear an oath to not harm the pixies and trow, and any who will fight for me. If the Dearg Due cross my path again, this oath will not protect them. I cannot completely cast aside my burden."

Sage moved closer, leaning near her shoulder. "It will not be your burden alone. Ealasaid will not abandon you. We can figure out the imbalance together."

She swallowed the lump in her throat, her gaze on the trow. "I will swear your oath with these conditions. If you agree, return Naoki to me, help me defeat Belenus, and I will not harm you. Ever."

The pixies above cheered. The trow before her leaned forward in a nod, but was not so quick to share in their joy. She could see in his leaf-green eyes that he had seen what lurked inside her, had seen exactly of what she was capable.

For a brief moment, she had seen it too, and it was utterly terrifying.

Branwen

*D*ays had passed, and Branwen watched on. Finn's dragon had been returned, and light faie were flocking to the western forest near Garenoch. The black dragon remained beyond the front gates, biding its time. The plan she'd made with Arawn had been derailed. Finn had refused to steal more magic from the faie, and instead was enlisting them into her army. Did she not care that things were growing more unstable? Was not her ultimate goal to balance the land?

She rolled onto her back atop the roof of the main estate. It was high enough that none would spot her as long as she remained pressed against the slope, out of sight of the guards atop the estate walls near the gates. A corner created by the western wing and the back part of the building created a nice crevice to cradle her body.

She remained on her back for a long while. She barely felt the sunlight on her face. It was as if nothing really touched her these days. She couldn't remember the last time she had truly *felt* it, and the memory seemed to fade more with each sunrise. Would she soon no longer remember the warmth of day?

A shadow moved across the sun. She squinted upward, not surprised to see Arawn standing over her.

"You should crouch down before someone sees you."

Shading his eyes with his palm, he looked out toward the back courtyard. "No one will see me. It is you who should be worried. You have failed me."

She couldn't really bring herself to care. Over the past days she'd sunk into a deep depression, wondering if her vengeance would ever be had. "It's not my fault Finn's too soft-hearted to steal magic from the trow and pixies."

Arawn continued to gaze outward. "Fortunately for you, one end is as good as another. As long as Finn can use them to defeat Belenus, it is all the same to me."

Not wanting to remain flat on her back, but unwilling to hop to her feet like a whimpering maiden, she lifted her upper body enough to lean on her elbows. "What about the balance in the land? Is it not the gods' job to fix it?"

"I already told you why we're really here. This is our punishment."

These gods were almost as infuriating as mortals. "You said this land is dying."

"Yes. From war. Too much power attracts destruction. The dragons are proof of that. War and hatred will destroy this land, and most of its inhabitants."

She stared up at him. "But what about the disappearing burghs? I thought that would be the end of things?"

Arawn snorted. "That, you naive little girl, is the work of the Ceàrdaman. They hope to guide Finnur toward some goal, though what that is, one can only guess."

"The Ceàrdaman do not have such power!" She slapped a palm across her mouth, her heart thudding as she waited to see if anyone below had heard her.

Arawn didn't seem to care. "Silly, silly girl. How can you hope to conquer your enemies when you do not truly know them? The magic of the Ceàrdaman was restored when the barrier broke. It was their goal all along, as you know. They are the ones shifting people and places to a different realm. A realm near enough and similar enough for the transition to be made with relative ease. As these occurrences seem to be centered around Finnur—where she will see them, or experience them herself—I believe their purpose is to guide her along a certain path."

Branwen's face burned with fury. Niklas had told her none of this, which meant he'd never trusted her at all. He'd been pulling her strings, just as she'd thought. She shook her head. As if it could ever be any other way.

Arawn glanced at her, then continued to watch the courtyard. "I'm glad to see you still hope for vengeance. I was beginning to think you'd lost your nerve."

"Never."

"Good." He smiled at something he saw below.

Branwen sat up and looked down. Finn was crossing the courtyard with Naoki trotting happy circles around her.

Branwen turned back to Arawn. "What would you have me do?"

"Our plans have not changed. Gain her trust. I don't want to end up on the wrong side of a faie army."

She blinked, and when she opened her eyes he was gone. She tilted her head, staring at the space he'd previously occupied. So the gods didn't care about balance, and the Ceàrdaman were responsible for the disappearing burghs. She sealed this new information close to her heart. If there was one thing Niklas had taught her, it was that knowledge was power. As long as she knew more than Finn, she could always remain one step ahead.

Bedelia

Bow ready at her side, Bedelia watched the forest, and the crest of the distant rock cliffs jutting up beyond the trees. Tired mages toiled nearby to expand the walls and prepare soil for planting winter crops like hardy neeps and winter squash. She wasn't sure how they could focus on such mundane tasks when the world was coming to an end, but she supposed people must eat. If they survived, they'd be glad crops had been sown in preparation—though Oighear's presence could mean the death of those crops and a critical wasting of seed stores. She shivered at thoughts of the Snow Queen, hoping she'd never return to Garenoch.

Sensing eyes on her, she turned to see Syrel approach, wearing the tan linen tunic and black breeches Bedelia had provided for her. The tan color did not suit her. It made her pallid, grayish skin seem even odder—though she did not seem to care about appearances either way. Her black hair had been freshly washed, and was pulled away from her face in a series of intricate braids, leaving the back loose, and her pointed ears bare.

Reaching her, Syrel stood at her side, her eyes scanning the distant forest. "What are you doing out here? I'd think the massive dragon out front is enough to ward off any malevolent faie." She tapped Bedelia's bow. "Not sure what you hope to accomplish with that."

She frowned. "I'd like to be helpful in some way, and fighting is all I know how to do."

Syrel looped her thumbs in the waistband of her breeches and rocked back and forth on her heels. "If we really wanted to be useful, we'd seek out more of the Aos Sí. An army of lesser faie is fair enough, but the Aos Sí are the greatest warriors this land has ever known."

Realizing she'd already deserted her task in favor of paying attention to Syrel, Bedelia whipped her gaze back to the rock cliffs, half expecting to see figures standing there, watching her in turn.

There was nothing there. Perhaps the dragon really was keeping the burgh safe.

Sensing that Syrel was still waiting for a reply, she huffed. "The Aos Sí no longer follow Finn. You know that. She cannot command them to help."

"But maybe they'd *want* to help. She did free them, after all. Some did not only follow her because she was the Oaken Queen. They could still be made to see reason."

"If that's the case, why hasn't Eywen recruited them?"

Syrel shrugged. "He's soft at heart. This is the first time the Aos Sí have experienced free will. As their former general, he probably doesn't want to take it away from them."

Syrel gasped, then held a hand to her heart, startled by someone walking up behind them.

Bedelia lifted her bow and whipped it around, then quickly lowered it. Eywen stood just a few paces away.

"I have looked for the other Aos Sí, actually," Eywen explained. "I cannot find them. None of our scouts who have actually returned have seen any trace of them." He eyed Syrel. "Which is why I was so surprised to see you, Syrel. You've done a fine job of avoiding me since your arrival."

Gnawing her lip, Syrel glanced at Bedelia, before turning back to Eywen. "I was hoping to prove myself invaluable before you could ask me to leave."

"Why would I ask you to leave?"

Shrugging, Syrel looked down at her boots, then seemed to force her eyes to meet his. "That's what you've always done."

They seemed to have forgotten Bedelia was even there. Eywen's mouth twitched into a brief frown. "For your own safety, you know that."

"You mean for the safety of *others*," Syrel corrected. "It was only one time, and it was an accident."

Now Bedelia was more confused than ever. All she could be sure of, was that this reunion was not something she was meant to witness. Eywen had seen his chance to corner Syrel, and he had taken it, regardless of her presence.

Eywen watched his sister for a long moment. "I suppose you will believe as you choose. I am not here to ask you to leave, but know this, should you cause mischief within this burgh, or should you have any hidden motives, you will be punished. I find it odd that you would so easily leave those you've traveled with since Oighear lost her hold."

Looking down, Syrel muttered. "I've never been one to frolic with the herd. You know that."

He smirked, and some of the tension of the moment seemed to ease. "Yes, I'm well aware. Now you should probably find some way to make yourself useful, and stop distracting Bedelia from her task."

Bedelia looked between the two of them, nervous to have attention drawn to her. She really should have walked away from the start.

At least Syrel didn't seem angry. With a quick nod, she smiled at Bedelia, then hurried off, not even sparing a formal farewell.

Bedelia watched her back as she retreated, wishing she had stayed.

Eywen cleared his throat, drawing her eye. "I do not know you well, but a word of warning. Syrel cares only for herself. She is not a bad sort, not really, but any who choose to care for her will be cast aside whenever it suits her."

She furrowed her brow. "Who says I care for her?"

He smiled softly, a knowing look in his eyes, then turned and walked away.

Bedelia watched him go, then turned back to her task, but soon found it too difficult to focus. She found her heart just wasn't in it quite as much as before.

Keiren

Keiren had always hated surprises. She had not expected to find an entire army congregating past the cliff's edge, let alone an army of Aos Sí. The immortal warriors had quickly apprehended her, and it had not taken much longer to ensnare Óengus, though the fool now had fresh bruises and a bloodied nose to show for it.

She had been wise enough, at least, to not fight the Aos Sí. Not without her magic.

The warriors tasked with keeping guard watched her and Óengus silently. They sat in the dirt side by side, ankles, wrists, and upper bodies bound. It was absolutely humiliating. A swath of red hair had fallen over one eye. With the other she saw only a sea of Aos Sí bodies so thick she could not see to the end of the camp—there were that many of them—and the only other route of escape was back down the cliffside. A trip that would kill them, bound as they were.

Occasionally a female Aos Sí passed, and their glares seemed even more intense than the males'.

Óengus had not once ceased to glare right back, and in between, he aimed his angry eyes at Keiren, which he was doing right now. "What have you gotten us into, sorceress?"

"As if you had a better plan."

"I had no plan at all. You said you could stop all the magic from shining, from searing my brain all the time."

"And I can." It was fortunate his magic sight could not see through lies. She had stolen what he'd referred to as "his shadow" once before, but once the in-between had rained its magic down upon them, there was no containing it.

Óengus snorted, letting loose a spattering of blood onto his silver moustache and beard, then grumbled, "Not if we both die here."

"If they wanted to kill us, they would have done so. Once Niklas arrives, we will be freed."

"Are you quite sure of that?"

"Yes." Another lie, but she was tired of his whining, and she just wanted him to shut up.

She noticed movement in one of the far tents made of dirty canvas, blending in with the bleak landscape and few scraggly trees. The flap opened, revealing three Ceàrdaman in white robes. The one in the center was Niklas.

"He was here all along?" she growled to herself. "That black-livered vermin!"

"Not so sure of anything, then," Óengus muttered.

She had no time to chastise him. Niklas broke off from the other two Travelers and approached. The Aos Sí guards stepped back, making room for him to stand before her and Óengus, his bald head gleaming in the murky sunlight.

"What a surprise," he purred. "I would have never guessed you'd enter a place without magic."

She straightened her spine, wishing she could stand. "I would have thought the same for you."

Niklas crouched down, placing himself at eye level.

He completely ignored Óengus. "Only in-between magic works here, my dear. If I will it into being, I am far from defenseless. Now tell me, why have you come?"

She was so humiliated, she almost didn't answer. "I need your help."

"And why would I give it to you?"

She sneered. "You know how useful I can be."

He rose, forcing her to crane her neck to look up at him. "Yes, that is true, but I need little help these days. You and the three queens saw to that. When you released the in-between magic, I became more powerful than any other."

"Then why do you hide up here, oh powerful one?"

Niklas laughed. "You know me better than that, girl. Why dirty my hands, when others do my work for me?"

"What do you mean?"

He grinned, showing sharp teeth. "Since you will not be leaving this place as you are, I will tell you. We have orchestrated a war. The gods, dragons, mages, mortals, and faie will kill each other. When they are finished, I will be waiting."

She swallowed the lump in her throat. Without her magic, he really could keep her here. Her father would die and she would be powerless to save him. "Waiting for what?"

He crouched again, this time closer. So close she could smell his stale hot breath. "When the barrier fell, we became what we once were, something akin to gods. Gods capable of traveling between realms, of shifting the very fabric of reality. Once war has ravaged the land, those remaining will need someone to guide them. Someone to create a new, and better, kingdom."

She knew the Travelers were mad, but she had never guessed just how far they would go. "And let me guess. In this new kingdom, you will be king?"

"Now there's my good sorceress. I knew you would catch on eventually." He stood, then gestured to the surrounding Aos Sí. "Bring her to my tent for interrogation. Leave the mortal where he lay."

Her arms were grabbed by Aos Sí on either side of her, hoisting her up, then dragging her along. She clenched her jaw, not bothering to fight. If she were to escape this, she'd have to wait for the exact right moment, and now was not the time. Let Niklas interrogate her. It would be a waste of his energy. Though she'd once prided herself on her far-sight and wisdom, now—well now, she was quite sure she wouldn't be telling Niklas anything he didn't already know. She'd fallen far from the woman she once was.

She glowered as the Aos Sí tossed her unceremoniously into the tent, gritting her teeth as her shoulder hit hard-packed dirt. This is what she got for finally growing a heart.

11

Finn

The hard chair back dug into Finn's shoulder blades. The room—meant for newly recruited mages—was far from the comfort she'd grown accustomed to in her chambers. Àed had been offered better furnishings once it was clear he intended to stay, but he had refused them, choosing to spend much of his time in the barren, uncomfortable room. It was almost as if he *wanted* to suffer.

She waited while one of the new mages, tasked by Sage with menial chores, served them hot tea then left the room.

Cupping her hands around her warm wooden mug, she looked Àed over. His skin seemed to sag from his bones, especially around his eyes, the orbs the things least affected by his aging. They still remained a light blue, filled with intelligence—if a little less gleaming than before.

She took a long breath, inhaling the gentle scent of oatstraw and nettle tea, then leaned her back more heavily against her chair. "Some of the scouts returned from the North this morning, but there was no word of

Keiren. Slàine's assassins are venturing further into reiver territory, but it may be some time yet before we hear from them."

Àed sipped his tea, then lowered the small wooden mug. "If ye hear from them at all, lass. I wouldnae depend on it."

She hung her head, her tea forgotten in her hands. "I am sorry. I do not know if we'll find Keiren."

Àed watched her for a moment, his brow furrowed. "Ye know, I regret livin' long enough to see the land in such a state. I would have been wise to pass on when I knew ye were safe. Keiren, I know she'll survive, she always do. But yer like a daughter to me too. I wish I could leave this life knowin' yer happy."

She straightened abruptly, sloshing hot tea onto her hand. "But I am happy! I have Iseult, Kai, and Anna. Eywen and Bedelia. Even if I must lose you, and you truly are a father to me, and my mother is long since gone, I still have a family. It is more than I could have ever hoped for."

"And this dragon magic in ye?"

She winced. She'd needed to talk to someone, and she felt, knowing all he knew, that Àed would not look at her any differently. "I do not know. I suppose I must learn to control it. For now, we have a plan." Her throat tightened. "A plan that must be enacted within the next five days."

They were running out of time. With the help of the pixies, word had spread quickly that any who agreed to serve her would not have their magic drained, and would be granted freedom once the war was over. But there was still much to navigate. Namely, figuring out how to ensnare Belenus long enough to defeat him—but not kill him—so they could give him to Ashclaw.

Àed watched the thoughts play across her face. "Ye should go, lass. Ye've much to do, and ye don't need to be wastin' yer time worryin' about me."

She agreed, she should go, but the thought wracked her with guilt. He seemed so aged, so feeble, she was not sure how long he would last.

Her decision was made for her by a knock at the door. She set aside her tea, then rose and answered it, finding Iseult outside.

He glanced her over quickly, assessing every detail for signs of emotional pain. "Branwen has returned. She's being guarded."

A spark of hope flickered through her. Honestly, she had not expected Branwen to return. Her hand on the door, she looked to Àed. "I asked Branwen to search for Keiren. Perhaps she has news."

He waved her off. "It's fine either way, lass. Go do what ye must."

She watched him a moment, so frail and weak. What if he passed away while she was gone? "I'll see you soon," she said resolutely.

"Aye lass, I willnae pass on while yer gone."

She looked to Iseult, worry clear on her face, but

there was nothing to do for it. He guided her out of the room, then shut the door.

Once they were far from Àed's room, he cleared his throat. "I do not think she searched for Keiren. She is up to something."

Though she felt a bit dizzy, like she was floating, she kept walking. "I agree. I simply hope we are wrong."

"We rarely are."

Her shoulders slumped. She had begun to always expect the worst, and she was almost always right.

Branwen

Branwen waited in the eastern guard barracks, gritting her teeth. She refused to acknowledge the assassins and mages eyeing her skeptically. If only the fools realized she'd come to the main gates as a courtesy, not wanting to startle Finn once again. If she'd wanted to sneak by them, they'd have been none the wiser.

It was purely by choice that she sat in the cramped room, with only a writing desk and chair, with two more chairs across from it, a small window—too small to climb through—and a few flickering lanterns.

She vaguely recognized one assassin, an older woman with steel-gray hair pulled back in a tight braid, and sharp eyes that seemed to catch every subtle movement. Slàine, she thought her name was. Maarav's mother figure.

Slàine crossed her arms over her fitted black vest and shirt underneath, leaning her slender hips against the desk.

Branwen glared. "Is there something you'd like to say?"

"Where have you been all this time, wraith?"

Ah, so the assassin knew who she was. "That is no concern of yours."

"You are here in our estate. It is indeed my concern."

The men in the room watched on silently, clearly deferring to Slàine.

She wished Finn would hurry up. She was beginning to regret her gesture of goodwill. She sighed. "After my brother was murdered and entire burghs disappeared, I grew concerned for my parents. I've been watching over the archive."

The corner of Slàine's lip ticked up. "Liar."

Branwen sucked her teeth. "Believe what you want."

"It's not what I believe. It's what I know."

Why did anyone keep this unpleasant viper of a woman around? "You know nothing of me, or my circumstances, so keep your judgements to yourself."

A knock preceded Finn and Iseult's entrance.

Branwen's shoulders slumped at their arrival, but she quickly straightened, not wanting Slàine to see her relief at the interruption—though a quick glance at Slàine told her she'd seen the movement.

The door shut behind Iseult, and the room fell heavily silent.

Branwen quickly realized it was upon her to speak. She looked to Finn. "I have important information to share with you—in *private*."

Finn stepped forward. She looked small and shabby in her loose tunic, with her unkempt dirty-blonde hair falling down to her waist. "Keiren?"

Noting the hope in Finn's voice, she realized perhaps she should have actually searched for the sorceress.

She chewed on her lip, glancing around the room. "No," she said finally, "but it is still a matter that requires privacy."

"Everyone within this room can be trusted," Slàine cut in.

Branwen gritted her teeth. "By you, perhaps, but not by me."

Iseult placed a hand on Finn's shoulder, some silent communication passing between them.

"It's alright," Finn said to Slàine. "Please leave us."

Slàine pushed away from the desk. "Anything going on within this estate must be reported to its rulers. Maarav and Ealasaid must know whatever information this wraith has."

Finn opened her mouth, but it was Iseult who spoke. "I agree, but you are not them. Now leave."

Branwen would have cowered at his tone, but Slàine just stood there, her face red. "Fine," she said finally, gesturing to the waiting men. "We've more important matters to attend regardless."

Branwen waited while they filtered out of the room, then looked to Finn. "Tension among the ranks?"

Finn laughed, surprising her. She hadn't been sure the woman was still capable of humor. "More like an overprotective grandmother nipping at fingers." She walked around the desk, then leaned against it. "Now what is this information you'd like to share?"

Branwen took a steadying breath. She'd need to speak carefully. Finn might not catch her in any lies, but Iseult would surely note the smallest misstep.

"I was visited by a man claiming to be the god Arawn." She wrung her hands, hoping to appear terribly pathetic. "I was stolen away by him, actually. He held me in a cellar and would not let me leave unless I agreed to help him."

Iseult and Finn locked gazes, then turned back to her. Finn spoke first. "And what did he want you to do?"

"He wanted me to speak on his behalf. He no longer wishes to follow Belenus, he wishes to help you."

Finn huffed, glancing again at Iseult, then back to Branwen. "Help me? He cursed Iseult and nearly killed him. He tried to trick me into sacrificing myself to Belenus." She shook her head. "Arawn is a snake. You would be wise to steer clear of him."

Iseult stepped back and leaned against the wall near

the door, his feathers yet unruffled. "What else did he tell you?"

She debated telling them the whole truth. If she told them the reality shifts were caused by the Ceàrdaman, Finn might go after Niklas immediately . . . except she had that black dragon outside the burgh, and a god after her. Diverting her now might get her killed, then Arawn would not go after the Travelers, and there would be no one else left to help her.

Finn and Iseult were both staring at her, and she'd realized she'd thought about her answer too long.

She let out a shaky breath. "If I tell you something, you must promise to speak of it to no one."

Iseult shifted his weight, looking bored. "You will tell us, or you will be cast out of the burgh. It is your choice."

She clenched her jaw. "Fine. Arawn plans to go against Belenus. He thinks that with your faie army and your ability to drain faie magic, you will be able to defeat him, for he no longer wishes to support his cause. He didn't want me to tell you, lest you believe it a trick."

Another moment of locked gazes. Branwen's heart thundered in her chest. Had she made a mistake? Would Arawn abandon their deal?

After a moment, Finn nodded, then looked back to Branwen. "You will stay within the estate. If you see Arawn again, you are to tell me immediately."

She blinked back false tears, though the quavering relief within her was quite real. "You will let me stay?"

Finn nodded, her gaze distant, as if her thoughts had already turned to something else. She rose from her perch on the desk. "Come with us, we will find you a room." She crossed the wooden floor to Iseult, who held the door open for her.

When both their backs were turned, Branwen grinned, stepping toward them. This had been easier than she'd thought. Now she just had to watch and wait. When the time came, she would only need to decide if she would soften Finn's views toward Arawn, or send her after Niklas. The power she desired was finally within reach. She would steer Finn wisely. She didn't care who else died along the way, as long as Niklas was one of them.

Keiren

Every minute felt like forever. Flat on her belly, wrists bound, Keiren's fingernails scraped across dirt and loose stones. Sweat soaked her silken black blouse and matted her crimson hair to her scalp. Niklas alone stood over her within the tent, but he was more than enough. She'd had no idea just how much power the Travelers had gained when the barrier fell. All this time, Niklas had hidden it well.

With ankles tied and her body wracked with pain, she was unable to sit up, but managed to barely lift her head. "I know nothing you do not know. Why torture me?"

He grinned. There was a sheen of sweat on his pale skin, but despite his exertion, she knew he would not tire soon. "Why not? Consider it retribution for the time I spent in service to you."

She coughed in the dirt, coming up with flecks of blood, then raised her eyes. "Your *service* was lackluster at best."

He stepped toward her, close enough that the hem of his long white robe brushed her cheek. "Are you aware that if I keep you here long enough, you will begin to age just like your father? You should be at the end of a mortal lifetime by now. Should we see how quickly it happens?"

Fear flickered through her. Her magic, stronger than her father's even in his prime, had sustained her many decades.

Niklas cut right to the heart of that fear. "After all your misdeeds, what do you think you will find in the afterlife?"

She licked her cracked lips, coating her tongue in dust. This was what she got for trying to do the right thing. "What do you want, Niklas. Why am I still alive?"

He crouched before her. "I want to strip away the layers guarding your soul, so you can finally become useful. Your magic, the magic of air and darkness, is exceedingly rare. It is one of the few things that could perhaps hold a god in place long enough to kill him."

Her eyes widened. "You intend to kill Belenus?"

"No. I intend for Finn to kill him. When she eats all of that magic," he grinned, "you've no idea what she will become."

She blinked at him. "After everything, it's still all about that blasted tree girl?"

He licked his sharp teeth. "Even I could not have predicted she'd survive this long, or that she'd be capable of harboring dragon magic, but it is all rather convenient."

The tent flap opened behind him, revealing three exceptionally tall Ceàrdaman, their bald heads draped with heavy gray hoods. She saw a flash of dimming sunlight behind them before the flap fluttered shut. Just how long had she been in this blasted tent? She'd lost track.

"Now," Niklas said, "open your mind to us. It is time we made you something different too."

She tried to pull away from his outstretched hands, but she was too weak. Her last thought was of her father, and how she'd failed him. Part of her hoped she'd die resisting Niklas, for whatever he had planned, was surely worse.

Óengus

Óengus sat in the dirt, his back hunched forward to ease some of the pain that always plagued him these days. His joints ached fiercely from being bound, far more than they would have once upon a time.

He was getting too old for this.

How he'd ever thought to charm a faie queen was absolutely beyond him now. Oighear was a fierce woman, and centuries old. It hadn't taken long for her to leave him behind.

He'd never stood a chance.

The Aos Sí around him spoke lowly in a language he'd heard Oighear speak a time or two, though most also spoke the common tongue. They silenced as Keiren's scream cut across the camp. For a heartbeat, all turned toward the tent where she was being held, then slowly, conversation resumed.

Óengus considered inching himself closer to the fire—a full day had passed, and the cold night would soon come—but he had an inkling he'd only be punished and tossed further away.

Keiren screamed again, and this time the Aos Sí hardly seemed to notice. The cursed sorceress probably had whatever was being done to her coming, but his spine still tingled with quiet rage. He'd tortured many men in his lifetime, but not women. The concept to him seemed inherently wrong.

He shifted his weight. As little as he appreciated Keiren's predicament, he should probably start thinking about escaping without her, before the Ceàrdaman turned their attention to him. Did they realize how many of Oighear's secrets he harbored? Did they care, or was she no longer a concern to them?

He watched the Aos Sí, memorizing every weapon, getting a feel for the order of the camp. Beyond that, he could see their dully glowing magic. It seemed their innate essence was not affected by whatever barrier silenced magic in this place. A good thing too, as it would help him distinguish their whereabouts in the dark. Nightfall would be the time to act.

Keiren screamed again, and Óengus winced. Nightfall could not come soon enough.

12

Anna

*A*nna sat in the grass of the courtyard, sharpening her daggers—though they hadn't seen much use recently. Still, it was all she could think to do. With Finn off gathering faie in the forest, preparing to march on Sormyr to draw out Belenus, everyone else was left waiting for the black dragon to attack. The mages spoke little, and the burghsfolk only in hushed tones. She wasn't sure if those outside of the estate were lucky, or unlucky. Lucky, because they did not realize the severity of the situation. They saw the dragon, yes, but they also saw the walls being expanded, and aided in the sowing of new crops. But unlucky . . . oh so unlucky, because most did not have magic. Many were women and children. They might not be on the front lines, but they would die just as swiftly as any mage.

A long hiss of whetstone on metal drew her eye, and she cursed herself for not paying better attention. Eywen now sat beside her, legs crossed, sharpening his sword. She found herself watching him longer than necessary, overcome by the compulsion to reach out and touch his impossibly soft black hair.

He eyed her askance, a small smile playing at his lips, making her realize she'd dropped her dagger to her lap.

Before she could react, he snatched it away and began sharpening it.

"I can do that," she snapped. "I'm particular about how my blades are sharpened."

His smooth movements across the blade did not relent. "Trust me, Anna, I've had centuries of practice."

She bit her lip. Infuriating faie. She found herself blurting out the question that had been burning a hole through the back of her mind. "Will you go with Finn and the faie when they march on Sormyr?"

"No."

She sat up a little straighter. "No?"

He continued to work her dagger. "I will do little good in that endeavor, nor will the other Aos Sí who have remained here. The goal is not to slaughter the mortals, but to draw Belenus out to Finn. My place is here," he finally looked at her, "with you."

She blinked at him, hoping to disguise her pleasure. "You know, I'm not one to sit out of a fight."

"Well if Finnur fails, you'll get to face that black dragon outside the gates."

The thought made her shiver. The green and bronze dragons had nearly destroyed the burgh, and it was only with Oighear's help that they were fully overcome.

Now they would not have Oighear, nor Finn. Only Ealasaid, and she was not sure the girl was up to the task.

Eywen watched her closely, her dagger forgotten in his nimble hands. "You're frightened."

She forced herself to meet his gaze. "Aren't you?"

He looked down at his lap, then lifted her dagger and began sharpening, even though the blade was now perfectly honed. They sat in silence, interrupted only by the rhythmic *schwip schwip* of the blade being sharpened, and occasional gentle gusts of breeze tinged with the scent of frost from the mountains. Finally, he answered, "I have known little fear in my life. From a young age, Aos Sí warriors are taught to not form attachments. The only loss we face is that of our own lives, not of others."

She waited for him to continue, pleased at another small revelation of his past.

He extended the dagger toward her, but held on as her hand wrapped around the hilt, touching his. Their eyes met. "I know that fear now—the fear of loss—and it is greater than any fear I could hope to ever feel. Part of me wants to spirit you away in the night, somewhere far from this land."

Her palm began to sweat around the dagger hilt. Slowly, he released it, and the tension eased.

She sucked her teeth, but her mouth remained unbearably dry. "I told you, I'm not one to sit out of a fight."

"I know, neither am I. I'm just wondering if you've reconsidered my offer."

She didn't have to ask what offer he meant. He wanted to bond with her, to share his immortality as Finn could with others. It would make her harder to kill—but it would also make him weaker.

"No, I will not do that to you."

"It is what I want."

She stood abruptly, dagger in hand, finished with the conversation. "I will not weaken you when the dangers we face are so great. If you die because of it." She shook her head. "The answer is no."

He looked up at her, his face impassive. "That is your fear then, weakening me?"

She sucked her teeth again. Her feet were telling her to run, but her heart would not obey them. "Yes, that is my fear."

"So you no longer fear the rest of it?"

She shifted her weight. She could run to the nearest estate building. Run inside and lock the door. She swore she'd never let herself get that close to another person, not after what Yaric had done. Her voice came out barely above a whisper, "No, I do not fear it. In fact, I *want* it, but I find my heart is too impulsive to be trusted."

He left his sword in the grass and stood, then gently took her hand. "Anna, if you do not trust your heart, what else is there?"

Her fingers twined with his, the movement feeling

far too natural. "There is my mind. It has never let me down."

She pulled away as a group of mages entered the courtyard from the main estate. She hadn't meant to let the conversation get this far, but with Eywen, she rarely seemed to be in control.

She cleared her throat. "Let's go find Kai. I want to make sure he isn't planning on following Finn to Sormyr." She turned and started walking away, leaving Eywen to pick up his sword and sharpening supplies.

"You know, it's his choice if he does!" he called after her.

Anna shook her head and kept walking. She might be a fool, but Kai was an utter idiot. At least the man turning her heart to pottage was in love with her. It was time Kai addressed his own love issues—hopefully in a way that wouldn't get him killed.

Never mind that she was far more comfortable focusing on her friend's heart than her own.

❧

Finn

The day had seemed impossibly long as Finn waited to slip away into the forest to the west of the burgh. When she finally managed it, she couldn't help but be pleased with what she found. Pixies darted around the trees overhead, none daring to come close and land on her shoulder like they used to, but at least they were there. The trow and pixies had done their job well, recruiting all manner of light faie. Trow were rooted all around, bucca hid in the bushes, and blue caps in the branches —their small humanoid forms barely visible through the light of heatless blue flames surrounding them. Even some red-furred grogoch peeked out from behind tree trunks.

There were more faie to come, but would it be enough? The light faie were formidable, but they were not predators—not for the most part at least.

Human footsteps sounded across dried leaves to her right, startling her. She relaxed as Kai reached her side, dark cowl pulled up to shade his eyes from the murky sunlight dappling the ground through the boughs.

"You followed me," she sighed.

"You shouldn't have come alone." His eyes followed the path of a nearby pixie, then glanced about at the other faie. "No dark faie?"

She shook her head, looking for a trow she might recognize. Spotting the one who'd orchestrated Naoki's kidnapping, she strode toward him, her steps light in her soft boots and suede breeches.

He seemed to cower as he reached her, if a tree could truly cower.

She stopped farther back than she had intended. Had she truly changed so much? They had not been so frightened of her when she had Dair magic. She forced her spine straight. "What of the dark faie?"

The trow's brow fell, almost obscuring his leaf green eyes. "They will not fight for you. They feel if they stand together, you cannot harm them."

They were probably right. Just because she could drain the magic from any who came near, did not mean she couldn't eventually be overwhelmed.

"Will we be enough?" the trow asked.

She shook her head. Speaking more to herself than to him, she answered, "You will have to be. We do not need to overcome Sormyr's soldiers. We must simply present enough of a threat to draw Belenus out." *And capture him. And feed him to a dragon,* she added internally.

Kai touched her arm, then gestured for her to walk with him, away from the faie, though she already knew what he was thinking.

Once they were alone, the trees silent around them, she sighed. "No, I do not know how I will capture him, but we must do something. Time is running out. We know he will protect Sormyr. When the faie attack, he will be forced to face me in this realm."

Kai nodded, his gaze distant, settling on nothing in particular. "You need more magic, don't you? You don't have enough to defeat him, and you don't know how to trap him."

She wrung her hands, kneading the hem of her loose tunic. "I fear I am simply not strong enough as I am. How can I hope to capture a god? Not even Ashclaw has managed to corner him. He can disappear in an instant. I need enough magic to hold him still."

Kai looked out at the forest, squinting at the sunlight. "Then perhaps tonight, we should let the dark faie find us. We can avoid it no longer. If they will not follow you, you must back up your claim to drain their magic. Use their folly to make yourself strong."

Biting her tongue against an instinctual rebuttal, she let his words sink in, then shook her head. "You're right. I know what I must do, but do you not think it is wrong?" It hadn't felt wrong, draining the Dearg Due's magic. It had felt right. And that was exactly what frightened her.

"I have no sympathy for the Dearg Due. Be it wrong or right, if it will help you to survive, I will stand beside you. But . . . it is your choice. The dark faie have already made theirs."

Turning to look back at the distant faie, she leaned her shoulder against his. "Thank you for always being on my side. Iseult does not understand."

"He worries for you. So do I. But I understand you have little choice in these matters."

She suddenly felt unbelievably tired. Her knees willed her to slump to the leaves, but she resisted. She could not rest yet. "I fear that if I drink down too much magic I will become something else. Something power hungry like Ashclaw. I fear that if I change beyond redemption, Iseult will no longer love me."

Kai put an arm around her shoulders, the touch seeming to steady her. "That will not happen."

"How can you be so sure?"

"Because even if you became something else, you'd still be you too, and I'd still love you. That is something I can guarantee, so I'm sure it will be no different for Iseult."

His words made her throat clench. She loved Kai too, in many ways.

"You do not need to reply. I know where I stand."

"I don't think you really do," she sighed, though she was unwilling to explain further. "Just know how important you are to me."

He squeezed her shoulders, then released her. "Let's go tell the pixies to spread word to the Dearg Due. Tell them to meet you tonight."

"Do you think they will come after what happened last time?"

He seemed to think about it as they walked. "Perhaps we should tell them to meet me? They've made it clear they still want me for . . . well let's not go into that. But if they think they have broken me down, it may draw them in. Tell them I'm willing to make a deal in exchange for your safety. Let them believe you fear they will attack and overwhelm you."

"I suppose we must try."

She sensed someone approaching their backs, but Kai turned before she did, always a little faster than her these days.

Branwen could have been Kai's sister in her black dress and deeply shadowed hood. Did the sunlight hurt her eyes as it did Kai's, or did she simply wish to not be seen?

"Arawn came to me again!" she blurted as she approached. "I thought you'd want to know immediately. Ealasaid said I'd find you here."

Finn narrowed her eyes. Had Branwen been spying on them? She doubted she'd rush out here with such urgency otherwise.

Branwen reached them, seeming out of breath, though Finn knew better. She was no longer the trusting fool she once was.

"What did he want?"

"He wants to meet with you. A place of your choosing so you'll feel safe."

She resisted the urge to glance at Kai as a new plan formed in her mind. She needed to know if she'd be able to trap Belenus. What better way to test her magic, than to trap a different god?

"Tell him to meet me in these woods tonight, when the moon has reached its apex."

Kai shifted beside her, ever so slightly. Perhaps Branwen had heard what they planned with the Dearg Due, but it didn't matter. All she needed was for Arawn to be near once the magic had been gathered. If her actions turned him against her, then so be it. Perhaps feeding him to Ashclaw would buy them just a bit more time.

Iseult

Iseult rubbed his brow. He'd searched for Finn within the burgh until nearly nightfall, but eventually *she'd* been the one to find *him*. And she'd come to him—come to them all, for after she'd told him her plan in private, she'd included Kai and Maarav—with an utterly mad plan.

They now stood around the long wooden table where they often took their meals, a few candles and a roaring fire the only light as night's darkness overtook the fortress.

"This is unacceptable." Though his words were low, devoid of emotion, Iseult felt a hurricane inside him. *This dragon blood had caused Finn to lose her mind.*

Finn looked to Kai and Maarav, the only others present at this meeting. Ealasaid had not had the time to come, which was regrettable. Perhaps she could have made Finn see reason.

It was Kai who finally spoke, watching Iseult like he was a spooked horse . . . or perhaps a cornered predator. "It is far less risky than facing Belenus without first testing her magic."

Iseult had the urge to reach for his sword. Though he could be irritating at times, Kai had at least always encouraged Finn toward self-preservation. As far as Iseult was concerned, the man was quickly becoming his enemy. "The Dearg Due nearly killed us all the last time we faced them. We escaped because Finn surprised them and they are strategic predators. They do not like acting without a plan."

Kai, Maarav, and Finn were all watching him, as if to say, *go on*.

He huffed, allowing a thread of well-controlled emotion to seep through, and spoke directly to Kai. "This time they will have a plan. They know what she can do, and they will see that she is present long before you will see any of them. If they choose to face her, it is because they believe they can overcome her. Do you truly want to become their possession?"

Kai's expression faltered, ever so slightly, and Iseult knew he had struck precisely the blow he'd hoped. Kai's deepest fear was being taken by the monsters who'd traumatized him.

Slowly, Kai shook his head. "It is a risk I must take. I truly believe this Finn's best chance of survival."

Iseult couldn't help but respect his answer, for he realized he'd misjudged Kai's deepest fear. He would put Finn's life above his own.

Still, he could not agree with this plan. This time, he turned to Finn. "Do you truly believe stealing their magic is without consequence? How different is it from stealing their souls?"

Finn blinked at him, stunned, and he knew he'd misspoke. He hadn't intended his words to bring up what she had done to his people. Something he knew she still felt great guilt over, even though she had eventually set it right.

Her mouth sealed into a tight line for an agonizing moment, then she spoke. "I cannot afford to leave the dark faie as they are. They will kill me if they are able, and their attack may come at the worst time." She sighed heavily. "Nor can I afford to face Belenus as I am. I am not strong enough."

"I will never agree with this plan."

A flicker of fire seemed to dance in her eyes. Her shoulders went rigid. "You don't have to, because you won't be coming regardless."

Iseult could find no words as she walked past, followed by Kai. His back remained turned from her as she exited the room, though he did not miss her sharp inhale, nor the soft sob that followed.

Then she was gone. His brother gave him a look that conveyed what they were both thinking. He was an utter fool.

Maarav shook his head, peering past Iseult toward the door. "You should go after her."

"There is no stopping her."

Maarav shook his head again, his gaze distant. "No, there isn't, but when she must be pulled back from the brink, you are the one who will be needed."

Finn

Finn, Kai, Branwen, and Naoki, wandered through the western woods near midnight. A pall of silent darkness smothered any words they might have to speak, leaving the only sound their trembling breaths and cautious steps. Finn had debated bringing Naoki. While the Dearg Due might be wary of the dragon, they might also sense something was off if she didn't come along, since Finn rarely ventured out without her. They might not come with Finn there regardless, but there was no way she was letting Kai wander the woods on his own. Not where the Dearg Due could easily steal him away. She knew if that happened, she would never find him again. The Dearg Due would make sure of it.

So yes, they brought Naoki, and they stuck close together. Branwen, however, she would have preferred to leave behind, but she'd sworn up and down that Arawn wanted her there. Finn didn't really care what Arawn wanted, as long as he showed up.

The moon flashed across Finn's path as she walked through an opening in the trees, then into the deeper woods, her mind replaying the events preceding her departure. Every replay ended with Iseult's tortured expression as she walked past him.

It brought her back to when they'd first met, when he had been distant. Cold and untouchable. But what else could she do? She could not sacrifice Garenoch for the sake of their relationship.

"Why would you want Arawn to meet you out here?" Branwen's question cut through her thoughts. "Surely these woods are crawling with faie."

"Are you scared?" Kai whispered to Branwen, to which he received no reply.

Finn continued walking until she thought they'd gone deep enough, casting away her thoughts and concerns, then stopped. If her presence, or Naoki's, prevented the Dearg Due from revealing themselves, then so be it. Part of her wished they wouldn't show. Part of her wanted to run back to Garenoch to ask for help . . . help that could easily get the ones she loved killed. She straightened her shoulders. Returning empty-handed was not an option.

Naoki stalked around the perimeter of the small clearing, her head bobbing up and down as she scented the air, quite likely unaware of all that was to transpire. Even so, Naoki could sense her tension and fear, of that she was sure.

"I find it offensive that you would bring a dragon to our meeting," a voice said from behind her.

The three companions turned, taking in a cloaked

form not ten paces away. Though his features were shadowed, Finn had no doubt it was Arawn. He was in his younger form, judging by his voice, which sounded singular and not like one hundred whispering voices all at once.

She stepped toward him. "You specified that we would meet in a place of my choosing, does that not include accompaniment?"

Arawn shrugged, then pulled back his hood, revealing his shoulder length black hair. His hooked nose cast a sinister shadow over his lips. "I suppose it does, but before we discuss matters, I'd like to know why you've set our meeting place where we might be surrounded by Dearg Due."

So they had come? She hadn't sensed a thing.

"Am I to prove my allegiance?" Arawn pressed. "This seems a risky way to go about it. What if I decide to let you die?"

Did he think she expected *him* to protect her? All the better, she supposed. "I am a busy woman, Arawn. Two meetings in the time of one."

"If I prove my loyalty here and now, you will ally yourself with me against Belenus?"

"I will."

Arawn flicked his gaze to Branwen, who nodded. "She speaks the truth."

Finn wasn't sure why Branwen was lying for her. Did she truly believe she would ally herself with someone who'd cursed the man she loved?

A soft humming emanated from the branches above, slowly increasing in volume in a sickly sweet song that instantly made her drowsy. Her eyes widened, their heavy lids quickly forcing them back down. She hadn't considered that the Dearg Due might enlist other faie, and she should have, given they'd done so before.

"Cover your ears!" she hissed, covering her own, but Kai had already fallen to his knees. Branwen stared dumbly up at the branches above.

"I suppose now is my time," Arawn drawled, raising his voice to be heard over her clamped hands. "I could easily entrap you while you sleep. Belenus could hold you captive until his work is done."

Though she couldn't block out all the sound, the song of the geancanach did not seem to affect her as strongly as it did in the past, but her eyelids were still growing heavier by the moment. "You lied about an alliance," she yawned.

Arawn stepped forward into a sliver of moonlight. "If I'm to save you now, as an immortal, you must *allow* me to curse you—mildly and temporarily, of course. I cannot curse an immortal without that being's cooperation."

"What?" she said, not fully understanding his muffled words. She looked to Kai. He was on the ground, but still conscious.

Arawn lifted his voice. "He is mortal enough that I

do not need his permission." He knelt down and touched Kai's forehead.

Kai groaned, then blinked up at Finn and Arawn. "Why can't I hear anything?" His words were slurred and awkward.

"You cursed away his hearing?" Finn questioned, knowing she was speaking too loud over her muffled ears, but she was beginning to panic. Her knees felt like pottage. She'd be on the ground soon. Naoki was already curled up, fast asleep.

"Yes, and if you do not allow me to do the same, I believe the Dearg Due will swarm."

"Fine," she growled. "Do it." She wasn't sure how to allow a curse, but she didn't flinch away when he touched her. In fact, she welcomed the touch. Anything to keep her from falling asleep at a time like this.

Her hearing deafened, except for a gentle whirring, making her feel like she was underwater.

Arawn's lips moved, but she could not make out his words. He turned from her, lifted a long fallen branch, then walked to the nearest tree, shoving the branch upward into the foliage. Something small and gray, slightly resembling a rock, tumbled down from the tree. The geancanach hopped to its scrawny feet, unfurling its bat-like wings as it scurried away into the underbrush.

Arawn whacked a few more trees with his branch, knocking down more geancanach. She imagined they were hissing and shrieking, but she couldn't hear a thing.

She simply took it all in, realizing how foolish she'd been. While she could easily defend herself against predatory faie, others like the geancanach would never attack head on, and she might not be immune to their gifts. Fully recovered, Kai stood and moved to her side, his mouth a grim line.

Once the trees were clear, Arawn approached, then poked her in the forehead with his index finger, likely harder than was necessary. With a loud *pop*, her hearing returned. He moved next to Kai and did the same.

Finn looked around for Branwen, spotting her curled up on the forest floor beyond Naoki, who now lifted her head with a yawn. "What about her?" she asked, gesturing toward Branwen.

Arawn sneered. "I'm not sure I could curse her even if she allowed me. Her life is no longer mortal, she's animated by the magic of the in-between. She'll have to wake on her own."

Kai sidled close to Finn's side. "Let's hope they didn't enlist any other dark faie. Fire elementals, for instance." He shuddered.

"Fire elementals aren't dark faie," she said distantly, scanning the woods for the next sign of attack. "They're simply chaotic. The only one who could command them before was Oighear."

Hissing laughter tickled her spine. She turned, spotting several pairs of reflective eyes.

"Surprising to hear such knowledge from one who would enslave us."

Finn focused on the source of the voice, spotting a wisp of white hair as it caught the moonlight. "I do not wish to enslave you, but it's my fault the land is in chaos. I must set things right."

"We think things are right as they are," the voice hissed, echoed by mutters and laughter of what seemed a hundred other voices.

"This night just keeps getting worse," Kai muttered.

Finn felt sick. She'd grossly underestimated the number of Dearg Due that would come. She'd only ever run into smaller hunting parties. Could she drain so many? Had she grown so arrogant that she'd endanger Kai not once, but twice this night?

"Stay where you stand." *Arawn*. She'd nearly forgotten about him.

She forced herself to not turn back. "Why?"

"I'm proving my allegiance, tree girl. Do not be so ungrateful and do as I say." He muttered words in another language under his breath. Another curse?

"Who is your new companion?" a hissing voice questioned. "Will he be as tasty as you?"

"Hardly," Arawn scoffed.

The Dearg Due hissed and chattered for a moment, then swarmed.

"Remember my words!" Arawn called.

Finn didn't move a muscle, except to prepare herself for attack. The first wave of the Dearg Due came into view, moving gracefully like deer. Soon they would be upon them, and she knew she'd never drain them fast enough.

They reached the clearing, then fell to their knees, shrieking.

Finn's eyes darted around for the source of their pain.

"He's cursed the ground around you." She jumped at Branwen's voice in her ear. "Do not venture forward."

Kai stayed near her other side. She turned just in time to halt Naoki from bounding past them into the horde of Dearg Due. They kept coming despite their sisters' agony.

"I would act quickly, Finnur," Arawn called out. "You may miss your chance."

So Branwen had been spying, and had spilled her plan to Arawn. Did he also know she would use this new magic against him? She lifted her arms, closed her eyes, then reached out to the magic of the Dearg Due. The ones hit by Arawn's curse were the first to be drained. They were nearly defenseless, and it was always wisest to pick off the weakest prey when one could.

Finn's eyes snapped open, her thoughts startling her.

"Don't stop!" Kai urged.

She inhaled sharply then closed her eyes, draining magic from more of the Dearg Due. They'd stopped swarming when they realized they couldn't cross the barrier.

"Flee!" voices hissed. "Abomination!"

The night was a shifting mosaic of tattered black dresses and white hair. Just as quickly as the attack had begun, it ended, leaving the three companions, a dragon, and a god alone in the clearing.

"You may move now," Arawn instructed. "The ground is no longer cursed."

She barely heard his words. Currents of magic like angry ocean waves swept through her. She needed more. She'd need much more to defeat a god. She never wanted to let this feeling go.

"Finn?" Kai questioned.

Kai's magic called to her. It was lesser than the Dearg Due, but it was still there. And she wanted it. She *needed* it. She started to drain his magic. He had no barriers in place, it was easy to steal.

He gasped, surprise in his wide eyes, then fell to his knees.

"What are you doing!" Branwen cried. She reached out toward Finn, then quickly recoiled.

Her fear was unwarranted. Branwen did not call to her predatory instincts. Her magic was different, not tasty. What called to her were the faie.

Kai looked up at her, his eyes bugging and his mouth gaping like a dying fish. "Finn," he rasped.

Arawn's laughter cut through her mind like jagged

glass, shattering the veil of hunger disguising her actions.

"No!" she gasped. She lowered her hands. What had she done? What had she been about to do?

Kai still stared up at her, but seemed unable to move. She fell to her knees in front of him. She held out her hands, but didn't dare touch him.

He watched her cautiously, his shallow breaths fogging the air between them. Finn's breath was so hot it seemed as if she was breathing smoke.

After a moment, Kai nodded. He seemed ready to topple over, but he was alright.

She looked up to Arawn. "You knew this would happen to me."

He grinned. "It's the price you must pay to defeat Belenus. You should be thanking me for making you strong."

Her horror was replaced by rage, like flipping a coin, it only took an instant. She rose, then stalked toward Arawn. She reached out her hands and called to his magic. He was her true target. His magic quickly answered, pouring out of him. Even just a taste of it was almost too much to bear.

"Good girl," Arawn cackled, even as he fell to his knees. "You're almost strong enough to defeat him, but there's one last thing you must figure out, and you'll need me to do it." He snapped his fingers and disappeared.

She stared at the space where he'd been. Even with

his magic weakened, he'd escaped so easily. She could feel Kai and Branwen's eyes on her. Even Naoki seemed frightened to approach.

She couldn't blame them. Even as the taste of Arawn's magic faded, she still wanted more. She wanted to cling to every last hint of that intoxicating warmth. Hunching her shoulders, she looked to Kai. "Please forgive me."

He watched her for a moment, shadows obscuring the lower half of his face. "Are you, you again?"

She nodded, clenching a hand to her stomach. She'd almost killed Kai, and it had felt wonderful. Even draining Arawn had felt wonderful, though he was right. She might be able to drain Belenus, but she'd need Arawn to trap him. That was a feat she could not manage on her own.

She stared at Kai with wide eyes, and finally managed to answer. "Yes, I'm me again, the only problem was, I was me the whole time."

***

Kai

Kai stumbled several times on the way back to the estate. What Finn had done . . . it was like nothing he could have imagined. It had to have been even worse for the Dearg Due. Part of him felt they deserved it, but part of him wondered if *anyone* deserved such a fate. It was like having your soul drained away. The very thing that made you, *you*. He hadn't realized how much his Dearg Due blood had become a part of him until that moment, but maybe it was partially the Dair blood running through his veins too. Maybe she had tugged at all of it. If Finn's people still walked the land, would she be able to do the same to them?

As they neared the gates, Branwen finally broke the silence. "You need to figure out how to trap Belenus. If you just drain him like that, he will easily escape."

Finn didn't answer. Kai could only imagine what she was thinking. Guilt had driven her to do horrible things once upon a time. If anything, guilt was her greatest weakness.

He forced his feet onward, longing for his bed, though usually he'd be awake most the night. "Arawn let you drain him to prove that you need him. If he can hold Belenus still for long enough, you can defeat him."

Kai looked at Branwen to observe her response to his comment. She glanced back with wide, innocent eyes, but he saw through the act. She was working with Arawn, and well aware that he planned to involve himself and become invaluable to Finn. The real question was, why? Why would a god side with Finn over another god, especially when not long ago, he'd proven himself her enemy? What had changed?

He stopped walking, then addressed Branwen. "Don't act like you don't know," he sighed, tired of the ruse. "What does Arawn really want?"

Branwen turned back to him with a frown. "I believe he just wants Belenus gone, and he believes Finn is his best chance of reaching that end."

Finn stepped away from Kai to face them both. "If Arawn does not care to harm the mages, then we'll work with him. We may not be true allies, but we have a common enemy, and we are stronger together." She glanced over her shoulder toward the gates, then back to Kai and Branwen. "After that . . . well, if Arawn is to become my enemy once more, I will know as much about him as I can gather. If I'm to hurt someone with this new—" her brow furrowed in disgust, "magic, then it will be him." She looked to Kai for a moment, her expression pained, then shook her head. She turned and continued walking, leaving no room for arguments.

Not that Kai had any to offer.

Kai and Branwen caught up, flanking her in silence. As they reached the gates, the guards quickly recognized them—and the feathery white dragon hurrying after them from the western woods—and signaled for the gates to open. Kai didn't see Ashclaw, but imagined he was nearby, *hunting*.

He looked up at the tall walls as he awaited entry, telling himself to keep quiet, but he could not banish Arawn's mocking expression from his mind. "So we will ally ourselves not only with a dragon, but a god," he muttered. "Not one enemy, but two."

Finn looked toward him, her brow furrowed. He'd

expected her to look tired, pallid, something . . . what she looked was wonderful, as if the magic had granted her endless energy and good health. The only hint that the experience weighed on her was the slump in her shoulders. The unsure look in her eyes. "Do you have any better suggestions?"

He chewed his lip, hoping an answer would come.

The gate had opened. The guards awaited their entry, eyes cast nervously outward into the dark night.

"No, I do not," he finally replied, "I just hope that no harm comes to you because of this."

Finn cast her eyes downward and walked past him through the gates. Her muttered words carried on the wind. "I'm not the one you should be worried about."

At those ominous words, he looked to Branwen, her eyes swarming with the worry he felt. Not quite allies, and not quite acquaintances with common enemies, but two people now sharing similar fears. Fears of what they'd just witnessed, and what might be soon to come.

⁂

Óengus

Óengus panted, unable to breathe fully with the bruising on his ribs. The sun had begun to rise, and he needed to get further away from the Aos Sí encampment.

If only he could move.

His cursed gifts had finally come to use, allowing him to escape the encampment by first judging Aos Sí positions in the dark. Then, with hands and feet bound, he was able to inch himself along with his heels. The only issue had been the route of escape . . . down the cliffside . . . with his hands and feet still bound. He knew he might die, but he would have died anyway if he didn't take the chance.

At least the bindings on his hands had snapped during the fall, along with a few ribs, and his shoulder ached horribly. Now he stared up at the first rays of morning, his mouth bone dry, and his body unable to rise. There was no point in rising regardless.

A shadow cut across his face, relieving his eyes from the light.

Keiren stood over him, her crimson hair billowing in the omnipresent cliffside breeze. She looked well for a woman who'd endured lengthy torture. Perhaps *too* well.

"How did you escape?" he asked, blinking up at her.

She looked down at him, her expression slack. She could have just as easily been looking at a carcass rotting in the sun. "That is not important. You must come with me now."

He glared at her.

She tugged at a thin leather strap cutting across her chest and cloak, bringing a water skin forward from where it had been resting against her back. She lifted it from her shoulders, then tossed it to him.

He caught it with his good arm, removed the stopper, and swilled water so greedily he choked.

She watched him for a moment, then continued walking, easily scaling the boulder shielding his body to continue on down the escarpment.

He took another swill of water, then sat up. His body resisted, but he managed to stand and hobble after her.

While he'd been fairly resigned to die on that cliffside, now curiosity won out. There was something very wrong with the sorceress. The Travelers had clearly done something to her mind.

No matter. He followed anyway. It wasn't like he had anything better to do.

14

Iseult

In the chamber he shared with Finn, Iseult sat alone, hunched over, elbows on knees. The bed beneath him offered no comfort, nor did the crackling fire in the hearth. He had let her go off into the woods to meet a god. He hadn't even tried to stop her—or to protect her.

Not that he could have done either.

Now time dragged on. It was well past midnight. She should have been back by now.

With an abrupt movement he left the bed and hurried to the door. He didn't care how many faie he had to cut down to reach her. He'd find her and bring her home—he shook his head as he grabbed the door-knob—not able to fully reconcile the idea of this place as *home*.

He opened the door then stepped back.

Finn stood outside, shoulders hunched, face smudged with dirt. A stray leaf clung to a lock of her hair.

He stepped aside for her to enter. "What happened?"

She walked inside. "Iseult I—" she lowered herself

to the bed, eyes downcast. "I nearly killed Kai, and I hardly even cared. The reality of it is only now beginning to dawn." She looked up at him, tears rimming her eyes. "There is something dark inside me, hungering for magic. I must finish this task on my own. I cannot risk hurting anyone else."

He sat down on the bed beside her, reached out, then let his hands fall. Something told him his touch would not be welcome. "You won't hurt anyone. You cannot do this alone."

She buried her head in her hands, bracing elbows on knees. "That is something you cannot guarantee. I need more magic to face Belenus. And when I drain his power away," she hesitated. "Iseult, I truly do not know what I will become. I may not be able to return to you."

His heart, seemingly still for so much of his life, skipped a beat. "If that is the case, you cannot go."

Her body sagged further. "If I do not do this, we all will die. There is no other way. I brought Ashclaw upon us. I must fix this."

Finally, he touched her, barely brushing his hand across her shoulder. When she did not pull away, he rested it more heavily upon her. "We will face the dragon instead. With you, Ealasaid, and the mages, it can be defeated."

"And Belenus will not only live, but he'll have the perfect opportunity to attack." She lowered herself further as her shoulders began to shake with silent tears, soon echoed by quiet gasps of breath.

He rose, then guided her to lay down on the bed. With the blankets pinned beneath her, he simply folded one half over her, tucking it up to her neck. "Rest now. Surely things will look different in the morning."

He stepped back. She did not question why he wasn't resting with her. She buried her head in her pillow and did not move.

It took every ounce of his bravery to step away. To risk that when he returned, she might be gone. But there was something he had to do, lest he lose the woman he loved forever.

Kai

A knock on Anna's bedchamber door turned Kai's attention from her. She'd been waiting for him upon his return from the woods, and had wanted every detail of the meeting.

"Do you think it's her?" Anna whispered.

"No." Kai rose from the bedside where he sat. The knock was too heavy for Finn's small fist, and the footsteps he'd heard, though light, had the feel of more weight to them. He was rather sure who he'd find outside, but part of him was still surprised to find Iseult as he opened the door.

Iseult strode into the room without hesitation, then turned, his gaze encompassing both Anna on the bed, and Kai near the door. "We cannot let her face Belenus. Not like this."

Kai shut the door behind him. "You know we have little choice in the matter."

Iseult's predatory glare as he spoke sent a shiver down Kai's spine. "She cannot take the magic of a god. She has admitted herself that she does not believe she will survive it."

Kai moved to sit on the bed beside Anna, hoping to ease some of the tension in the room, though Iseult remained standing, as rigid as the sword at his hip.

In truth, he shared Iseult's worries, but even so, he felt Finn's best chance of survival was to become more powerful. If it drove her to become a destructive force, well, he'd be there, ready to pull her back. At least she'd be alive. That was truly what mattered.

Iseult, however, did not seem to share in this sentiment.

"What do you propose we do?" Kai sighed.

"I'm going to talk to Ashclaw."

Anna let out an abrupt laugh, more shocked than amused. "You? You think you can talk to that beast of darkness outside the gates? Only Finn can talk to dragons."

Iseult turned his cool gaze to her. "This dragon is different, it speaks clearly in her mind, unlike Naoki. I will speak to the dragon. We do not need its protection here as much as Finn needs its help in defeating Belenus."

"Iseult," Anna said more calmly, "that dragon will eat you."

"If Finn will not return to me, I have nothing else to lose."

Kai bit back another sigh. He loved Finn too, he would do all he could to save her, but he knew if she were to perish, she would wish him to continue fighting, to protect those who still remained. "Finn already walks a cliff's edge. If you go and get yourself eaten, it might just be the thing to push her over."

"I do not intend to be . . . eaten."

Did the fool truly think he could face the black dragon and survive? Kai glanced at Anna, who seemed just as dumbfounded as he, then turned back to Iseult. There was clearly no stopping him. "So what do you want from us?"

Iseult's expression shifted just a hair, showing the anguish hiding deep inside. "You will remain by her side at all costs. Protect her, for as strong as she is, she is not always capable of protecting herself."

"You know I would do that without you asking. Why are you really here?"

Iseult was silent for a long moment. He looked to Anna, as if debating whether or not she should leave the room. Seeming to dismiss the idea, he finally spoke. "Finn is consumed by dragon's blood. Too much of it runs through her veins. If I fail, and she takes in too much magic, there is only one thing that will bring her back. Humanity."

Kai leaned back, quickly catching on. "But if she's consumed by too much magic, she may not wish to save me."

"I believe she will, no matter how far she has gone."

Anna whipped her head back and forth between them. "What in *Tirn Ail* are you two talking about?"

Kai kept his eyes on Iseult as he explained, "If Finn becomes too consumed by magic, Iseult wants me to mortally wound myself so she'll be forced to save me. She will have to take in more of my humanity, in exchange for her magic blood."

"You idiot!" Anna hissed. "Don't you dare consider that. You're part faie now anyway. You won't give her just mortal blood."

"I'm mostly mortal. I believe, if she actually chose to save me, it might work. It might dilute the dragon magic just enough." He turned to Iseult. "But you know, such a feat would weaken her, and beyond that, she may choose to let me die."

"She will not. And weakened is better than lost to us forever. I must go now, before she wakes. Will you swear to me you'll be there if she needs you?"

Would he? Would he mortally wound himself, taking the chance that she may or may not be in the right mind to save him?

Was it even really a question?

He nodded. "I will."

Anna shook her head as Iseult turned to leave.

"Blasted stupid men," she muttered. "Why do we let you plan anything at all?"

Kai tended to agree with her. Iseult's plan was utter madness, but it was already in motion. It had been set into motion the day Finn saved Naoki.

Kai could only hope she'd care enough to save him too.

Finn

hispers skidded across the halls of the Garenoch estate. Some had seen Iseult leave the gates in the darkest hours of night. He'd gone in the direction of the dragon, the way no others dared venture. It had been too dark that night to see what occurred next. All the people of Garenoch knew, was that he had not returned.

And the information had spread like wildfire. Finn was well known as ruler of the faie, mother of a dragon, and dear friend of Lady Ealasaid—and to see her consort disappear late at night, on his own, never to return? To the minds of many, it could only spell trouble.

Ignoring the whispers, Finn walked through the halls of the main estate in search of Ealasaid, needing her and Maarav to find Iseult. Her stomach clenched painfully at the thought of his name, wanting to find him herself, but she could remain in the estate no longer. Tomorrow was the final day. If she did not feed Belenus to Ashclaw, many would die. Today she would travel the forests with Naoki, gathering magic and faie.

Then at sunrise the next morning, they would march upon Sormyr. She could ride on Naoki's back to make it there swiftly, and many faie had already been instructed to gather in the forest near the Gray City. There they would await her command.

She was not far gone enough to lie to herself about what she was doing. She knew the people of Sormyr were mostly innocent. Belenus was something of a savior to them. Their crops were plentiful, the city safe. Many who'd lived in poverty all their lives were now flourishing. Kai's family . . . she shook her head and picked up her pace. She had failed him there too. She hadn't figured out how to find them in that other realm. There hadn't been time. She didn't even know if they were still alive.

This time, even more lives depended on her. She could not fail again.

She caught sight of someone coming up an adjoining hall as she hurried past an alcove. Recognizing Sage, she stopped abruptly, then stepped back into sight as he reached the intersection. "Do you know where Ealasaid is?"

Holding his simple staff in one hand, Sage gestured in the direction she'd been headed. "She's in the war room. I was just on my way to meet her."

Sage fell into step beside her. She'd not seen him since they'd gone looking for Naoki in the forest. Now he was dressed for battle, in red robes labeling him as a fire mage. The colors made the different magics easier to coordinate when mages worked together, though as Ealasaid's general, Finn doubted there were any mages unaware of Sage's flavor of magic. Though he was young, appearing even younger thanks to his close-cropped dark hair, he was more powerful than most.

"I meant to thank you," she said abruptly, "for encouraging me to ally myself once more with the faie."

He glanced at her as he walked. "Thank me when you defeat Belenus, for if you fail, I might come to view you as my enemy."

She supposed she deserved that. "I did what I thought was right at the time. The dragon has guarded the burgh as promised."

"From all of our many attackers?"

She huffed. She could not have foreseen the relative quiet the burgh had enjoyed over the past nine days, but perhaps she should have. Belenus had tried to lure her in before. Despite his threats, he didn't seem willing to risk his soldiers on repeated attacks of a well-armed burgh.

"I know you did what you thought best," Sage said as they reached the closed double-doors of the war room. He rested his hand on one ornate knob as he turned toward her. "And you've been here to save us before, I've no doubt you'll do all in your power to save us again. But this is the only home many of us have ever known. If we were feared for our minor magics before the barrier fell, we are absolutely abhorred now for the powers we have accumulated. At least a few years ago there were other places to run. Now this burgh is all we have, save sailing to another continent. The forests and marshlands are overrun by faie, and Migris is in ruins. Without Migris' soldiers up North, the reivers creep further from their borders into our lands. I don't imagine the port towns along the River Cair will last much longer, and we cannot flee to Sormyr, for obvious reasons."

She stared at him. "What are you trying to say?"

He met her gaze evenly. If he feared her, as many had come to do, it did not show. "I'm not trying to say anything, Lady Finnur, I'm trying to beg. I beg you, do not fail us. I know you have other concerns. I know you fly with dragons, and run with faie. I know you are not entirely of this world, but we are. Please do not forget that our lives depend on you. We may survive the black dragon on our own, but we will not survive the gods."

Her mouth went dry. Did he not realize she already knew that? Could he not comprehend the fear and guilt she lived with every single day?

Not waiting for an answer, he opened the door, which was just as well, as she had no idea what to say. She might have been consumed with many other things, but she'd never forgotten about the unnamed faces depending on her. In fact, she clung to them, because she knew if anything could keep her as human as she could be, it was the innocent lives at stake.

Finished blinking at Sage's back as he entered the

war room ahead of her, she followed. Ealasaid and Slàine were the only other occupants, leaning over a massive map spread across a long table. Ealasaid wore tan breeches and a loose black blouse—she must not be meeting with anyone other than Slàine or Sage this day —and Slàine was dressed in her usual black. She looked sharp and deadly, but most of all she looked tired. Finn echoed that tiredness from the bottomless pits of her soul.

Ealasaid nodded to Finn, but her attention was mainly on Sage. "Some of Slàine's scouts have returned. Reivers have come down from the North. They would like to speak of terms."

Finn looked to Sage, gauging his reaction, as it was the last thing she'd expected to hear.

It seemed Sage felt the same. "They actually want to speak terms with us? How many clans, and how large?"

"Two clans," Slàine explained. "Two of the largest."

"And they expect to enter the burgh?" Sage balked.

Slàine snorted. "Hardly. We will speak of an alliance on neutral ground, nothing more."

Sage stepped toward Ealasaid, clearly dismissing Slàine. "What could the reivers possibly gain from an alliance? It is a trap. It has to be."

Slàine smiled smugly at his back, though he could not see. "The reivers fear the Ceàrdaman, and the Aos Sí. Both have encroached upon their lands in great numbers."

The tiny hairs at the back of Finn's neck prickled at

the mention of the Ceàrdaman. There had been few sightings of them since the barrier fell. Those who knew what was good for them had worried over what they were planning, and when that plan would finally be revealed.

Before more information could be divulged, Ealasaid turned her attention to Finn. "Forgive me for becoming engrossed in this most recent news. Are you preparing to depart?"

Suddenly nervous, Finn nodded. This may very well be her final goodbye, and it seemed so lackluster, and somehow unimportant.

Reading her expression, Ealasaid strode across the room, leaving Sage and Slàine to bicker amongst themselves. She wrapped her arms around Finn, holding her tight. "Please, be careful."

Finn bit back tears. "Iseult—" she managed to say, but could speak no more. He had gone to see the dragon, and had not returned. Now that light had washed over the burgh, *neither* had been spotted again. She could not even question Ashclaw before she left.

Ealasaid squeezed Finn tighter. "I know, I heard. We will try to find him."

Finn didn't argue that perhaps *she* should be the one searching for him. They both knew there was no time.

With a sound that could have been a gasp or a sob, Finn pulled away. "I swear to you, I will do all that is within my power to save the burgh."

Ealasaid smiled softly. Being a mother had changed

her. Sometimes, like now, she almost made Finn feel like a child, though she was over a century older than the woman standing before her. "I know you will not fail us. Now go."

Finn turned away before Ealasaid could see her tears. She'd promised Anna and Kai she'd say goodbye, but if it was going to be like this, she could not bear it. She left the war room without another word. Ealasaid could deal with the reivers, for she was the lucky one. Finn would gladly face one thousand bloodthirsty reivers to avoid the task ahead.

She hurried down the hall, away from the eyes of Sage, Slàine, and Ealasaid, all boring holes into her back. She had no weapons save her belt knife, and no supplies save a water skin, a single meal, and the suede breeches, linen tunic, and fur-lined cloak clothing her body. She would need nothing else.

She exhaled a sigh of relief as she exited the estate. The front courtyard held a few mages, but none with whom she'd ever spoken. Kai would be resting at this time in the morning, and Anna was nowhere to be seen. She could make her escape without goodbyes. It was better this way.

She jogged across the yellowing grass, mentally summoning Naoki to join her outside the burgh. Though the trek was longer than riding Naoki over the wall, she'd leave through the front gates, where she was unlikely to see anyone else she knew.

Before long, she was outside the burgh. Her hot

breath fogged the cool morning air, like the smoke of a fire dragon pouring from her lungs. She shook her head, she had to stop summoning such imagery. It only made things worse. She hurried west, where she knew Naoki would wait.

It didn't take long for Arawn and Branwen to appear on either side of her. No one spoke. They all knew what lay ahead.

They reached the woods to find Naoki waiting at the border, and someone was standing beside her. From a distance, Finn's first thought was Iseult. Her heart plummeted to her knees, for just a moment, then they were near enough to see clearly. It was Kai. He must have seen Naoki leaving the courtyard.

He rested his back against a tree, arms crossed, face shadowed by his cowl. "You didn't think you could leave me behind, did you!" he called out.

She jogged ahead of Arawn and Branwen to reach him first. "Yes," she panted, "actually I had." Then why was she so relieved to see him?

He nodded toward those approaching behind her. "You can't trust those two to watch your back."

She clenched her fists. As much as she wanted him to come, she could not risk his life any further. "Kai, we will face countless dark faie, the Gray City's soldiers, and a god. You cannot join us."

Naoki chittered, then lowered her head to bump Finn's arm with her beak.

"You see?" Kai pressed. "She wants me to come."

"Let the mortal come," Arawn said from behind her. "It is no difference to me, as long as he does not slow us down."

Kai pushed away from the tree. "Naoki can easily carry us both."

"You might die!" Finn hissed.

Kai shrugged. "So might we all. You are free to risk your life as you wish, and so am I."

And so was Iseult, the words hung unsaid, but she could not face them now. She was fully aware when he left their chambers last night, and so anxious to enact her plan, she hadn't questioned why. After he was gone, she used the opportunity to find Branwen and inform her they would depart in the morning . . . She'd *let* him go. If Iseult was gone—he might not be, she assured herself—but if he was gone, it was her fault, and she could not live with that pain. Once her task was done, she would be needed no more, and she could give in to it.

"We are wasting time," Arawn grumbled.

Finn glanced back at him. "Fine." Then back to Kai. "You can come. Now let us begin. We have a long way to travel."

She moved toward Naoki and climbed atop her back. She knew that short of using violence, she could not prevent Kai from joining her.

If he wanted to see her become a monster—a ravenous beast, hungry for magic—then so be it.

Anna

Anna found Eywen just as he was exiting the main estate, his artful faie features grim. His face brightened as he spotted her hurrying across the courtyard to meet him.

She threw up her hands, billowing the sleeves of her loose white blouse. It was too cold to be without a cloak, but she hadn't thought to grab one. "That blasted Finn left this morning without a word, and she took Kai with her!"

Eywen stopped before her, his dark eyebrows raised. His whitish skin looked sharp against his battle clothes, similar to what the assassins wore at such times, a mixture of black linen and leather—though there should be no battle until tomorrow. His hand alighted on her shoulder. "I'm sure if Kai left, it was of his own volition. Finn would not take him willingly."

Anna sneered. She knew it was so, but she was still profoundly irritated. To be left behind without a single farewell? She might not ever see either of them again.

Eywen squeezed her shoulder. "It is done, there is no use worrying about it now, and we have other pressing matters that require our focus."

Her shoulders relaxed beneath his touch. She let out a long breath. "Such as?"

"Such as the Lady of this burgh holding court with a band of reivers."

She inhaled sharply through her teeth. "They actually found some?"

His nod draped a lock of black hair over his eye. "Some of Slàine's scouts, yes, and they lived to tell the tale. If we are to believe the reivers, my people have gathered in the North, alongside the Ceàrdaman. The reivers fear they will claim their lands."

Anna searched his face for any hint of emotion. She knew he cared deeply for his people, as twisted as their pasts had been. "Why would the Aos Sí be with the Travelers? That makes no sense at all."

Eywen lifted one shoulder in a half shrug. "They have lived their entire lives under the thumb of one master or another. Perhaps in the Ceàrdaman, they have found new leadership."

She shivered, and it had nothing to do with the cool wind, carrying with it the scent of rain. It tugged at the loose strands of hair falling free from her braid, chilling her cheeks. Though she knew it was irrational, the wild cold wind felt like a portent of things to come.

"We will find out more tonight," he assured. "I intend to join the meeting with the reivers."

"What if it's a trap?"

He shrugged. "We will have mages and assassins in our midst. We will not be easily overcome."

"I'm coming with you."

He smirked. "I thought you might say that."

"You won't try to stop me?"

He shook his head, then guided her to walk at his side toward the front gates of the estate. "Nowhere is safe for you, not anymore. After you left to find the Dearg Due—" he shook his head. "Whatever dangers we may face, I'd like you where I can see you."

She furrowed her brow as they walked. "I can't decide if that's sweet, or if you simply don't trust me to take care of myself."

"Let's go with the former."

"Where are we going?"

"To the front gates. I'd like to check in on the construction of the new walls."

She shook her head, but kept walking. "That seems a useless task at a time like this."

"You need a distraction, my love, and we will not meet with the reivers until nightfall."

She almost stopped walking out of sheer stubbornness, but with a slight nod to herself, she continued on. Eywen had come to know her well, perhaps better than most. Just like before, she was not sure whether to find it sweet, or vexing. She settled on both, which she could admit, if only to herself, was the way she liked it.

Ealasaid

Though she'd been quite sure of her plan to enlist the

reivers, Ealasaid found her nerves getting the better of her as day slowly gave way to night. She paced around her room, debating shucking the fine sapphire blue velvet dress she wore in favor of breeches. The dress made her look like a queen, but might the reivers respond better to a warrior?

Moving to check on Elias in his bassinet, she thought back to her first encounter with reivers. Conall, their leader, had enlisted mages to fight for him, assuring them he'd keep them safe. It had been nothing more than a ploy to overtake a ruined city and give reivers a place to gather so they could expand southward. Scarred by her early life as a mage, and destroyed over the news that her family had been killed, Conall had easily swayed her to his side.

She remembered the bloodshed of the day An Fiach attacked the ruined city. Did these reivers plan that for Garenoch too? She told herself the burgh was strong, and with the new fortifications springing up every day, soon they'd have the space they'd need to raise livestock and grow food without worrying about nearby faie. She told herself she was just as strong as the burgh she'd built up, but something deep inside her quaked in fear over the impending meeting.

She shouldn't be worried, she'd have Sage, Maarav, Slàine, and several others to watch her back. She'd have Eywen and perhaps Anna too. Just the mere sight of an Aos Sí warrior was sure to make the reivers rethink any hidden machinations. There would be ten on her side, and ten on the reivers. With magic, they should have no trouble overcoming the reivers, even if they came with more than the proposed amount.

So why did she feel so blasted nervous?

Someone opening the door drew her attention. The only person who'd open the door without knocking was Maarav, and by the gods she was glad to see him now. He always knew how to dampen her nerves.

He peeked his head in, his gray-green eyes quickly landing on her. He opened the door fully, and stepped inside. He bristled with weapons across his back and at the hips of his black breeches, though she knew there were far more weapons than what met the eye.

He offered her a half-smile. "Are you ready, wife?"

She looked down at Elias. "I hate to wake him."

"I already asked the healers to come. They will be here soon, along with the mages you requested to protect him."

She peered over her shoulder at his tone. "You think me over-cautious?"

He laughed. "Hardly, wife. We cannot be too careful. Now we must go. Elias' watchers will arrive shortly."

She stroked Elias' cheek, then moved toward the door. Suddenly she regretted the dress. She wanted to be able to move swiftly, to run back to the burgh if need be.

Maarav held the door open for her. "'Tis only a meeting, and we have scouts out. If the reivers come with more than ten, we will retreat. Now is not the time to entertain conflict."

She spotted Nira, a trusted healer, walking toward them down the hall with many others. She trusted each of them—perhaps not as much as she trusted Maarav and Slàine—but she could not expect any others to love her child as much as his father and grandmother.

"Let's go," Maarav urged quietly, nodding to the healers and mages as some entered the room, and others stationed themselves outside.

Ealasaid allowed herself to be coaxed away. She looked up at Maarav as they walked. "Why am I so nervous? My palms are sweating." She wiped her palms on her dress, but it did not seem to help.

He stopped walking and turned toward her, taking both her arms in his hands. "Do you not want to go? It was your idea to seek an alliance with the reivers, but it is not too late to turn back."

She shook her head. She was being silly. "No. I know we must go. We cannot rely on Finn alone to protect us. The stronger the burgh is, the more food and supplies we have, the better."

He nodded, then continued walking, though she noticed him glancing at her from time to time as they left the estate and moved toward the gates where they'd meet their party.

Darkness seemed to squeeze the exterior of the estate like a fist, forcing out the last traces of daylight. The night felt heavy, like it might rain, or perhaps even snow. The portentous feeling in her gut increased with every step. She found herself reaching out for her magic from time to time, just to reassure herself that she could drop any reiver where he stood.

They reached the gates. Slàine, Sage, and the others were already there. They would walk through the burgh and exit the main gates together, with archers and mages watching over them from above. They had scouts in the woods. They would know about any possible traps long before they were sprung. In these dire times, no risks were to be taken.

By the time they reached the main gates, icy droplets fine as mist coated Ealasaid's face, wetting her loose curls. As they waited for two stablehands to reach them, towing horses from the stables near the inn, Maarav took her hand. She'd soon have to drop it—she didn't want anyone to see her looking weak—but for now, she interlaced her fingers with his, and squeezed as tightly as her smaller hand was capable.

Manned by the sentries above, the gates opened enough for them to exit, just as the horses reached them. Ealasaid was given a tall white mare, a bit too sizable for her small frame, but she understood why the choice had been made. A ruler should sit above her subjects. It was fortunate few subjects stood witness to Maarav boosting her into the saddle.

A shiver ran through her as they rode through the open gates and into darkness flickering with torchlight, the flames hissing with steam from the rain. To the east were further fortifications, but out here, they might as well be on their own, save the archers watching them from overhead.

Slàine was the first to speak. "To the northeast we will meet our scouts, then we'll continue on toward the meeting place." She looked past Maarav to Ealasaid. "If anything seems amiss, you'll turn that horse around and flee. We will guard your back. Do not forget that you are more important than any of us."

The words made her sick. She knew it was her place to turn and flee, but if Maarav was in danger . . . some things came before being ruler, at least to her. He met her gaze for a moment. She was sure he knew exactly what she was thinking, but he knew better than to argue.

Seeming to believe they were all in agreement, Slàine gestured to the two assassins joining them, Rae and Isolde. With his dark skin and close-cropped hair —both highly uncommon on the continent—Rae nearly blended in with the darkness. She realized she'd never had the time to ask Rae his history, all she knew was that Maarav trusted him more than most. It wasn't a surprise he'd been chosen to risk his life once again to protect her. Isolde, however, was a surprise. Small of stature and with mousy brown hair, Isolde seemed anything but imposing, but her skill with poisoned daggers was comparable to none. Would they be poisoning reivers tonight?

Ealasaid didn't have time to ask as the two assassins

kicked their horses forward, spurring everyone else into motion. Next in line went Slàine and Sage, then her and Maarav, followed by Eywen and Anna, then two more mages of Ealasaid's choosing. The two mages in the back should be able to avoid attack long enough to protect those in front with their magic, though Sage, on his own, was highly skilled in close combat. He'd set to learning every form of attack and defense since he'd arrived at the burgh, more dedicated to their cause than most anyone else, perhaps even Ealasaid herself.

They rode on into the quiet darkness, accompanied only by the light patter of rain, and the gentle stomps of the horses' hooves. Before long they met with the scouts, learning that all was as it should be, only ten reivers waited at the agreed upon destination. Perhaps they really had come to form an alliance, something Ealasaid realized she hadn't trusted until just then.

Slàine's scouts dispersed, prepared to blend in and prevent any incoming attacks from behind. Ealasaid didn't see the black dragon anywhere, which worried her. They should still have one final day left. Where was Finn now? Would she reach Sormyr and capture Belenus in time?

She forced her thoughts away from Finn, needing to focus on the present. As they neared the meeting place, she could hear hushed voices speaking in a foreign tongue. The reivers.

Maarav gestured for Ealasaid to halt. She would

stay back while Slàine and Sage approached the group, hopefully triggering any trap that might be waiting.

Ealasaid would have stopped regardless—her heart was in her throat, nearly choking her. She recognized one of the reivers standing in the distant clearing.

"Conall," she breathed.

"I recognized him too," Maarav whispered. "Do we continue on as planned?"

But it was too late to turn back. The reivers had spotted Slàine and Sage. They gripped rough-forged weapons tightly, waiting for the pair to reach them. The reivers' heavy fur cloaks added to their wild appearance, as if they were half-animal, half-man. Did they know what Sage was? That he could burn half of them to ashes before they reached him atop his mount?

Hushed conversation. Tense moments. Those behind Ealasaid could hardly be breathing with how silent they were. Isolde and Rae stood still as statues—watching everything and nothing all at once—on either side of the clearing.

The tension seemed to ease like a storm finally breaking as Slàine motioned them forward. No hidden dangers had been spotted. It was time to find out what sort of treaty Conall had in mind. She could hardly believe it would be good. No one so power-hungry would enter into a deal that benefited him less than anyone else involved.

Conall's gaze landed on Ealasaid, seeming to recognize her as she neared on her horse. He looked the same, wild blond hair faded to whitish gray, stout frame, and light eyes, gray if she recalled correctly. She didn't recognize the nine reivers fanned out on either side of him, though she hadn't taken the time to observe others in the ruined city long enough to know if any had accompanied Conall since that time.

Conall raised his voice. "I was surprised to hear you yet lived, lass. You must have cast away your foolhardy nature to survive so long."

"I have cast away nothing," she said as she reached the reivers. Her party fanned out on either side of her, remaining on horseback, though the reivers were on foot. "And I myself am surprised. How did you reach the South so quickly?"

Conall smirked. "Having the Still Folk and Prowlies invade one's lands can light a fire at one's boot heels."

Slàine cleared her throat. "He means the Ceàr-daman and Aos Sí."

Conall gestured in Eywen's direction. "Though I see you've got a Prowlie problem yourself."

The other reivers watched on silently. She briefly wondered if they were more like her people than she believed, constantly threatened and willing to act out in violence to protect the place they called home.

She shook herself. No, they were not alike. The reivers were invaders, bandits. They killed and took what was not theirs to take. She needed to remember that. "Let us cut short these . . . pleasantries. We are both in need of allies in these dire times. Speak your terms."

The reivers shifted at her tone. She found her eyes darting toward Sage. He would be the first line of defense should something go wrong.

To her surprise, Conall burst out with laughter, cutting through the eerily silent night.

Her body sang with tension. She waited as the laughter died down, expecting sudden attack . . . or a dragon swooping down. There were other dragons hunting the land besides Ashclaw. They might hesitate to attack a burgh brimming with mages, but just a few out here on their own . . . she'd been so concerned with the reivers, she hadn't considered that possibility.

"You look like you've seen a phantom, lassie," Conall's words brought her back to present matters. "Or perhaps you're simply a spooked mare, frightened to be away from the protection of your burgh."

"Stop toying with her," Slàine hissed. "She could easily end you where you stand, and you know it. Now speak your terms."

Conall continued to grin, his eyes darting back to Ealasaid. "Our women are not fighters. They tend our fires, skin our kills, and care for the young. With enemies invading our lands, we can no longer leave them unattended."

Ealasaid narrowed her eyes. What did that have to do with anything?

"Terms," Slàine pressed. "Speak them."

Conall's grin finally wilted as he shot Slàine a fiery glare. "We want you to allow our women and wee ones inside your walls. Protect them, and we will protect you in turn. The Still Folk are planning something, and I will not have our bairns left vulnerable."

Ealasaid wanted more than anything to seek advice with her companions, but she could not appear weak. "How can we trust that you will protect us?"

"You will have our women and children inside your walls, lass. How can you believe we would not?"

She supposed he had a point. "We'll need more from this bargain. We will be offering you much more than you offer us."

"Our numbers are great," Conall growled.

"Our strength is greater," she countered. "We have a surplus of weaponry, we can outfit your fighters, but in return, your primary objective will be securing supplies for the burgh. Food, wood, and components for medicine."

He huffed, and the others around him seemed to bristle. "You'd have us work as woodcutters? Gatherers?"

"Are your children's lives not worth the price?"

It was difficult to tell in the moonlight, but Conall's face seemed to be turning red. She worried she'd pushed him too far, and there would be no alliance at all.

"Fine." Conall's words were tinged with malice. "But know this, lass. An oath to a reiver is as good as blood-binding. You may control the elements, but my folk have a special brand of magic running through the veins of us all. In blood there is power, do not forget it."

Ealasaid's mouth went dry. The reivers had no magic. Everyone knew it . . . but they were a secretive race. Most known about reivers was little more than legend.

"We have a deal," she breathed. "Your women and children may enter the burgh, but no warriors. Not a single one. You will coordinate with my general on what supplies must be gathered, and in what manner. How soon will your people arrive?"

Conall snorted. "Your woods are thick, soldiers on the road few, even An Fiach no longer hunts the faie."

"Meaning?"

"Our women will await entry at your gates at first light. A small group of warriors will be sent to meet with your general."

First light? She'd thought it would take weeks. The burgh was close to bursting with inhabitants as it was.

"All will be accommodated." She was pleased her voice did not tremble, because truly, she had no idea how she was going to make that happen.

Conall nodded. "Then let it be so, lass. We'll speak again soon."

The reivers turned without another word, leaving their backs vulnerable. Though what reason did she have to cut them down? She was the one who deserved to be stricken for not telling them of Ashclaw, who could well attack just as the women and children arrived. But she couldn't say as much, lest she risk this new alliance.

She felt rooted in her saddle. More lives on her conscience. More lives depending on Finn.

Maarav moved his horse close to her side. The reivers had disappeared into the dark trees. He lowered his voice to the barest whisper, "I hope you know what you're doing, wife."

She turned wide, worried eyes to him, conveying what no one would want to hear.

Did she know what she was doing? Now, more than ever, she most certainly did not.

16

Kai

Kai finally understood what Anna was talking about when she spoke of people *shining*. She could see the faintest glow of magic from a person, even from a distance. Now he understood just how blinding it could be.

The night had been long. Many dark faie were hunted down. With Arawn's help, they had fallen easily. It might have been humorous except for the reality of what was happening. Finn was draining something akin to faie souls, and her demeanor had become almost unrecognizable in the process.

Now, under the soft light of morning, they neared Sormyr. He couldn't remember the last words Finn had spoken, they seemed so long ago. All he could focus on was the immense shine emanating from her. He wondered if he could see it because of his faie blood, or if others could see it too. Branwen and Arawn seemed unfazed.

Kai watched Finn's back as she peered out from the edge of the forest, Arawn at her right, and Naoki—crouched to fit beneath the lower boughs—at her left.

Branwen, perhaps feeling as far away from current events as he, sidled closer, then leaned near his ear. "What are they doing?" she whispered.

He clenched his jaw and shook his head, even though he knew just what they were doing. They were plotting their attack. The forest behind them, though silent, felt heavy with the presence of countless light faie. Trow, pixies, bucca, grogoch . . . they all awaited Finn's command.

Could Belenus sense what was coming? Could the city folk, supposedly safe within the faded basalt walls, know what peril awaited?

"Now!" Finn's voice rung in his ears. The forest seemed to wake up. Pixies swarmed over his head.

He stood still through the swarm, glancing at Branwen as she fell to her knees and covered her head, then up to Finn as she swung herself atop Naoki's back.

"No!" he reached forward, for what good it would do. Naoki had already launched herself out from the trees, then up into the sky.

Arawn turned back to him with a smirk.

Kai's breath came out in a huff. "She was supposed to wait until Belenus was lured out."

"He's already coming." He lifted his hand, snapped his fingers, and disappeared.

Stunned with how quickly it had all happened, he looked down to Branwen, crouched beside him. Trow and other slow-moving faie ambled past them, but the immediate chaos had died down.

She came to her feet, pushing her russet hair back from her pale face, then looked out toward Sormyr as the first screams erupted from the farms. The faie filled the fields all around, approaching the city.

Branwen and Kai both stood awestricken, neither able to move. He didn't see Finn or Naoki anywhere.

He could barely register Branwen's voice as she spoke. "I thought the point was to lure Belenus out. If he's already coming, why are they still attacking? Why did Finn tell them to charge?"

War horns sounded from the high walls. Shouts of men filled the air as the soldiers rallied.

He shook his head. "I don't know, but if I wasn't certain before, I am now. Finn isn't Finn anymore." He turned fully to Branwen. "You have to help me find her."

She looked out toward Sormyr, chewed her lip, then turned back to him. "No. Nothing has changed. She must still face Belenus, and we must not interfere."

He scanned the fields as the first of the soldiers clashed with the faie. Swords struck against nearly impenetrable bark. Axes moved too slow to swat down pixies. Archers rained arrows down from the walls, but many of the faie were impervious. It seemed so . . . wrong. These were peaceful faie, only acting to ensure Finn did not harm them. Deep down, Finn would not want this. She was blinded by dark faie magic.

"Branwen," he said, turning back to her. "I do not know what your aim is, but can you not see that this is wrong? There are innocent people out there." He gestured toward the city. "The faie were only supposed to attack long enough to draw Belenus out to protect them, but he is not protecting them."

Branwen stared outward. "No one is innocent, not really."

The dappled sunlight suddenly felt too hot on his face, his chest constricted. "What has become of you?" he hissed. "Does nothing remain of the scholar I once knew? Your brother would be ashamed."

His words seem to finally elicit a response, though not the one he was hoping for. She whirled on him, producing a dagger from within the folds of her black cloak like magic.

He barely managed to duck out of the way. If he'd been only human, he would have died right there. Before he could recover, Branwen charged again.

He flung up a dagger of his own, parrying her strike. "What are you doing fool woman!"

"You know nothing of my brother! He died because of you!" She charged again, too fast for a human, and once more he parried. "Because of her!" She tossed her free hand toward the city, toward the area that to her, symbolized Finn.

"He died because he trusted the Travelers," he growled, this time parrying her blow more quickly.

"No," she spat, her body trembling. "He had no choice in his circumstances." She swung again, but this time with less fervor.

He easily swiped aside her strike, now under-standing just where Branwen played into things. "He had no choice in his circumstances, and neither did you. And for that, someone must pay, is that it?"

She panted, the dagger now held loosely, forgotten in her hand. She watched him like he was a predator ready to take her down, but not like she was afraid. He could see in her eyes that she wanted death.

He lowered his weapon. "Vengeance and death will never sate the fire burning in your heart. They will only stoke it."

She stared at him. Sounds of battle increased near the city, but he could not look away. If she would not help him find Finn, all would soon be lost.

Branwen's expression stiffened. "Perhaps you are right, but I cannot let my brother's killer go unpun-ished. Niklas must pay."

"Niklas isn't here," he said evenly. "The only ones paying are innocent people."

She bared her teeth. "If I interfere, Arawn will not help me bring Niklas to justice."

He stepped forward, sensing she was done attacking him. "Then I will help you, I swear it."

Her fist clenched around her dagger, her jaw rigid. She seemed to teeter on the fine edge between action and resolve.

He debated just leaving and searching for Finn himself, then her expression crumbled. "Fine, I will help you find her. They are still in this reality for now. If they move to another, we will not be able to follow."

His body flooded with relief. The fight was far from over, but at least they still had a chance. "Thank you."

Her gaze was sharp enough to slice skin. "Do not thank me. If you break your promise, I will kill everyone you hold dear." She turned and darted forth from the trees, heading west toward the sea.

He had no choice but to follow. There was never really a choice. Not for him, not for Branwen, and most certainly not for Finn.

Finn

Finn stood atop the jagged cliffside, next to Naoki and Arawn. Sormyr seemed small below her. *Everything* seemed small. The faie. The humans. *Death*. The conflict seemed distant and far away, having little to do with her. The pounding waves, down the cliffside at her back, drowned out the sounds of battle. Icy winds nearly lifted her from her feet, whipping her cloak out behind her.

Her hand rested on Naoki's neck for support as she peered at Belenus. He stood roughly ten paces away, his embroidered white coat glinting in the cool sunlight.

Wind gusted her hair back from her face. "It is time to end this."

Arawn was nearly forgotten at her side. Distantly, she knew she needed him, but all her senses were focused on consuming the magic of the god before her. With so much magic, she could set *everything* right. No one would ever threaten her again.

Belenus sneered, his features somehow remaining ethereally handsome even in the ugly expression. "You believe you can best me, dragon girl? You are no match for a god, not even with the traitor at your side."

She looked to Arawn. It was time for him to uphold his promise. She could see his magic coursing through him like tiny snakes emanating with dark light. It called to her.

"Remember who the enemy is," Arawn muttered. "Are you ready?"

"So this is truly how it shall be?" Belenus laughed, his crisp blue eyes on Arawn. "Allies for so long, now enemies?"

Arawn glared. "You know I never shared in your vision. In your dreams you are always king, and everyone else merely pawns, including me."

Belenus spread his legs, crouching slightly, braced for an attack, though he held no weapon.

Arawn took on a similar stance. "Be ready," he hissed to Finn, "you won't have much time."

Magic erupted from both gods, so bright it was nearly blinding. Finn staggered back, for a moment too stunned to even remember what she was doing there. Everything she had done came rushing back. Countless dark faie crumpled at her feet, begging her to stop. The light faie taking lives—and losing lives—below.

The fresh memories stole her breath. Arawn and Belenus hadn't physically moved, but Arawn's brow was already coated with sweat from a battle of magical wills. They silently warred—Arawn holding Belenus in place, and Belenus attempting to escape him.

Belenus seemed less sure now. "How did you grow so powerful?" he said through gritted teeth. Wind— both magical and earthly—whipped his white hair around his head.

"I have always been so," Arawn spat, "if anyone had ever cared to look." He did not remove his eyes from Belenus, but Finn knew his next words were for her. "Do it now, I cannot hold him for long."

Belenus' eyes snapped open further. His body jerked slightly, but he seemed unable to move.

Naoki pressed her belly to the rocks, ready to pounce.

"Now!" Arawn shouted.

Finn gestured Naoki back. Her dragon was not strong enough to consume a god. But Finn was. She walked through currents of magic toward Belenus.

"You should have never threatened those I love." She reached him. "That was your first mistake."

He panted, struggling to move even his mouth. "They will love you no more once they see what you've become. Devouring my magic will destroy you. There will be no going back."

She knew his words were true. But she had to do this. She'd changed who she was with the first dark faie she'd drained. She had long since passed the point of no return.

She began to consume his magic. It poured through her veins like fire and ice.

Fear shone in Belenus' eyes. True fear.

She drank it up. In the distance she heard the beat of wings, too large to be Naoki. She turned to see Arawn behind her on his knees, sweating and struggling to hold Belenus still, even with his power half drained. A large black shape grew even larger behind him, swooping down from the sky.

It all happened in the blink of an eye. Ashclaw touched down, shattering the edge of the cliff with his mighty talons and casting boulders toward the city below. He rose up behind Arawn, weakened from his battle with Belenus.

Arawn looked up, horrified, lifted his fingers to snap himself out of existence . . .

Ashclaw's steaming maw dove down, trapping and swallowing Arawn in one bite. Naoki skittered back, frightened.

"No!" Finn screamed. She had to finish Belenus before he escaped, but a rider slid down from Ashclaw's neck.

"Do not do this," Iseult yelled over the wind. "Do not leave me!" His words carried to her ears, seeming to rattle every bone in her body.

He walked toward her past Ashclaw.

She glanced at Belenus, on his knees, panting and beaten. She should finish him now, but she felt herself reaching out toward Iseult.

Iseult's eyes went wide. "No!" he shouted, just as reality seemed to shift around her.

Everything blurred, went black, then white, then black again. Her body slammed down into snow. Wind whipped flakes violently above her, stinging her visible skin as she sat up with a groan. The first thing she managed to make out through the blizzard was a flash of fiery red hair. A hand extended down toward her, and she took it.

Keiren's face became clear as she stood. "Are you well?"

"Why?" Finn gasped. "Why have I been brought here?"

"Ouch," a voice said from behind her.

She turned around. "Kai?"

Kai and Branwen were both rising to their feet just a few paces away.

"We were coming to find you," Kai explained, "then suddenly we were whipped up and tossed here."

This wasn't right? Where was Belenus? Where were Ashclaw and Iseult? "Who brought us here?"

"I did," Keiren said to her back. "Niklas and I made a deal. He gave me the ultimate power I always desired. I'm sorry, but it had to be this way."

The blizzard slowly faded, until everything was still

and silent. Belenus stood not far off in the snow, watching them. Near him, stood Niklas.

Belenus watched Finn warily, then flicked his eyes to Niklas. "It seems I am in the debt of the Ceàrdaman. Why did you save me?"

Finn shook her head. She didn't understand. Keiren was working with Niklas? They had both brought them here?

Niklas swiped flecks of melting snow from his bald head, then shook out his gray robes. "I did not save you. I witnessed Finnur failing to complete her task. My sorceress possesses the magic of air and darkness, and I have empowered her with the magic of the in-between. You will not be able to escape her." He walked away from Belenus to Keiren's side.

Her eyes on the god, Keiren smiled wickedly.

Belenus began to lift one hand, then stopped halfway. His jaw tensed, but no other part of him moved. Keiren's gaze was concentrated on him, holding him still. He was a rat in a trap, a rabbit in a snare. Finn licked her lips. Soon it would all be over.

Niklas turned toward her. "It is time to finish this."

She nodded. It was time. She loved Iseult for what he'd tried to do, but this was the only way to keep him and everyone else safe. Belenus had to die. If he died fully, where she could not feed him to Ashclaw, then so be it. She would become strong enough to defeat even the mightiest of dragons.

She walked toward Belenus through the snow, holding out her hands.

"Finn wait!" Kai's voice. She'd forgotten he was there.

She turned to see him standing back with Branwen.

"Do not come near," she warned. "I may not crave Branwen's in-between magic, but your Dearg Due blood calls to me."

His jaw went slack, and she turned away. Perhaps, to him, she no longer seemed herself, which was well. It was easy to let go now. She finished her approach toward Belenus and began draining his magic anew.

It was time to end this.

It was time to end everything.

Kai

Kai struggled against Branwen's grip where she'd managed to tug him back into a small copse of snowy trees. For a waif of a girl, she was *strong*. "Let me go fool woman! I must stop her!"

Branwen wrapped her arms around his chest and let her weight drag him downward. "You idiot! If you wound yourself now, she will not save you."

He froze for a moment, surprised by her words, then he remembered what she was. She could flit about unnoticed by anyone, even Iseult. She'd been spying when they came up with their plan.

He resumed his struggles, dragging her through the snow. "I have to try!"

He could see Finn's back, and beyond her, Belenus, now on his knees. Someone crept up behind Finn, their identity obscured by gusts of snow. This someone had silver hair, so not Keiren or Niklas, who stood out of sight.

Kai opened his mouth to shout a warning, but Branwen hopped to her feet, then kneed him in the groin, dropping him to the snow. The last thing he saw was a silver-haired man, raising the pommel of his short sword over Finn's head.

He took just a moment to relearn how to breathe, then swiped his feet around, kicking Branwen's boots out from under her. She landed hard in the snow, and he managed to scurry away, his gut revolting against the pain.

As he staggered out of the trees, he first noted Finn, lying on the ground, unconscious or dead. Óengus stood over her, his sword now sheathed. Beyond him stood Keiren and Niklas, facing each other as Belenus struggled to his feet.

"Why!" Niklas wailed, his attention on Óengus. "Why have you ruined the scene I so perfectly created!"

Silver flashed in Keiren's hand, then she shoved a dagger into Niklas' belly. She pushed it upward with a grunt, searching for his heart.

Niklas' mouth gaped open and closed like a dying fish out of water as his eyes rolled toward her. "Why?" he rasped, sputtering up blood. "I gave you so much power."

Keiren placed her free hand on the dagger with the other, shoving further, coating her pristine white hands in blood. She sneered. "One thing you've never under-stood about mortals, Niklas, is that we can grow and change. I no longer fear my death, not like I once did. Power means nothing to me anymore."

Bracing herself, she gave the dagger a final shove,

then pulled it out in a spray of blood coating her black clothes and melting the snow at her feet. Niklas fell to the ground, dead.

Someone grabbed Kai's arm, gently, not tugging him away.

He turned to see Branwen. She was smiling softly. She'd finally found her vengeance, if not by her own hand.

Óengus walked away from Finn, and Kai tugged free of Branwen's grip, rushing toward his fallen friend. He fell to his knees in the snow and checked her pulse, then slumped over her in relief. She was alive. Óengus had merely knocked her unconscious.

Suddenly remembering there was a bigger problem, he hopped to his feet, then stood in front of Finn. Belenus, not quite recovered, but able to walk, approached.

Kai drew his dagger, knowing it would do him little good. He could never have imagined that this would be the way he would die, at the hands of a god.

"Not so fast, god," Keiren growled. She wiped the blood from her hands onto her black cloak, then moved toward Belenus.

Belenus flicked an irritated glance her way. "What is it *now*? Finnur's actions have declared a personal duel between us. I am within my rights to finish her."

He began to turn back toward Kai, then stopped mid-motion.

Keiren swayed toward him, leaving Niklas' body

forgotten in the snow. "The in-between magic will leave me soon, now that Niklas is dead," she explained, "but I am not yet powerless. I can still hold you immobile. Make a deal with me here and now, or I will kill you."

Suddenly Kai's world was encased in blackness. It had to be Keiren's magic. She controlled air and darkness. Such thick, suffocating darkness. He knelt beside Finn, fumbling until he gripped her limp arm. He tried to fight against the magic, but stood little chance. Soon it consumed him, and all the world was roaring blackness.

❦

Finn

Finn awoke to a cold beak nudging her cheek. Her eyes fluttered open. Her body was icy and numb, creating an indent in the snow. Someone else lay beside her.

Naoki's head came into view. She chittered down at her mother.

With a painful breath, Finn sat up. Seeing Kai beside her, she shook him, fearing she'd drained his magic.

Hot tears welled behind her eyes as he groaned, then sat up, rubbing his forehead, then swiping his hand back through his damp hair. A few paces away lay another form. Black dress and russet hair. Branwen.

Finn cast a final glance around. Belenus and Keiren

were gone, but Niklas' body remained. She looked up to Naoki. The snowy land seemed to be dissipating around them. Everything blurred and shifted, as if not entirely real.

Suddenly Branwen was at her shoulder, though she hadn't seen her rise. "We need your dragon to take us out of here, *now*. Niklas was the ruler of the Ceàrdaman, he held much of their power, and he created this place. With his death, his magic is unraveling."

Kai helped Finn to her feet, and they all gathered around Naoki.

Finn shivered, clinging to her dragon's neck, with Kai clinging to both of them. "I'm not sure if she can transport you," she chattered. "You have no dragon blood to travel between the realms."

"This realm will soon be no more!" Branwen called from the other side of Naoki. "She need only carry us back as it breaks!"

"What of my family!" Kai rasped. "Are they in this realm? What will happen when it breaks?"

Finn didn't have time to answer him. She managed a single sob, mourning the lives of his mother and sisters, then they were moving, too fast to see. She clung to Naoki against the wind trying to tear her away. Naoki only had to flap her wings a few beats, then they ended up in another field of snow, but this time, they were in their own realm.

Before them stood Oighear the White in all her glory, with an army of faie at her back.

Finn

Finn scurried to her feet, brushing snow from her tunic and breeches. Her head ached horribly, but otherwise, she felt full of life and energy. Much of Belenus' magic coursed through her, but she had a feeling it would not remain forever. This must be why dragons constantly hunted. The magic sustained them, but it was just like food, it would wear off eventually, and they would need more.

Gusts of snow swirled around Oighear, rippling her silken white cloak and gown. Anger seemed to emanate from her tall form. The faie—trow, pixies, all faie Finn had brought with her—were utterly still behind the Snow Queen. Far beyond she could see smoke billowing up from Sormyr, but the city was little more than a speck in her sight, and the sound of the ocean was near. They must have been transported directly south—far south—from the cliffside where she initially faced Belenus. The city was to the northeast, and the border of the forest not far from the shore.

She could feel Kai and Branwen standing close

behind her, while Naoki crouched a few paces to her left.

The drawn out silence was enough to drive Finn mad.

As if on cue, Oighear cleared her throat. "What happened with the god?"

Finn eyed her cautiously. "Shouldn't you know? You were working with him, after all."

"I work with no one, my only concern is for the faie, my people. I saw an opportunity to aid them, and I took it."

If Oighear was so concerned, Finn thought, perhaps she shouldn't have treated the faie with such retched disregard in the past. Although, she supposed now she was no better.

Finn steeled her gaze. "I was unable to trap Belenus or kill him. Arawn is dead, and with him my only chance of defeating any god. The magic I've gathered is slowly fading, even now. I have failed." Her gut clenched at her own words. She had failed in her bargain with Ashclaw, but he'd been here, not attacking Garenoch, and with him was Iseult. But where were they now?

Oighear watched her for several long moments. "The faie have done as you've asked, the soldiers of Sormyr were defeated. It will take long for those within the city walls to recover."

The sick feeling increased. Part of her abhorred what she had done, deep within, but on the surface she was still dancing on waves of power. "Yes, they have fulfilled their oath to me."

Oighear lifted her nose. "Then you shall release them, and you shall keep your oath to harm none of those who joined you this day."

Finn's eyes darted across the waiting faie, so many standing out in the open that it was almost jarring to see. Her gathered power would fade eventually, and Belenus still lived. She would need the faie again.

"No, they agreed to follow me, and my task is not yet done. But I will keep my promise. I will harm none of them, and I will protect them to the best of my ability."

Fresh snow picked up around Oighear, seeming to manifest from thin air. Her icy eyes were sharp like cracked ice. "They. Are. Mine."

Finn shook her head. Oighear was frightening, but at least for now, she was stronger than the Snow Queen. "They belong to no one. They are bound to me simply by oath. Not possessions, but allies." She lifted her voice to address the faie. "Do you all understand!"

The rows of faie shifted at her words, but none replied.

Oighear sneered. "You know faie are more loyal to their oaths than any others. But I have no oath to you, Dragon Queen, and so on this day, you have become my enemy."

The beating of wings signaled Ashclaw's arrival. Finn

glanced northward as he landed far from the waiting faie. Cautious, or simply wanting a clear place to touch down? Finn dared to watch him for a moment, searching for a figure atop his back, then swayed in relief. Iseult was with him, now on his feet, walking her way.

She wanted things settled with Oighear before he reached her. It was clear by the snow coating the land that Oighear had fought with the faie, pitting herself against Belenus and the mortals. Had she hoped to regain their loyalty?

Finn shook her head as she looked at Oighear. "I think we're done here."

Oighear watched her for a silent moment, her eyes seeming to search every part of her, both inside and out. Her shoulders straightened as she lifted her nose. She seemed to find Finn lacking. "The desolate winter is the balance to fertile summer," she said lightly. "You'll see that in time. The faie are meant to be mine. If they are not, all will be destroyed."

Finn shook her head. "The imbalance was a lie. Belenus just wanted to rule over this land and was trying to use me to eliminate all threats."

Oighear sucked her teeth. "How many deaths will it take for you to see the truth? Great power must be controlled."

She turned to Iseult as he reached them, Oighear's words lingering in her mind. *Great power must be controlled.* But by whom? For any who could control forces like the faie would be controlled by none. She and Oighear were leaders, not pawns.

She turned back to Oighear, who was now watching Ashclaw as he stalked near. "Your allies may be mighty, Dragon Queen," she muttered, "but your heart is weak."

She turned with a flourish of her white cloak and walked away, trailing snowflakes behind her. She didn't so much as glance at any of the faie, her people no longer.

Finn looked to the faie, then called out. "Our fight is finished this day! But be ready, the war is far from over!"

She could feel Kai's eyes on her back. Supporting her, or judging her? Her mind felt filled with rich, lustrous honey, tasting of Belenus' power. Wonderful, yet dangerous, for it clouded her perceptions.

The faie dispersed, and she was left to face Iseult. Yet he looked past her to Kai. "What happened?"

Kai stepped forward. "Belenus lives. Finn is still herself . . . sort of."

Finn glowered at Iseult. "I'm right here, and I should be furious at you for bringing Ashclaw to attack Arawn." She glanced at Ashclaw, who kept his distance, watching them all, and waiting . . . but waiting for what? She huffed, turning back to Iseult. "And just how did you manage that?"

Iseult was so still, he seemed a statue in the slowly melting snow. "I suspected that the dragon could understand the mortal tongue, even if his maw cannot form the words. I told him of your plan, and proposed that first eliminating Arawn would be the only way he could consume both gods. For if Belenus was defeated first, Arawn would become your ally, and allowed to live."

She glanced warily past him toward Ashclaw. "But what of the bargain to protect Garenoch? The ten days are up, and Belenus yet lives."

"You have bought yourself extra time, dragonkin," Ashclaw's voice sliced through her mind. "The God of Curses' power will sustain me for some time now. I can afford to wait. I am interested to see what you will do next."

Iseult, Kai, and Branwen all watched her, unable to hear Ashclaw's words.

She shook herself, like a bird settling its feathers. Her mind grew a little clearer. "You couldn't have known he would grant us more time," she said to Iseult.

"I did not know it until this moment."

Anger washed up, but she pushed it back down. "You risked Garenoch to save me?"

"Garenoch was risked the moment you made your deal, but the burgh is strong. Ashclaw had not yet attacked for a reason. It was not worth the risk."

Ashclaw's tail thrashed, then slammed into the ground, sending the sodden, icy soil trembling. Kai and Branwen stepped back further from the dragon, though he was not yet near enough to strike.

"Your mate should watch his tongue," Ashclaw

growled in her mind. "Attacking so many mages is a risk, yes, but I would bet all odds on myself."

Finn opened her mouth, then closed it, unsure of what else to say. There was still much to do, but for today, they were safe. "We should return to Garenoch. Ealasaid will be waiting to hear the news."

Kai, standing behind her now with Branwen, touched her shoulder, drawing her gaze. "If that snowy realm is gone, unraveled by Niklas' death, do you think my family—" he seemed unable to form the final words.

She shook her head. "We will visit the area of their farm on our way back." She selfishly hoped they were well, that they had been returned safe and sound. Self-ish, because her deepest hope was that Loinnir had been returned to this realm too.

"I will carry you to the burgh, dragonkin," Ashclaw's voice cut in. "I am far faster than your small dragon, and you are heavy upon her back. She is weary from her journey. She needs rest."

"Why?" she asked out loud, drawing the gazes of her companions.

Only she received the answer. "We are allies, for now. You nearly defeated Belenus. I have faith you will do so again."

She looked to Iseult, then to Kai. "Ashclaw has offered to return me to Garenoch. The journey would take us many days on foot, and Naoki is too tired to carry me. I should let Eala know that no attack will come today by tonight, and I can return to you with horses."

Kai nodded. "Go. We'll head toward my family's farm." He shook his head, then raked his hand back through his hair. "To the place their farm once was. We can await you there. We'll be fine."

"We?" Branwen said from behind him.

"We," Iseult agreed.

Finn looked to him. "You aren't coming with me?"

"I will await your return with the others."

If there were unexpressed meanings behind his words, she could not decipher them. And so, she simply nodded. They were both alive for now—and both obviously angry. They could discuss things further later.

She looked to Kai. "My thoughts will be with you. I hope you find those you seek, unharmed. Naoki will protect you until I can return."

"I never agreed to go with anyone!" Branwen whined as she turned away.

Finn barely heard Branwen's words. She didn't just feel like she was turning away from Iseult and Kai for a short time—for just the time it would take to reach Garenoch and return with horses—she felt like she was turning away from yet another lifetime. She had left her life with the Cavari behind, and now, she might be forced to leave yet another.

She wasn't sure how many lifetimes she would have to live before she finally found peace.

Branwen

Of all the companions Branwen could have found herself traveling with, Kai and Iseult were two of the last she would have ever imagined. They walked on either side of her, silent and brooding, their thoughts on their own troubles, which had nothing to do with hers. The presence of Finn's dragon was even more comical, slinking through the desolate fields, clearly weary. They had walked through most of the day.

Branwen's boots swished through the grass, far enough from the battlefield that no snow had touched this earth. Her primary problem now, was that she had no idea what to do with herself. Niklas was dead. Her vengeance had been carried out. So what in Tirn Ail was she supposed to do now?

Kai stopped walking and pointed. "My family's farm should be just around that bend. Just a few more paces, and we'll know if it has been returned, or—"

Branwen exhaled in relief. The long walk had actually tired her. She couldn't remember the last time her bones felt so weary. Was Niklas' magic leaving her already?

One glance at Kai tore her away from her own thoughts. He had slowed, seeming fearful to move on, and she could guess why. What if they neared, and his family's farm was not there? Or perhaps even worse, what if it was, but the people missing?

A long-forgotten empathy cracked her heart, she understood his trepidation all too well. She found herself reaching out to him, then quickly recoiled, scolding herself for caring. Caring led to pain. She glanced at Iseult, hoping he hadn't seen. His eyes were focused on the fields.

She let out a silent sigh. "Let's get this over with. Better to know now than—" but Kai had already started walking, braver than she, and it was his family on the line, "to draw it out," she finished, mostly to herself.

She hurried after him, her heart thundering in her chest. Late afternoon sunlight cut across the golden fields ahead. She had no idea what Kai's family's farm looked like, but found her eyes searching the field for any sign of inhabitance.

When Kai started running, she hurried along just behind him, with Iseult and Naoki close behind. He ran toward a humble abode with a small pigpen build against one wall. Beyond that were more fences, likely for sheep, but there were no sheep to be seen. The home seemed utterly still.

Even tired, she was still faster than she used to be. She reached the front door just behind Kai, and Iseult just behind her. Naoki veered off, curiously circling the house.

Kai threw the door open and stepped inside.

Hands trembling, Branwen followed. Warmth emanated from within. She wasn't sure how she'd missed the hint of smoke from the chimney, and she could tell by Kai's stunned expression that he had missed it too. Around a small table in the center of the home, sat a plump older woman and three young girls.

Kai fell to his knees with a soft *thunk* on the floorboards.

"Kai!" the youngest girl squealed as all three rushed toward him.

Branwen backed against the wall, suddenly uncomfortable being there. Tears streamed down Kai's cheeks as his sisters hugged him. The plump woman—his mother she supposed—remained back at the table, smiling and swatting at the tears glistening in her lashes.

Iseult watched the scene for a moment, then stalked outside, likely more comfortable waiting with the dragon.

"We had to eat snow!" the youngest girl exclaimed. "And we ate all our sheep. We thought we'd be there forever! We lost your friend's pretty white horse too. We didn't mean to, she just trotted off one day."

Kai clung to his smallest sister. Knowing just a bit of Kai's history, Branwen guessed the child was but a babe when Kai left his family behind, but they seemed bonded none the less.

Feeling another welling of emotion in her blackened heart, she backed out of the door to wait with

Iseult. Though once she saw him standing outside with the dragon, she decided to wait on her own.

She wondered how these latest turns of events would effect the land. Those who'd survived the snowy realms had been returned. Many dead in Sormyr. Armies of faie allied with the mages . . .

She shook her head, walking out into a field by herself. None of it had much to do with her. She would probably die now that Niklas was gone. She'd expected it all along. It had been his magic that animated her. The magic of the Travelers. Now—did she feel herself weakening already? She wasn't sure, but it could only be a matter of time.

She wouldn't tell Kai or Iseult. She could not stand to feel their lack of caring. No one had seemed to care when her brother perished. So she was quite sure none would care about her.

❦

Finn

"You must teach your dragon to consume magic," Ashclaw's voice echoed in Finn's mind.

She pressed herself against his scales, avoiding the whipping wind pushing hard against her.

"She doesn't need it!" she called out, unsure if Ashclaw could hear her words as she heard his.

"She has sustained herself on your magic since she

came to this realm. It is why your bond is so strong. But sustaining her weakens you. It weakens you both."

"Why do you care?" she thought, and was shocked when he answered.

"You are the only other dragonkin I know capable of consuming gods. When this realm is dead, we will hunt together in other realms."

"Dead?" she gasped, nearly losing her grip on his scales.

She wasn't sure if he actually heard her over the wind, or if he'd read her thoughts again. "Realms attract dragons when they are ready to die. We are harbingers of the end."

She silenced her thoughts, unsure of what he could pick up on.

"You will come to understand as your new magic leaves you. You will hunt for more, and you will understand."

She remained silent, but could almost feel the air of contentment radiating from Ashclaw. He was serving his purpose here, and all was going according to plan. The gods would die, and this realm would die, but there would always be others.

Ealasaid

"This is absurd!" Lady Síoda wailed.

Ealasaid watched with crossed arms as Síoda and Gwrtheryn gathered their possessions. "Perhaps, but this is the way it is. If you will not share a building with reiver women and children, then you will have to share with mages."

Lady Síoda dropped the silks she'd been pulling from a dresser drawer with a huff, then stormed to the other side of the room where her husband was fussing with a box of jewelry. She towered over the nervous, trembling man, whose movements only became more inept with her presence.

Síoda's height and girth had once seemed imposing to Ealasaid too, but she was a frightened young mage no longer. She'd led An Solas to the estate, where they had turned into something else all-together. They had become a community, intent on protecting their walls and their brethren. It was more than Gwrtheryn had ever managed for the burgh of Garenoch.

Maarav and Eywen waited behind her like twin pillars. Maarav, because he feared Síoda might throw a vase at his wife's head, and Eywen, because they'd all agreed the sight of an Aos Sí warrior would speed the would-be nobles along.

Maarav leaned down near her ear. "We should not keep the . . . ladies waiting. They may not be fighters, but they are still reivers. They could cause a ruckus."

She sighed heavily. As promised, the reiver women and children had arrived early that morning, escorted only by Conall and one other male, both of whom had been left outside the gates.

She'd almost been as shocked to see Conall as she had the previous night, leaving himself vulnerable so close to the burgh and its mages. Perhaps she could trust him as an ally, as he seemed to trust her. He trusted her, at least, to not strike him down on sight.

"There," Lady Síoda hissed, stuffing the last of her velvet dresses into a trunk. She locked the lid, then hoisted the heavy trunk by its handle with just one arm before approaching Ealasaid. She sneered down at her. "You'll come to regret this, little mage."

Maarav laughed. "Are you no longer thankful for being alive, then? Would you rather take your chances outside the walls with the faie?"

Síoda's gaze darted up to him. "Are we truly better off here, waiting to be attacked by dragons and gods?" She looked to Ealasaid in time to catch her surprised expression, then smiled wickedly at the effect she'd had. "You believe just because we are trapped here, that we have no spies. I hadn't thought you that *dense*."

"What do you mean?" Maarav growled.

Síoda laughed, while her husband stared at his feet, as far from the altercation as physically possible. "I mean that you're a fool if you believe all within this burgh are loyal. Many still shiver with disgust at your unnatural magics, and your alliance with the enemy," she nodded toward Eywen. "Some day they will speak out, and you will not be able to strike them all down."

Ealasaid's face flushed. She'd heard no rumors of rebellion, Síoda must be lying . . . but she couldn't immediately brush off the idea. She'd been busy with the mages and the faie, the non-magical humans of the burgh could have been plotting right beneath her nose. They could easily be lured in as spies for Belenus. They could even help him plan an attack—

Síoda's smug look forced Ealasaid's fear aside. That would be dealt with later. She straightened her spine, then looked Síoda square in the eye, though it was to Eywen she spoke, "Escort Lord Gwrtheryn and his wife to the holding cells. I want Slàine to interrogate them."

Síoda's face fell. "You cannot do that!" she gasped. "We *own* this estate. We own this entire burgh!"

Ealasaid stood her ground. "You own nothing, Síoda. And your spies will soon learn that I do not tolerate traitors. Slàine will extract their names from your venomous lips, and I will feed them to the dragon myself."

Síoda's face went snow-white. Behind her, Gwrtheryn looked like he might lose his morning meal. Ealasaid almost felt bad for the terrified man, but his wife could rot in a cell for all she cared.

"On second thought," she lifted her hand before Eywen could advance, "lock them in separate quarters. I will speak with Gwrtheryn myself."

Eywen and Maarav both moved past her to escort Síoda and Gwrtheryn away. There were more guards waiting just outside the door should either put up a fight.

She watched on, hiding her discomfort as the pair were ushered out the door. Next, she'd see that the women and children were given rooms in the mostly-empty building, then she'd pay a visit to the one-time ruler of Garenoch.

She hated that she'd had to threaten him—he was selfish and sheltered, but not quite malicious enough to be fed to a dragon—but Síoda's words had shaken her to her core. She'd witnessed firsthand what hatred toward mages could breed in even the smallest villages. What started out as flames of fear, could easily turn into a wildfire. No one knew what had become of An Fiach, but the roots of the organization could begin anew, right within the walls she'd built to keep them out.

Finn

The sunlight was fading by the time Finn and Ashclaw neared Garenoch. She'd instructed him to land far out of sight. It would leave her quite the walk back to the burgh, but Ealasaid might be expecting Ashclaw to attack soon, and she didn't want to risk arrows being loosed her way.

Ashclaw touched down amidst a meadow speckled with ancient oaks. She recognized the meadow instantly, and felt sick as too many memories and worries collided all at once. Feeling cold and sore, she slid down from the dragon's back.

She spun a slow circle, her eyes searching the dying light, and—

There. Right there. The spot she'd been rooted as a tree. She knew if she turned around, she'd see Àed's small hovel not far off. Àed, who'd rescued her and accompanied her to Garenoch. Without him, she might have never found all the others she now considered family.

And she'd left him to die alone while she'd been too concerned with faie, dragons, and gods.

Not wanting to see the hovel, and too sad to keep her feet, she sat in the grass, entirely overcome.

"You have a long walk," Ashclaw muttered in her mind. "You must begin plans to capture Belenus."

"I know," she sighed, still staring at the spot she'd once been rooted as a tree. Part of her longed for that solace, but she knew there was no going back. This life had shown her many horrors, but many wonders too. She'd found far too many things worth fighting for.

Ashclaw watched her for a moment, then snorted smoke. "Very well. When you are ready to act, return to this place, and I will find you."

She didn't speak as he prowled away through the trees, likely searching for a suitable spot to run forward and launch himself skyward once more.

His departure was a relief. She stroked her fingers through the cool yellow grass. She knew she needed to rise and make way toward Garenoch. They'd all be waiting for news, and it would be a long walk to reach them.

Yet, she could not make herself stand. In that moment, she felt the most peace she'd known as far back as she could remember. For once, she was alone, and though Belenus' magic still swam through her, nothing called to her for destruction. There was no one here to elicit her hunger.

A flash of glittering white caught her attention, right past her original rooting place. She narrowed her eyes, not really fearful, but curious.

A white horse walked into view, its coat seeming to shine as dusk gave way to night. From its forehead jutted a gleaming white horn.

Loinnir had no need to hide her true form with no mortals near.

In a heartbeat Finn sprung to her feet, rushing toward the unicorn. She could hardly believe she was real. Loinnir ambled toward her, never one to rush. They met in the middle, near Finn's rooting place.

Finn ran her hands up Loinnir's smooth forehead, ruffling the silken mane around her horn. "I've really needed you here," she murmured, only just realizing it in that moment.

Loinnir bumped Finn's arm with her muzzle, as if to say, "I know, but only now could I reach you."

Finn leaned her forehead just below Loinnir's horn, her hands smoothing across the unicorn's cheeks. She still felt so very tired. "I'm not sure I can continue on. The sacrifice is too great." Her confession surprised her, buried deep inside until just then.

Loinnir went still for a moment, then let out a long huff of steaming breath. "You will not give up," she seemed to say, "not this time."

It was in those sensed words that Finn finally realized, this lifetime was not the first time she and Loinnir had met. She had seen her once long ago, when she was just a young girl, within the fortress of the Snow Queen.

That was a time when she would have done

anything for her people, the Cavari, and beyond them, the Dair. She was born to be their queen, and with that came great responsibility and sacrifice. Her life was never to be her own.

No one had understood her pain, but that night at Oighear's fortress, when she had first glimpsed Loinnir within a stall, their eyes had met. It was only for a moment, but Finn was sure the unicorn knew her struggle, and her desire to be free.

Yet, Finn had been defeated. She'd gone on to do her people's bidding. When she did not follow their will, it had ended with the death of her daughter.

Loinnir nudged her, letting her know it was time to act.

"You're right," she breathed. "I must fight for the lives I've chosen to protect."

Loinnir stomped her hooves, pulling back and eyeing Finn with one glittering eye. It was that same look the unicorn had given her from her stall, well over a century ago, as if saying, "You choose to sacrifice yourself so readily."

Finn eyed her back, knowing just what the unicorn wanted her to say, but unable to agree. "My life is not worth the lives of so many others."

Loinnir stomped her hooves again. "Perhaps not, but it is worth *something*. It is something worth fighting for."

Finn took a steadying breath. Either she was going

mad, or she could actually understand Loinnir's thoughts.

She supposed it didn't really matter, as they were the words she needed to hear. She approached the unicorn and scrambled atop her back. Loinnir was an ancient being, far more ancient than Finn. More than anyone else, she understood Finn's dilemma.

She laced her fingers through Loinnir's mane, then leaned forward near her neck. The unicorn took off like an arrow, just a streak of glimmering white in the night.

As cold wind buffeted her face, Finn's mouth set into a grim line of determination. She'd always been willing to sacrifice for others, but perhaps the time for sacrifice was over.

Now—now was the time to fight.

Ealasaid

Gwrtheryn had aged so dramatically since their first meeting, Ealasaid almost felt guilty. He was a man consumed with fear, and she had brought war to his burgh . . . what *used* to be his burgh. At the rate things were growing, they'd soon be a great city. Not as large as Sormyr, perhaps, but they could have easily competed with Migris, were the port city not in ruins.

Gwrtheryn clung to the bars of his cell, his lined

face gleaming with sweat in the torchlight. It wasn't hot in his cell, nor the narrow corridor in which Ealasaid stood—alone, for fear Gwrtheryn would not speak in front of other mages or assassins.

She lifted her nose, standing proudly. "Tell me everything you know, and you will be freed."

Gwrtheryn glanced around warily. They were alone, but he had no way of seeing into the cells on either side of his. "But my wife—"

Ealasaid lifted her hand to cut him off. "Your wife is another matter. She is being questioned separately in another part of the estate."

She noted the slight slump in his shoulders at her words. Did he fear his wife's wrath should he speak against her?

He gripped the bars so tightly his knuckles turned white. "You'll protect me from her?"

Her eyebrows lifted. Perhaps this went far deeper than she realized. "That all depends on what you tell me here and now."

His eyes darted around again, then landed solidly on Ealasaid's face. Well, solidly on her nose, he didn't quite meet her eyes. "They've been planning it since the dragon attacks. Meetings in the dead of night, though I know not how he gets past the walls."

"Who?"

"A tall man, shining white hair like the finest silk. Uncomfortably handsome. Síoda fawns over him."

Her eyes widened. She wasn't sure if it would be a

help or a hindrance to tell him that his wife was fawning over a god, though it would easily explain how he'd gotten past the walls. "What are they planning?"

He licked his cracked, thin lips, glancing around again. "I do not know for sure. My wife thinks her meetings private. She doesn't realize that I've followed her more than once when she creeps out of our chambers at night. All I can say is that they plan a fatal strike toward the mages."

Her blood turned to ice. This was why Belenus had not attacked. He'd been plotting a way to wipe out the mages that wouldn't risk droves of his soldiers.

She shook her head. She could not trust this one man's words alone. "Why are you willing to tell me this? You hate the mages."

A flicker of heat shone in his eyes, letting her know that he wasn't entirely broken. "I hate my wife more."

There was so much fire in his words, she couldn't help but believe him. She withdrew a key from a pouch at her belt, then stepped forward to unlock his cell.

"You would free me with no guards present?"

She paused her movements long enough to look up at him with a smirk. "I could drop you before you could blink, old man. Remember that in these coming days."

She finished unlocking the cell, then opened the barred-door.

He remained within, watching her warily. "What are you going to do with me?"

"You will be given a comfortable room, guarded at all times, and you will tell me absolutely everything you know. Even small things that may seem unimportant."

He wrung his hands for a moment, then finally stepped out of the cell. Still, he watched her warily.

"What is it?" she sighed impatiently, worried about her mages.

He shook his head, still watching her. "It's odd, I have always feared magic, but I find the effect is beginning to wear."

"What changed?"

He shrugged, still clutching his hands together. "Perhaps it was spending so many seasons watching so many mages receive more kindness than I have ever known." He shrugged again. "Or perhaps it's just that nothing is scarier than my wife."

She sucked her teeth, warring with the sympathy his words elicited in her. "When all you give is hate, that is what you will receive in turn."

He looked down at his feet. "I suppose I deserve that."

"Let's go," she sighed, gesturing for him to walk ahead of her. She had no time to sympathize with old broken men. Her mages were in danger, and a single viper of a woman held the key to their survival. Síoda might have broken her own husband, but her tactics were nothing compared to the wrath Ealasaid was about to rain down upon her.

Finn

Twelve days had passed since Loinnir had found Finn in the woods and returned her to Garenoch. She'd given Ealasaid the good news that Ashclaw would not be attacking, but found a burgh frantic with activity, and reiver women and children inside the estate. Apparently, Belenus had been plotting against the mages, which was no surprise. She only wished she had been able to do him in when she had the chance.

Concerned with these new developments, she, Eywen, and Anna had made haste bringing horses to Kai's family farm. Reaching Iseult, Kai, and Branwen took five days, and another six to bring them back to the burgh, though they did not come back alone.

Doubling up on horses, Kai's family returned with them. The debate whether to bring them had been long, but in the end, Finn and Kai both agreed they could not leave them vulnerable to Belenus' vengeance. If he learned of their existence, they could be used against Finn.

She now walked down the stone corridor toward

er room, having seen to it personally that Kai's mother and three daughters were comfortable for the night. More than comfortable, she would say. Even Lanis, the eldest, had struggled to hide her awe at the estate, at the mages running to and fro, and at the black-clad assassins watching silently as the newcomers walked past.

Finn was almost disappointed the journey was over. Perhaps she could have asked Ashclaw to transport them all, and it could have been done with long ago, but after their last conversation, she wanted to be nowhere near the great beast.

She stopped outside her chamber door, unprepared to face the reason she'd not wanted her travels to come to an end. She and Iseult had not had much time to speak alone since the events at Sormyr. She could reluctantly admit that the lack of time was her own doing, for when they finally spoke at length, she feared what he might say.

"Are you planning to enter?" Iseult's voice, soft behind her. She'd thought he was inside, but he'd likely been out patrolling the walls.

She turned, placing her back against the door. "I'm not quite sure yet, to be honest. What do you think?"

"Go inside, Finnur."

Moving her back from the door, but keeping her eyes on Iseult, she turned the knob. Rarely could she read his expression, but now? He seemed as foreign as a distant land, as still and dark as the deepest recesses of the sea, only imaginable by the blackness viewed from a safe depth.

She swung the door open, then stepped inside, finally turning her back to him. What might he think of her, after all she'd done. Monster? Beast?

Dragon?

His touch on her shoulder startled her. She felt unable to face him, a fawn caught in the predator's gaze.

"Finn," he said again, his voice soft. "Will you not even face me?"

She turned abruptly, surprised by his tone. "I am only reluctant to face you, for fear of what I might see in your eyes."

But there was no fear in his eyes. No repulsion. "You are not upset?"

Her lips parted. "Because of Arawn you mean?" She had been angry at first, but that had long since waned.

He nodded. "I know I foiled your plan, but I could see no other way. I know I am selfish, but I cannot lose you."

She laughed, though it was bitter, like broken glass scraping across stone. "I've been avoiding you this whole time because I feared you would no longer want me after what I've become. I am no longer the creature you fell in love with. I am not noble, not kind." She flourished her words with her hand.

He caught her wrist. "My love is not conditional."

He seemed almost offended, and it shocked her more than anything up until this point.

She shook her head, at a loss for words. "Iseult, so many innocent people died because of me. I had already drawn Belenus out, but I still let the faie attack. I wanted to deal him an even greater blow. He threatened me with an army, and I destroyed it with one of my own. Now that the magic has faded, I can see that it was wrong, but in the moment, it didn't *feel* wrong. It felt like I had power, and that was all that mattered."

He watched her for a painfully long moment, the chamber so silent she could clearly hear the distant voices from the courtyard.

Finally, he seemed to settle on an answer. "This will not be the last time you stand on the brink of darkness, staring down into an endless abyss. You will see it many more times, I am sure. It is what you are now."

She blinked at him. Was this it? Was the rejection she'd been waiting for finally here?

"You may stand at the cliff's edge," he continued, taking her hands in his. "But you will feel a weight at your wrist." He moved one hand along her skin to slowly encircle her wrist. He squeezed lightly. "That weight will be my hand, keeping you here with me."

She hadn't realized the nerves she'd been stuffing down until that moment, as her body began to tremble. She wanted to fall into his arms, but she couldn't. Not yet. "Your weight may not be enough. You may be pulled into the abyss with me."

"Then so be it. Any world without you would be far worse."

Her breath hitched. Could she do this? Could she truly risk dragging him down with her? She thought of Loinnir, now safe within the estate, then fell into his arms, shaking with relief. Although underneath it was fear. She knew what he offered was something she could not ask, but she was not strong enough to turn it away.

Bedelia

"Still itching for battle?" Syrel's voice startled Bedelia from her thoughts. She'd spent most of the last several days atop the new walls of the burgh, trying to make herself useful, though her bow now rested against the parapet, useless, and they'd seen no sign of dragons nor soldiers.

Bedelia crossed her arms, clad in a heavy winter tunic, then turned toward Syrel, who'd acquired more fitting clothes somewhere, black breeches and a billowing sapphire blouse that matched her eyes. "On the contrary," Bedelia corrected her, "I'd be content to never see battle again."

Syrel's eyes glittered, starkly contrasting with her pallid skin and loosely flowing black hair. "Liar. You like to be useful, and fighting is what you know how to do."

Bedelia searched for any hidden meanings in Syrel's words, Eywen's warning still lingering at the back of her mind. She could admit now that she'd avoided Syrel recently, if only to process how she felt. "Why are you here?"

Syrel's smile faltered. "I just came to see you. I apologize if my presence is unwelcome." She stepped back.

Bedelia held up a hand, flustered. "No! Please, that's not what I meant."

Syrel's shoulders seemed to relax as she regained the step she'd taken away. She turned her gaze outward, toward the eastern forest and the cliffs beyond. "I fear what my people are planning, and the Ceàrdaman," she said, her voice low. "I haven't spoken to my brother about it, he thinks me a mischief-maker, and little more."

Bedelia watched Syrel's lips quiver, and almost expected tears to fall, though none did. "What do you think they are planning?"

Syrel shook her head. "I cannot say, but if they are with the Ceàrdaman, nothing good. They are so conditioned to blindly follow power, many of them have lost any sense of honor."

Bedelia wasn't sure why Syrel was telling her any of this, but part of her was overwhelmed with gratitude that she trusted her enough to share. "I hope it is not what you think. I hope they can all find peace."

Syrel turned wide eyes toward her. "Many of them have named you enemy in the past. Why would you care?"

Her words came out before she could reconsider, "Because *you* care."

Syrel smiled. That genuine smile wiped the last remnants of Eywen's warning from Bedelia's mind. She startled at the touch of fingertips on her hand, then relaxed as Syrel laced her warm fingers with hers.

Together they looked out beyond the walls, for what, Bedelia could not be sure. But they were looking together, and she found that was quite enough reason to continue.

Kai

Days had passed since the events at Sormyr, and things seemed quiet. Unusually so. Kai felt uneasy walking through the burgh. After the merrymaking—brought on by Ashclaw's disappearance—had died down, a certain tension had manifested. Burghsfolk spoke in hushed tones, their eyes darting about nervously, especially when mages were near.

Having gone to visit Anna and Eywen at the newly-constructed walls, he now hurried back to the estate, his hand always hovering near his dagger.

The burghsfolk had always looked at him askance—he looked a bit too faie these days—but it had never been like this. Just what was brewing, and how much did Ealasaid know? He knew the prior lord of the burgh had been taken on as an advisor, divulging some scheme by Belenus, but Kai hadn't had a chance to speak with Ealasaid or Maarav about the matter. They seemed eternally busy, and Finn was already dealing with far too many issues of her own.

As he neared the estate walls, a flash of black skirts

caught his attention. Had someone just darted behind the nearest building at the sight of him?

Having had enough of whispers and sidelong glances, he veered sharply to the right, going around the front side of the small home, quiet at this darkening hour. With his feet light as feathers, he crept around, finding someone kneeling behind the slats of a small chicken roost.

He watched her for a moment, almost regretting that it was her. He hadn't spoken to Branwen since they'd returned to Garenoch. In fact, he'd hardly seen her at all.

"Is it really necessary to hide from me?"

She startled, then hopped to her feet, facing him. "Who says I was hiding?"

He crossed his arms and sighed. "So you just really like kneeling in chicken droppings?" He extended one arm toward the tall wooden box behind her, which occasionally emanated with sleepy clucks.

She scowled. "Really, I'm shocked you even noticed me. Most do not."

He'd noticed it too, how eyes seemed to naturally avert from her, but he'd had no trouble spotting her here and there the past few days. "What are you doing out here anyway?"

She glanced over her shoulder, seeming to plan her escape route before turning back to him. "Leaving."

"To go where?"

She shrugged. "Does it really matter? I've done what I've set out to do. It's finished."

He knew he shouldn't trust her, but the pain in her eyes was too obvious. Too *raw*. "Well if you've finished what you needed to do, you may as well stick around and see what happens next?"

"Why?"

Fool woman. Couldn't she see he was doing his best to be nice? "You could make a life for yourself here."

She scoffed. "Just as you have made a life for yourself? Running around, risking peril, and for what? I see you wandering about alone just as much as I."

He lifted his hands in surrender. "I shouldn't have even tried with you. Flit away if that is your choice."

Though he'd given her permission to leave, she didn't move. Instead, she watched him like a hungry rabbit, hoping he'd feed her and not eat her. "I think—" she hesitated, "I think now that Niklas is gone, I am dying. It was his magic keeping me alive, and now it is slowly leaving me. It is better for me to go now. I can't bear for others—others who care nothing for my life —to watch."

His mouth fell open, but she clearly wasn't jesting. He shook his head and stepped forward. "There must be something we can do. Finn—"

She shook her head, holding up her palms to keep him back. "No. I've been living on borrowed time, but at least it gave me my vengeance. It is alright."

"But—"

She shook her head to cut him off, then stepped toward him. She reached up on her toes and planted a light kiss on his cheek. "Thank you for caring," she whispered.

And just like that, she was gone.

❄❄❄

Àed

Though Àed's eyes were closed, he felt as if he could see the stars glittering beyond his window. It was a peculiar sensation, one he'd never experienced, even in his younger years when his magic was the strongest. At times, he felt like he was leaving his body, and it was as easy as drifting off to sleep. He'd begin to drift away, then something would jolt him back, perhaps his deeply ingrained survival instinct, cultivated during his many years of life.

He sensed a feminine form leaning over him, cloaked in darkness. Perhaps a phantom, come to lure him to the grave. His eyes cracked open, just enough to see delicate, long-fingered hands cradling a glowing red gem as big as the figure's two palms put together.

The gem lowered toward his chest, bringing the scent of herbs and smoke with the figure's closeness.

A familiar voice whispered, "I'm sorry father, I cannot stay. I fear you will not forgive me for what I have done."

He was too weak to respond. The gem touched his chest, and the magic of a thousand ages rushed through him. He shot upright, blinking back tears as his eyes darted around the night-darkened room, but he was too late. He was alone.

⁂

Iseult

Iseult sat at a table in the inn, far from the fire, cast half in shadow. He did not naturally flock to crowds, but knew this was likely the last place anyone would search for him. He needed time to think, and to plan.

He reached for his untouched dram of whiskey, then slowly recoiled, having no real desire for the drink, though the other patrons did not seem to share that sentiment. Word had spread that the black dragon was gone. They were all safe . . . for now.

He sat back in his chair and watched the loud, blad-dered burghsfolk. Mead and whiskey seemed to be the only thing the burgh wasn't short on these days, though if they succeeded in growing new crops, food stores might recover by the end of the next growing season.

Iseult pushed thoughts of the burgh's well-being from his mind. This was not his home, and not what truly mattered to him. He had succeeded in his plan, to a degree. His risk in approaching Ashclaw had resulted in Arawn's death, but it had not stopped Finn from eating Belenus' magic.

Perhaps it was for the best—the magic did make her stronger—but she had survived this long by following her heart. Now he feared she was guided by *other* instincts. He would love her regardless, but he also wanted to save her. He just had to figure out how.

His eyes caught a glimmer of silver hair. He clenched his full dram of whisky so hard with his fingertips, the pewter was in danger if warping.

Óengus approached him, no fear in his eyes, no caution in his gait. He stopped before Iseult's table.

Iseult did not reach for a blade. He knew he was faster than Óengus. If violence was called for, he would cut Óengus down before he could blink.

Instead, he looked up at him. "What are you doing here?"

Óengus looked thinner than he used to be. *Older.* His winter cloak and suede breeches threadbare. "Waiting for a friend," he explained. "I'm surprised to see you here. *Alone.*"

"Which friend." More a demand than a question.

Óengus pulled out a chair and sat across the table from him. "That's of little import. I assure you, we mean no harm. For now."

Iseult's fingers itched to fetch his sword. "You were there in that snowy realm with Keiren. You hit Finn over the head. I should kill you now."

Óengus rolled his eyes. "It was just a small bump,

and if you ask me, it was for the girl's own good. She's gotten herself in way over her head. You should just be grateful Keiren brought along Kai and the wraith to make sure Finn safely awoke in time."

Iseult stared. Kai had told him what happened, that he and Branwen had been suddenly snatched up and transported, but that they had all been consumed by darkness when Keiren faced the god. So perhaps the sorceress had really been interested in Finn's wellbeing. The trio were all still alive, after all. There was still just one thing he did not understand. "And you? Where do you come in? The last we saw of you, you were with Oighear, and she is our enemy."

Óengus laughed. The sound would have been startling if the common room wasn't already awash with shouts and laughter. "You and I are fools, my friend, to ever think we could belong with these immortal women. They know so much more than we ever will."

"I am nothing like you."

Óengus leaned forward, bracing his elbows on the table. He lowered his voice, "Then what are you doing here alone, while your tree girl is resting within the estate?"

Iseult gripped the tabletop. He'd never been one to give in much to blind rage, but it seemed always just beneath the surface these days. "I will ask one more time, what are you doing here? What does Keiren plan?"

Óengus shrugged and leaned back. "The sorceress

loves her father. As I've said, you have nothing to worry about. As for what she plans next, I suppose I'll find out eventually."

"You are not one to act without motive," he accused.

Óengus laughed. "The barrier breaking changed us all, my lad. Once upon a time, I would have been at the center of a brewing war, now I find myself on the periphery. I am old, not the fighter I once was. I suppose now, I'd like to just live long enough to see how it all ends."

Iseult watched him for a long moment. Normally, he'd believe nothing Óengus said, but he'd displayed not a single hint that he was lying.

Iseult's shoulders relaxed, just a touch. "I suppose you and I are in the same situation, then. It seems all I can do now is wait, and watch."

"You're not the idle type, lad, don't fool yourself. You'll fight for her until your dying breath. Perhaps you are wiser than I in that matter. I suppose we won't know for sure until the end." He snatched Iseult's forgotten dram of whiskey and drained it in one swill.

"You speak as if it will be the end for us all."

Óengus smiled, if the bitter crook of his mouth could be called a smile. "You may not feel it yet, but some of us see far more than others. Ask your friend Anna. It's as if the land has a heartbeat. It's been drumming faster and faster, like a rodent's pulse, just before the viper strikes. It may not be the end of us all, but it will be the end of something."

Óengus' shoulders straightened suddenly, though Iseult could not divine any change in their surroundings. He stood. "My friend is ready to go now. I've no doubt I'll be seeing you soon."

With that, Óengus turned and walked away, and Iseult made no move to stop him. He waited a time, with the merrymakers standing near the hearth-fire casting looming shadows all around him, then finally stood to return to the estate.

He didn't need Anna's magic to tell him that chaos was at its breaking point. He could feel it building, like a mighty wave ready to crash upon the shore.

EPILOGUE

*B*eneath the eastern prison in Sormyr, a group of men gathered with torches. All watched a single man, his hair shaved unusually short, his face littered with scars of battle. All men had heard tales of him. He'd toppled giants, battled mages, had even faced a dragon or two.

Radley eyed them each in turn, just twenty men, but more would come. Perhaps some of the tales about him had been embellished, but he would not correct them. These men needed a strong leader if any mortals were to survive.

"Listen," he said, and all fell silent. There was no need to raise his voice here. In the underground tunnel, all sound carried. "The thing we've always feared has finally happened. The faie have formed an army, and Sormyr nearly fell—*would* have fallen, if the faie had not relented. I've little doubt we will never understand why they did not murder all within the walls of the city. They are bloodthirsty animals, incapable of seeing reason. The mages who tolerate them are just as horrible. Abominations of nature!"

The men muttered words of agreement, then once again fell silent.

"I have spoken with the Ceàrdaman." He waited at another expected outburst of murmurs. To most, the Ceàrdaman were faie. Radley agreed with the majority, but at least the Travelers were sentient. They could be reasoned with. Alliances and treaties could be made.

The men quieted again, waiting to hear more.

"I am told their leader was slain, but their people yet stand in strength. They will make An Fiach great again."

At the mention of their fallen organization, the tone of the men's mutters changed perceptibly. Any who had survived service had been appalled when the organization had disbanded, settling into the ranks of Sormyr's soldiers when it became too dangerous to roam the countryside in search of faie to hunt.

Radley knew without a doubt they would join up again when the moment came. "Are you with me, men? Will you face mages and faie alike to save the lives of the few mortals who remain?"

More muttering. "But the Ceàrdaman?" one questioned. "How can we trust them?"

Another anticipated question. One for which he'd already prepared an answer. "We have no choice. You saw what the faie can do. Our strength as men alone is not enough."

Silence weighed heavily as the men thought it over. His palms began to sweat. Had he been too bold? Would they skewer him where he stood for even considering an alliance with the Ceàrdaman?

Gazes locked around the small space, as one by one the men nodded. The first one who'd spoken finally turned to Radley. "If the Ceàrdaman can grant us strength to kill the faie, then we will be strong enough to kill them too—when the time comes."

His words made Radley squirm. He doubted even with newfound strength any man here could defeat one of the Ceàrdaman—he'd recently seen first hand what they could do—but their agreement was all he needed, for now.

For now, they would fight, and these battles would lead him to what he truly desired. He'd been searching for a particular faie all along. He saw her once at Garenoch, then again at the recent battle. He'd watched her at the head of the faie, and had spied as she fled to the woods.

Yes, he'd sought the Snow Queen since he was a boy. His peers had mocked him, and told him she was only legend. But he knew, he knew by his grandfather's stories of Oighear the White, who had pillaged his ancestor's estate, in one fell swoop lowering nobles to beggars, with none willing to help should they incur her wrath.

Generations later, he'd felt the effects of the Snow Queen's icy grip in seeing his mother begging for scraps. In seeing dirt and muck kicked in her face for even being alive.

His mother was long gone now, but Radley had not forgotten. With the help of the Ceàrdaman, and An Fiach, the Snow Queen would finally pay.

Branwen

Branwen stroked her fingers across the roughly carved stone. She was no mason, but she'd done her best to provide a memorial for her twin brother. His actual body had likely been left for the wolves, torn apart and forgotten. Hers would be the same, deep in the woods where she now sat, a bushel of snowdrops in hand.

She placed the flowers on her brother's marker, then curled up on the ground. Over the past days, she'd felt the magic of the in-between slowly leaving her. It had been Niklas' will that animated her, and now that he was gone, his spell—for lack of a better word—was unraveled.

She breathed the crisp night air, for the last time she was sure, and spared a final thought for Finn, Kai, and all the others still fighting. She wasn't sure who had it better. Life was a gift, but to her, so was death. She was so very tired.

She closed her eyes, ready to join Anders, wherever he was.

"You've been a busy little wraith." Words startled her back into awareness.

She cracked open her eyes, beholding Belenus, as glittering as a shining star in the moonlight. "You are too late to do me any harm, god. Go away."

He tilted his head, trailing pure white hair across his chiseled cheek. "Part of you is still mortal, girl. Part of you can be touched by me. I can offer you a new life."

She pressed the side of her face against cold soil. "I do not want it. Leave me be."

She squeezed her eyes shut as he crouched beside her.

His words were soft, barely audible. "I fear you have no choice. It is not for mortals to question the will of gods."

He placed his hands upon her and began to chant in an ancient tongue beyond her comprehension. Starlight seemed to trickle through her veins, cold, yet bright.

In that moment, she understood why mortals had once worshipped the gods. For as cruel and terrible as they seemed, inside they were as vast as the stars in the sky. As unstoppable as the rising sun.

And as vengeful as a the greatest maelstrom in the darkest expanse of the sea.

When the fate of the elves rests on the shoulders of an antisocial swamp witch, will a common enemy be enough to bring two disparate races together?

The Empire rules with an iron fist. The Valeroot elves have barely managed to survive, but at least they're not Arthali witches like Elmerah. Her people were exiled long ago. Just a child at the time, her only choice was to flee her homeland, or remain among those who'd betrayed their own kind. She was resigned to living out her solitary life in a swamp until pirates kidnap her and throw her in with their other captives, young women destined to be sold into slavery.

With the help of an elven priestess, Elmerah teaches

the pirates what happens to men who cross Arthali witches, but she's too late to avoid docking near the Capital. While her only goal is to run far from the political intrigue taking place within, she finds herself pulled mercilessly into a plot to overthrow the Empire, and to save the elven races from meeting a bloody end.

Elmerah will learn of a dark magical threat, and will have to face the thing she fears most: the duplicitous older sister she left behind, far from their home in Shadowmarsh.

Continue reading for a sneak peek at book one in The Moonstone Chronicles!

SNEAK PEEK AT THE WITCH OF SHADOWMARSH

Elmerah checked the shackles on her wrists for the hundredth time. What a load of *dung*. How in Ilthune had lowly sea pirates been able to afford magic-nullifying wrist bonds? The ones on her ankles were just simple iron. She would free herself from *those* easily enough if she had access to her magic...which, she didn't.

The heavy iron hurt her wrists and squeezed her boots uncomfortably at her ankles, not to mention the steady *drip drip* of water leaking in from the deck above her head to add to her annoyance. She leaned her back against the wooden wall of the small cabin near the ship's bow, her temporary prison. Her long legs, clad only in thick tights, erupted in goosebumps.

A few other women shared the space with her, their heads slumped in the swinging lantern light. That her fellow captives were all women, and all young and fairly beautiful, told her one thing. They were on their way to be sold into slavery of the worst kind. Although, how the pirates intended to keep a witch like herself tethered for long was beyond her. The bigger question was, *why?* She was at least a decade older than the young girls, though she felt herself not horrible to look at. Her black hair and bronze skin hinted at her Arthali heritage, and she was curvy enough to be considered feminine, though her height and well-muscled frame scared off most male suitors.

Not that she'd been looking.

She shook her shackles again. The ship swayed gently, the sound of the choppy sea above muffling the soft weeping of her fellow prisoners.

Elmerah sneered. She'd never been one to weep, and she sure as Ilthune's lance didn't consider herself a victim. She was a temporary hostage, nothing more. As soon as she managed to rid herself of these shackles, she'd teach the sea pirates a lesson. They'd rue the day they decided it was a good idea to turn an Arthali swamp witch into a slave.

She glanced at her nearest fellow captive, barely illuminated by the swaying, lone lantern. The girl had long white hair like spider silk, and bony, angular features carved into perfect alabaster skin. Her downcast eyes dominated her small face, and pointed ears jutted out from beneath her hair. She was a Faerune elf, one of the Moonfolk. Elmerah knew that if the girl turned her large eyes upward, they would glint in the darkness. Faerune elves could see just as well at night as they could during the day. They were fast too, with incredibly agile hands that could send a dagger into your chest before you could even blink.

Agile hands, Elmerah thought, glancing once again at her shackles. Perhaps this girl could be of use to her.

"Psst," she whispered, scooting closer to the girl.

The girl startled and glanced upward, and sure enough, her eyes glinted like moonlight. Her loose white tunic made her look like a ghost.

"Yes?" she asked softly, seeming to regain her composure. Poor girl couldn't have been more than eighteen.

"Come over here," Elmerah whispered. "I need your help."

The girl narrowed her eyes, then clutching her shackled hands to her chest, she scooted along the floor until she was sitting side by side with Elmerah.

Elmerah lowered her head toward the girl. "Search my hair, I should still have some pins left in there." She *hoped* she'd had some pins left. Even after the pirate caught her unawares and cuffed her, she'd put up a fight. The man had ripped a clump of her hair out in the struggle. She'd made up for it by kicking out two of his teeth.

The girl's fingers tugged through Elmerah's matted hair.

She cringed. She needed a bath.

"You smell like a swamp," the girl muttered.

"Well you smell like fairy dung," Elmerah grumbled. Never mind that the girl actual smelled like a crystal clear brook surrounded by wildflowers. Elves always smelled pleasant, except perhaps the Akkeri. The sea-riders smelled a bit like rotten fish.

"There," the girl whispered, pulling a hairpin free. "Now what do you want me to do with it?"

Elmerah lifted her head, then held out her cuffed wrists. "Get these off me and I'll make these pirates *pay*."

The girl's eyes widened, as if finally just *really* seeing her. "You're Arthali," she gasped, retracting the pin toward her chest.

Elmerah fought the urge to sneer. Pureblood Arthali had been exiled from the Ulrian Empire over three decades ago, but old fears ran as deep as the Kalwey Sea. "Yes," she hissed, "so you know I can back up my claims."

The elf girl met her gaze for several seconds, then lowered trembling hands to Elmerah's cuffs. "Arcale protect me," she muttered as she inserted the pin into the keyhole.

The girl's words inspired Elmerah to take a closer look at her garb. The white tunic, embroidered with little silver moons, topped fitted white pants. Her brows raised in recognition. These pirates really were idiots. They'd not only kidnapped an Arthali witch, but a Faerune priestess. If the elves ever found out about this, every last pirate would surely meet a swift end.

The pin clicked in the lock.

Elation filled her as she pulled off the cuffs, then hurriedly pumped magic into the benign shackles around her ankles, which soon clicked open. She stood, then looked down at the Faerune priestess.

Seeming to sense her hesitation, the girl glared. "You said you'd get us out of here."

"Actually, I said I'd make these pirates pay."

The girl's glare deepened.

She'd be a fool to get involved with the elves, but— she huffed out a long breath, then held a hand out to the girl. "Hold the cuffs away from your body."

Still staring up at her, the girl obeyed.

Elmerah pushed magic into the cuffs. They fell away from the girl's wrists, then clattered to the wooden planks, followed by the ones at her ankles.

The girl stood, a full head shorter than Elmerah "Now the others," she demanded.

Elmerah glared down at her. "Weren't you just trembling in your boots about freeing an Arthali witch? Are you sure you should be making demands?"

Her glare did not waver.

"Fine," Elmerah hissed. "They'll prove a worthwhile distraction, if nothing else."

She made her way around the small cabin, freeing the other women one by one. There were six in total, eight counting herself and the elven priestess. Some of the women stood, but others remained slumped on the floor, *broken*.

The elf girl watched her expectantly.

"I've freed them," she grumbled. "If they're not willing to help themselves now, there's nothing I can do. Now I'm off to murder some pirates."

After a moment, the elf girl nodded. She marched across the small space away from the lantern's light and retrieved something from a dark corner, then returned to Elmerah with a long oar in hand, taller than the girl holding it.

"You Moonfolk really can see in the dark, can't you?"

She nodded. "Yes, now let us go enact our vengeance."

Elmerah smirked. Perhaps she'd made a wise choice in allying herself with the girl after all. She made her way toward the rickety wooden steps leading up to the deck. A heavy padlock dangled from the trapdoor above.

She made quick work of it, overwhelming the metal components with magic until they snapped. Leave it to pirates to only buy enchanted shackles and not a padlock. They were in *way* over their heads.

The women had all herded together behind her, those who'd stood on their own now supporting those who'd refused.

"What's your name?" Elmerah asked the elven girl as she reached her side.

She gripped the oar tightly in her hands. "Saida Fenmyar."

"Elmerah Volund," she introduced. "Are you ready, Saida?"

Saida nodded.

Elmerah tossed the trap door open, landing with a loud *thwack* on the deck above. She rushed up the final steps, angry magic coursing through her veins. Only three of the men were on deck, all turned toward her with jaws agape.

She kicked the nearest one right in his hanging jaw, darting in and stealing his cutlass before he hit the deck.

"I thought you'd use magic to attack them," Saida said, facing the other two men just a few paces off as the other women ascended behind her.

"I'm saving it for their leader," Elmerah explained. "Plus, I was really feeling like I needed to kick someone in the face."

The other two men neared, weapons drawn. Their dirty faces and ragged loose clothing hinted to their status as lowly crewman. "Oi!" one of them called out, "the prisoners are loose!"

More men would be on deck soon. They needed to act fast so they wouldn't be overwhelmed. Elmerah lifted her cutlass, ready to fight, but Saida was way ahead of her. She launched herself at the men in a graceful leap, swinging the oar like a staff, her white hair streaming behind her. One man tried to counter, but his weapon was effortlessly flicked away, right before the oar swooped back around and smacked him with the broad side on the back of his head. The other man got the narrow side straight in his gut, knocking the wind from his lungs.

Elmerah would have liked to continue watching but more men had swarmed the deck, their legs braced wide against the swaying of the ship. She counted them, weighing their odds before realizing she'd be out of magical energy by the time this fight was over. The other women huddled together near the trap door, their eyes squinted against the occasional gust of heavily salted air. *Useless.*

She lifted the cutlass toward the cloudy sky, filling it with more of her magic than she should have been expending, but she wasn't about to risk someone shackling her once more. Her power surged into the blade to the point of bursting as the first man charged her.

A rumble in the sky echoed her guttural growl. She really shouldn't be doing this, but it was too late to go back now. If she moved the sword, the lightning might be attracted to her instead.

The bolt hit the blade, absorbing into the metal. The man stumbled away, eyes wide. Too late for him as well. She whipped the blade downward, sending a bolt of lightning straight toward his chest. It hit its mark, then bounced to the next man before hitting the far wall of the above-deck cabin where it dissipated.

She spared a quick glance toward Saida, who'd stayed near the women, protecting them with her oar, then turned back as more men charged her. One had a new set of shackles in hand.

"Get them 'round her wrists!" a finely dressed man shouted from a safe distance.

Her lip quivered with a snarl. She'd found the captain.

Still bursting with energy, she whipped the sword toward the men, tossing them aside with electrical currents. She surged forward, slicing any who'd not fallen with her blade. One man's cutlass neared her throat, then fell away as an oar thunked down upon his sweaty brow.

"My thanks!" Elmerah shouted, slamming her shoulder into another pirate and sending him overboard.

She turned toward another, brandishing her blade flickering with elemental sparks. She must have looked quite the sight, given a wet spot soon formed on his breeches. He tossed his cutlass aside and willingly followed his fellow pirate into the sea.

Her snarl still in place, she turned toward the captain. He was attempting to unlock the cabin door behind him, but his trembling hands were fumbling the key. She stalked toward him. Saida stood back with her oar in hand and several men lying broken at her feet.

The captain glanced over his shoulder at her approach. His blue eyes widened. With his shiny black hair and clear complexion he was almost handsome.

Unfortunately, the stain of capturing slaves made him ugly.

His little metal key clattered to the deck.

Cutlass still in hand, Elmerah knelt to retrieve it. She stood, dangling the key in front of his face. "I believe you dropped this."

"Please don't kill me," he whimpered.

Her smile broadened. "Did you really think it was a good idea to kidnap an Arthali witch? My people are well known for showing little mercy."

"I was just following orders. Please, I'll tell you everything. I'll tell you who hired me and you can go after her."

Her? Now that was interesting.

"I'm guessing any information I might want is contained in the cabin behind you," she gestured to the locked door with her cutlass. "I'm not seeing any reason to spare you."

Footsteps sounded behind her, then Saida appeared at her side. "We'll take him back to my people. He will stand trial for his crimes."

Elmerah snorted. "I'm not going anywhere near the elves." She turned back to the captain, offering him the key. "Unlock it. Let's see what you have inside."

The captain snatched the key, then unlocked the door with still trembling hands. "Thank you," he muttered. "Thank you for not bringing me to the elves." He pushed the door open.

His thanks sent a disgusted shiver down Elmerah's spine. She turned and gave Saida a subtle nod.

The oar came down. The captain crumpled.

Elmerah glanced back at the waiting women, then to Saida. "Have them tie up any who still live. I'm going to take a look around."

Saida nodded, then returned to the women as Elmerah stepped over the prostrate captain into the office.

The furnishings were sparse, but high quality. A heavy oak writing desk dominated the far wall, stationed next to a bed with a proper mattress topped with vibrant silks and fluffy feather pillows. While the bed appealed to her tired body, she was more interested in the desk, and what information its drawers might contain.

She marched across the room, fighting her sluggishness as her adrenaline seeped away. She'd used far too much magical energy calling lightning to her new cutlass. It would have been easier with an enchanted sword, but her weapons had been left behind when she was kidnapped.

Swapping the cutlass to her left hand, she opened the middle drawer. Ink, bitterroot with a pipe, and blank sheets of parchment. Useless. She opened the next drawer. Empty. Why even have a desk? When the third drawer revealed only a few clean handkerchiefs, she turned back to the rest of the cabin. She could hear Saida outside directing the other women to bind all the men, but she still wanted to act fast. She'd like to be far away on one of the smaller boats long before the ship reached shore. *If* it reached shore. She would be highly surprised if any of the women actually knew how to sail.

She narrowed her gaze at one of the floorboards near the bed. It was slightly raised from the others.

She stepped toward it, then halted, feeling dizzy. She'd used *far* too much power. She'd be lucky to make it to shore on her own at all.

"Are you well?" a woman's voice asked.

She turned to see Saida peeking into the cabin.

"All the men are bound, but we should decide what to do soon. If I'm not mistaken, we are headed toward Galterra."

"The Capital?" Elmerah balked, swaying on her feet. She shook her head. "It doesn't matter. Could you check that floorboard?" she pointed. "I'll take whatever is hidden down there and depart on one of the smaller boats."

Saida marched across the room and knelt, easily prying up the floorboard with her fingertips. She withdrew a stack of rolled documents, set them aside, then withdrew three large leather pouches of coin.

Elmerah stepped forward, then snatched two pouches of coin from Saida's hands and affixed them to her belt. Next she retrieved the folded documents from the floor and placed them under her arm. After a moment of debate, she tossed her new cutlass aside with a dull *clang*, then approached the unconscious captain in the doorway. Sure enough, a far finer cutlass was at his hip. She slid it from his belt, considering skewering the man with his own blade, but walked out into the open air instead. A storm was brewing further out to sea, and she really wanted to start paddling before it was too late.

Saida hurried out after her, then past her. "There are four extra boats," she explained. "We should all be able to reach shore easily enough." She retrieved her oar from one of the women, then turned back to Elmerah. "It would be best to have four women per boat, everyone can row."

Elmerah stalked past her toward the lower cabin where they'd been held prisoner, the pouches of coin jangling at her hips. "I told you, I'll be leaving on my own. The rest of you would be wise to take only one boat, and take turns rowing. It is more tiring than you think."

Saida followed her as she descended the stairs into the cabin. "If that is true, then how do you intend to man a boat on your own?"

"It's tiring for weak young girls," Elmerah muttered, groping about in the darkness for the oars. "Not for me."

Saida stomped a few paces past her, reached into the darkness, then handed Elmerah an oar. Her elven eyes glinted in the near dark. "There's no need to be difficult. We're all in this together. Surely once we reach Galterra we will be offered aid."

Elmerah raised an eyebrow at her. "Have you ever *been* to Galterra?"

Saida lifted her nose into the air. "Once, with an envoy. My clan was signing a new trade agreement."

Elmerah held out her hand expectantly for another oar, which Saida soon offered her. "You saw the Capital on its best behavior," she explained. "I advise you to don a hood as soon as you reach shore. Keep your hair and ears covered, and don't let anyone see your eyes at night."

Saida's dainty jaw dropped, but Elmerah had no more time to explain things to her. She herself would wear a hood if she decided to enter the Capital. While she might not stand out quite as much as an elf, her height and coloring would give away exactly what she was, a pure-blooded Arthali, not the half-breeds still allowed in the Empire. Many would steer clear of her, but others would view her as a challenge. Oars in hand, she turned and walked back up the stairs.

She heard the clatter of oars behind her, then thunks coming up the stairs after her, but didn't turn to look. If the girl wanted to carry oars and make herself responsible for the other women, that was her choice.

Her own oars in hand, she strode toward the side of the ship, then stopped in her tracks. She would have palmed her face if she had a free hand. She'd need someone to help her lower her boat down to the sea.

She turned back with a huff to see Saida handing out oars to the other women. A few of the men still alive had come to, and were groaning and pleading to be set free. She would have kicked them into silence if she had the energy. Cursed Ilthune her limbs were tired.

"Hey elf girl!" she called out. "Why don't you let the others row into Galterra to report what has happened, and you and I can find some quiet place far from the docks from which to disappear."

Saida approached, her brow furrowed. "I thought you wanted to go alone."

Elmerah shifted her oars to lean against the deck, then brushed a clump of salt-saturated hair from her face. "If you'd like to take your chances in Galterra, be my guest. I'm just trying to help you."

Her gaze narrowed. "Show me how to lower a boat for the other women, then I'll go with you, but only to the shore. After that I'll head toward Galterra to send word to my mother."

Elmerah fought her shoulders as they threatened to slump in relief. Saida was a bit scrawny, but she could still help her row . . . not that she'd *ever* openly admit to needing the help.

"Please," a nearby man groaned. "Just untie us. We can help you lower the boats."

Elmerah found she suddenly had enough energy to land her boot against his ribs.

After a pained *oof*, he kept his mouth shut.

"Let's go. I want to reach the shore before the storm hits."

Saida nodded, then moved past her toward the waiting women.

Elmerah watched her go, though her thoughts were no longer on the elf girl. Rather, her thoughts were on what in the name of Arcale she was going to do when she reached shore. Without the use of a ship, it would take her weeks to reach home again. She had no food or travel supplies, and no time to search the ship for such things if she didn't want to get stuck in a tiny boat in a storm.

She patted her belt pouch. At least she had coin, and if she could find a place to rest, she could regain enough energy to protect herself. She just needed to get through a single night, then she'd be fine . . . At least, that's what she kept telling herself.